About the Author

Neil T. Eckstein was educated at St. Olaf College, Luther Seminary, and the University of Pennsylvania. He served several Lutheran parishes as pastor and taught at Wartburg College and the University of Wisconsin, Oshkosh, from which he retired as Professor Emeritus in 1988. Since then he has served as "Senior Mentor" visiting professor at California Lutheran University for six semesters. From 1973 to 1992, he served as founding director of the Winchester Academy, an adult education center now operating at Waupaca, Wisconsin. He edited the Winchester Academy *Round Table* and other publications. He also authored *The Marginal Man as Novelist* (Garland Press, 1990). His alma mater, St. Olaf College, honored him with a Distinguished Alumnus Award in 1988. He was born in the house that "Jacob" built for his parents, and today he and his wife can view "Terje's" old farmstead from their living room window.

Neil T. Eckstein

September 1997

Norton's Folly

*Norwegian Immigrants and Yankee Neighbors
on the Wisconsin Frontier, 1849-1857*

by

Neil T. Eckstein

Grandview Books
5555 Grandview Road
Larsen, Wisconsin 54947

Published by:

Grandview Books
5555 Grandview Road
Larsen, Wisconsin 54947

ISBN 1-57502-487-X

Printed in the USA by

MORRIS PUBLISHING

3212 East Highway 30 • Kearney, NE 68847 • 1-800-650-7888

Acknowledgements, etc.

I wish to express my deep appreciation to certain persons for their assistance in getting this story told. I am grateful to my wife's kinsman, Olav Smedsrud of Vikersund, Norway, for sharing the Heddal troll story and the *Draumkvedet*, and to my late kinsman, Øystein Klingenberg of Stathelle, Norway, for good information about sailing ships. I am grateful to my seminar class at California Lutheran University for reading and reacting to a rough draft version of the manuscript in the spring semester of 1996. I am also indebted to several early readers of the manuscript, especially to Robert Berner and Polly Zimmerman for some good editorial assistance. Finally I wish to thank my wife, Marie, for her patience and support, and my daughter Jane and my son Jim for their assistance in formating the manuscript upon the computer and assisting in the publication of this novel. A special thank you to Jane for providing the sketch of "Norton's Folly" which appears on the title page.

I found it necessary to use a few Norwegian terms in the narrative, and I have included a glossary of those terms on page 255. I also found it necessary to alter the spelling of a few names to accommodate English-speaking readers. For example, the Norwegian *Anne* would be pronounced Anna, not Ann, so I chose to write the name as Anna. Also *Anne-Marie* is read by English-speaking readers as Ann-Maree, so I have written it as Anna-Maria, the way it would be pronounced by Norwegians.

Neil T. Eckstein
April 1997

Norton's Folly

Chapter Titles

The Onset of a Strange Fever

High above the shore line of the blue waters of Bjorvatn stood the two old log long-houses and the clustered farm buildings which belonged to two farms that shared a common *tun*. They had once been a single farm, but in the late 1600's a magnanimous owner defied the time-honored law of *odel* and divided his estate into three nearly equal parts: The two parts that shared the common *tun* for his two sons, and a third part some distance away for his daughter and her landless husband. And so the descendants of those three families continued to live on the three farms, growing ever more distant in their cousinage as the generations passed, but sharing the sustenance provided by these rocky and forest-lined acres and enjoying a kind of idyllic isolation from the pains of the larger world beyond.

A feverish restlessness was defined tragically for young Terje Larsen when he was only nine years of age. One beautiful morning in early June of 1805, Terje and his older twin brothers, Christian and Knut, ventured out onto the lake in a rickety old skiff which they had used dozens of times before. They each had a fishing pole, and Terje suddenly had a large trout on his line. In the excitement, he jostled the boat in such a way that it inexplicably capsized, throwing the three lads into the lake's yet-chilly water.

They were not far from the rocky little island in the lake, and Christian and Terje swam to the island without any difficulty, but for some unknown reason Knut did not make it. Ironically, Knut was the best swimmer of the three, and the two boys on the island hoped for some minutes that Knut had played some kind of trick on them, choosing to swim under water to the back side of the island. But it soon became apparent to the boys that Knut was nowhere to be seen. They began to yell frantically, hoping to attract the attention of someone up at the farmsteads on the hillside above them.

At last Ole Bjorvatn, their neighbor and distant cousin, heard the persistent cries of the boys and sensed that they must be in some kind of trouble. He hurriedly summoned their father, Lars Bjorvatn, and the two men rushed to the shores of the lake. Immediately Lars perceived that Knut was missing and sensed the very worst. Ole and Lars hastily rowed out to the island in Ole's sturdy boat, and heard from the boys the horrific news that Knut must have drowned in the lake. The two men and the two boys immediately began a futile search, hoping against hope that Knut had reached shore at some yet undiscovered site. But their searching was all in vain.

They next summoned some neighbors, and soon the shore of the beautiful and placid little lake was lined with dozens of people who came to lend a neighborly hand to the desperate search.

Day moved into the short June night of semi-darkness, and at sunbreak the searchers began again, but still with no luck. Another night came and went, and early in the morning of the second day the bloated body of young Knut Bjorvatn was pulled from the lake.

Terje never forgot the greenish white color of the skin and the look of terror which was frozen into the yet-opened eyes of his brother. He nearly fainted at the sight and had to go behind a tree to vomit. He felt the reassuring arm of his mother embracing him; but he also sensed at the same time a glare of resentment, if not downright hatred, in the eyes of his brother Christian. The twin brothers, Christian and Knut, had just celebrated their eleventh birthdays, and they had been inseparable as companions and friends. They often seemed to regard their younger brother Terje as a pesky intrusion upon their cozy and self-sufficient twosome.

Shortly after this tragedy Terje decided to run away from home. At age nine he was hardly responsible for this irrational decision, but at the time it seemed perfectly rational for him to leave his family and move to a greater world beyond the confines of Bjorvatn. Of course he only got a few kilometers beyond Bjorvatn when a distant neighbor took him in, fed him, and with a firm but kindly hand returned him to his parents. Perhaps this was the true beginning in Terje's life of that restless and strange fever that seemed to haunt him forever.

As the months passed, the resentment of Christian toward his brother seemed to harden, and their parents began to take note. To be sure, it had been the sudden movements of Terje that had caused the capsizing of the fragile little boat, and they tried to reason with Christian that Terje had intended no harm. But the admonitions of the parents only seemed to accentuate the resentment of Christian against his younger brother.

At last the parents, desperate and despairing, decided it might be best to separate the two boys for a time; and Terje was sent to Arendal to live with his Aunt Marit who lived in a small cottage alone most of the time because her husband, Mads Monsen, was a sailor and was gone at sea for long periods of time. Mads and Marit were childless, and Marit was delighted to have a child to pamper and look after. Terje developed a great fondness for his generous aunt; and his days in Arendal were happy and carefree, especially on those days when he was free from the firm discipline of his schoolmaster. He watched with great interest as sailing ships came into Arendal from distant ports, and he chatted with friendly sailors about their adventures in distant lands. It was at this time that Terje first heard the word "Amerika," but he had no real notion of what or where "Amerika" was. He also heard about "Afrika" and the "Spice Islands" and many other exotic and distant places.

Yet, happy as he was in Arendal, Terje missed Bjorvatn and his family. While Terje was in Arendal, his mother gave birth to yet another sibling, a tiny little bundle who was christened Knut, perhaps in an attempt to fill the tragic gap in their family caused by the death of the other Knut. In the years to come, two more siblings would join the Bjorvatn family.

After two years with his Aunt Marit, Terje returned to Bjorvatn. At first he seemed to be an outsider, but he soon discovered that he was loved and accepted. Even Christian seemed friendly and glad to see his brother, and the two developed a kind of uneasy camaraderie. But always the memories of the first Knut haunted their relationship.

After his confirmation at the Herefoss Church, Terje apprenticed to a cobbler in Arendal. Once again, he stayed with his Aunt Marit. As a younger son he would not inherit, by *odelsrett*, the ancient farm Bjorvatn. His brother Christian was the appointed heir. Of this there could be no doubt. Terje needed to have a means of livelihood, and the cobbler's trade seemed a good opportunity for him. Those four apprentice years in Arendal were pleasant for Terje, in spite of the long hours which he often labored at the shoemaker's lasts and the tongue-lashings which he sometimes had to endure from his impatient master who always demanded perfection from his apprentices.

But these were restless times. Napoleon's armies were on the march throughout Europe, and the reverberations of that marching reached even to remote Norway. Upon his eighteenth birthday Terje joined the Norwegian army and reported for duty at the fortress in Christiansand. The year was 1814, a most decisive year for Norway and for all of Europe. The British fleet had blockaded the Norwegian coast; and, at Eidsvold, Norwegian politicians and patriots took advantage of this blockade to declare their independence from Denmark after over four hundred years of rule from Copenhagen.

These were heady times and vast changes seemed to be occurring everywhere. Independence for Norway was the battle cry of the day, and the soldiers at Christiansand were swept up with enthusiasm for this cause. Terje could recall standing at stiff attention as they were addressed by a Norwegian colonel who tried to explain to his troops the real significance of what had been accomplished at Eidsvold. There were the hopes that Norway would, after so many centuries, have her own king, just as in ancient times. But those hopes had to be tempered by reality as Norway was forced to accept the Swedish king as her monarch. However, the people consoled themselves, we may have to share a king with our Swedish brothers, but we now have our own parliament. We are now a nation among nations, not a mere province of another nation.

Terje could recall standing at stiff attention once more in the fortress in Christiansand, this time because of the presence of a high-ranking Swedish general who came as the representative of their new Swedish king. Never in his life had he felt so impressed with the presence of high rank and the pomp of high ceremonial.

Terje stayed in the Norwegian army at the fortress in Christiansand until his twentieth birthday. Upon his release from the army he returned to Bjorvatn for several years. His father, Lars Bjorvatn, was ill and could no longer undertake heavy labor. His brother Christian now took over the operation of the farm; but he needed Terje's help, at least for some time, before more permanent arrangements could be made for the operation of the farm.

For many years the forests at Bjorvatn had supplied an abundance of birch and other hardwood logs which could be put into the farm's charcoal kilns and then marketed to the ironworks at Froland. Their father, Lars Bjorvatn, was still able to tend the fires at the kilns and drive wagonloads of charcoal to the ironworks, but he often needed Terje's help to load and unload the charcoal. For several generations this charcoal enterprise had earned hard specie-dollars for the folks at Bjorvatn.

After Terje had worked at Bjorvatn for nearly three years, his father suddenly took desperately ill; and, within a matter of less than a week in a sickbed, died. After the funeral, a settlement was made by which Christian inherited the farm, but needed to care for his widowed mother and his younger siblings until they were able to fend for themselves.

Thanks to the charcoal enterprise and the thrifty habits of Lars Bjorvatn and his ancestors, there was a surprisingly large supply of specie-dollars locked away in an old iron-clad small chest which had been carefully hidden under the kitchen floor boards. This allowed Christian to make a cash settlement to Terje and his other siblings, according to careful instructions which had been spelled out by their father before his death. As a result, Terje suddenly found himself with more money than he had imagined he would ever possess.

His mother and his brother Christian counseled him to use this money wisely and not waste it frivolously. His brother suggested that Terje now had enough money to make a good down payment on a small farm and could use his skills as a cobbler to supplement his living from the farm. Over a period of years he could use some of the money he could earn as a cobbler to retire the mortgage on the farm. This seemed a sensible plan to Terje, but he felt it would be better to work for several more years as a cobbler in Arendal, living in as thrifty a manner as possible, in order to add to the sum of his inheritance.

He also reasoned that he was a single young man, painfully shy around eligible young ladies, but he would need a wife if he were to operate a small farm. Then, too, he would need to look very carefully to see if and when a good small farm would be available for purchase. Some very poor farms in remote locations could perhaps be purchased at any time, but one might need to search carefully to find just the right small farm in a suitable location. They did not come on the market that frequently.

And so Terje returned to Arendal, living once more with his Aunt Marit and her usually absent husband, Mads Monsen. He was able to live with them rent-free in exchange for helping with household chores. Terje put in long hours at the cobbler's bench, intent upon adding to his savings as rapidly as possible.

One day, about four years after his return to Arendal, his Aunt Marit had a visit from her husband's cousin who lived in the Birkenes parish. This cousin, Thea Flaa, came to Arendal to consult a physician and brought along her young daughter, Anna Tøvesdatter, who had just celebrated her nineteenth birthday.

At once Terje perceived that perhaps his aunt and her husband's cousin had some notion that Terje and Anna should meet and get to know each other. Previously his aunt from time to time had tried to match Terje with young ladies of her acquaintance in Arendal, but her match-making efforts were always in vain. In fact, the more she made these attempts, the more Terje resisted, often to the embarassment of all parties concerned. But this time it was a bit different. Thea Flaa and her daughter stayed right in the cottage with Terje and his aunt, so there was no avoiding the situation; and Terje tried to make the best of it, taking pains to be as friendly and pleasant to the two visiting ladies as possible.

Frequently he was left alone to converse with Anna because the two older ladies had their own agendas, and he discovered that Anna was a very pleasant and witty young lady. They took several long walks together, and upon one occasion Anna slipped her hand into Terje's large open hand. Gradually Terje's natural shyness around girls was overcome, and Anna had the ability to tease Terje and make him laugh, putting him at ease. All too soon, the time came for Anna and her mother to return to Birkenes. At the last moment Thea Flaa spoke to Terje and his aunt:

"Thank you both for a very pleasant visit. Now you must both come to visit us at Birkenes. Terje, you should be able to get free from your cobbler's bench for a few days late in September. Your Aunt Marit would like so much to have you bring her out to our farm for a nice visit before the cold weather comes."

While her mother was talking, Anna smiled at Terje coyly, slipping her hand once more into Terje's leather-stained hand. And so the courtship began.

After Anna and her mother left, Terje discovered that he really missed Anna. In fact, he decided that September was yet a long way off; and he sat down at his aunt's table, borrowed her pen and ink, and wrote a brief letter to Anna, telling her how much he enjoyed meeting her and how much he was looking forward to seeing her again in September.

The September visit came and went all too quickly, and by this time Terje realized that he was hopelessly in love with Anna and that she had given every indication that she reciprocated. When he wrote his second letter to Anna, shortly after his return to Arendal from the visit to Birkenes, it was a letter that included a proposal of marriage. In fact, he showed the letter to his Aunt Marit before sending it, just to make sure he had chosen the right words. Aunt Marit gloated with satisfaction after reading this letter. Her work as a matchmaker had been successful.

After several more letters had been sent, it was agreed that the wedding should take place in Birkenes next June, after the spring crops were in and the weather was likely to be pleasant for the wedding festivities. Now it was also time for Terje to get serious in his search for a suitable small farm.

After speaking to a number of people about his desire to purchase a small farm, and after investigating several properties that were for sale, he discovered that in the Austre Moland parish, adjacent to the old Longum estate, there was a small farm called Skredderstua which could be purchased quite reasonably. The buildings had been neglected and needed repair because the house had stood vacant for several years. The elderly widow who lived alone in the house had died, and she had no heirs, so the disposal of her property was left to the courts.

Terje spoke to the judge who was in charge of the disposing of the property. They agreed upon a good price, thus avoiding the necessity of a public auction. The judge had confided to Terje that this procedure was a bit irregular, but he was busy with so many other affairs that it was convenient for him to proceed in this manner.

And so in April of 1824 Terje found himself the owner of Skredderstua. He was able to borrow some money from his mother and some additional funds from his Aunt Marit and her husband, Mads Monsen, who were pleased to be able to help their young nephew get a start in life. These funds supplemented his own inheritance and savings so that nearly the entire payment could be made to the judge in specie-dollars.

From April until June, Terje worked feverishly to prepare the little house for his bride. He also had to put in the crops, but he would wait until after the wedding to begin stocking the farm with animals. He knew that Anna would bring to the farm two cows and one horse from her father's farm in Birkenes as a part of her dowry. That had been agreed upon when the marriage plans were made.

And so Terje, earlier beset with restlessness, now settled down with Anna on their little farm. They approached their future with optimism and hope, but their hopes were dashed twice early in their marriage when Anna suffered miscarriages, and she began to wonder if she and Terje were destined to remain childless. But then, in 1828, she gave birth to a vigorous little son who was christened

Elias. The very next year her Jacob was born. Then the rest of the children came -- Maren and Kittel and Anna-Lovisa and Anna-Maria and finally little Klemet. The little cottage at Skredderstua bulged with life, and Anna Tøvesdatter relished her role as mother to this growing brood. But one great sorrow blotted her happiness when little Anna-Lovisa suddenly, at age three, developed a high fever and within a few days died. For weeks and months Anna was devasted with sorrow, and the loss of this lovely child left a permanent scar in her soul.

As the years passed, the older boys grew into young men. Elias took over more and more of the farm work, relieving his father to devote more time to his cobbler's bench so that some extra income could be earned. Jacob had a natural talent for carpentry, so Terje arranged that he should be apprenticed in Arendal to a ship's carpenter as soon as he had been confirmed at Austre Moland Church.

Life seemed to go smoothly enough for Terje and his family, and he and Anna often spoke to each other how fortunate they had been. Oh, to be sure, some years the crops failed to produce their expected harvest and now and then a cow or horse would get sick and die, but these reversals were not unusual and one learned to take some of the bad with the good.

But in 1847, and again in 1848, there were devasting failures of crops in the entire parish and in many of the neighboring parishes. The storehouses were emptied of their abundance, and there were only meager harvests to replenish the storehouses. Children on many of the farms began to look gaunt and hungry. The failure of the potato crop was particularly devastating for many families, and as one listened to the conversations in the churchyard on Sunday mornings, more and more the word "Amerika" was heard. A new restlessness swept over the land, and groups of people trickled past with their wagons and possessions on the road leading to Arendal to board a ship that would take them to the distant land of promise and plenty -- "Amerika."

Terje, too, felt a new restlessness. He had been forced to go to Bjorvatn to beg a supply of potatoes and other provisions from his brother. The potato blight had not devastated the crop at Bjorvatn, perhaps because of its isolated distance from other farms. It was humiliating for Terje to beg from his brother, and he felt a bit of condescension in his brother's attitude. He did not share his feelings with Anna, but Terje began to have restless thoughts about his own future and the future of his family. It was, however, Jacob, his second son, who was stricken with that strange fever most intensely.

It was all the fault of that wretched and wizened old sea captain, Nils Prebensen of Arendal. If he had treated young Jacob Terjesen decently during the third year of his apprenticeship as a ship's carpenter, young Jacob might not have succumbed to the America Fever, at least not as quickly as he did.

Jacob served his apprenticeship under the direction of Dietrich Gunderson, a veteran ship's carpenter, also from Arendal. Dietrich was a paragon of patience and had tolerated both the blunderings of young Jacob and the bad temper of Prebensen, captain of the *Neptune*. The ship was a sturdy little brig that sailed regularly from Arendal to Rotterdam with tightly packed holds of Norwegian lumber for the timber-hungry Dutchmen; and it returned to Arendal with barrels of exotic Dutch goods for the warehouses of local merchants and speculators.

Captain Prebensen was a vile man indeed. His tongue was laced with curses and his breath reeked of halitosis and schnapps. Even old Dietrich agreed that Prebensen was the worst skipper he had ever sailed with during his many years at sea, but he had signed aboard the *Neptune* because of a promise he had made to the widow of the late Nicholas Bruun, owner of the *Neptune*, that he would stay aboard for three more years.

In spite of Prebensen's shortcomings, he was a superb seaman; he had weathered the worst that the North Sea was capable of inflicting upon intruding sail ships; and he was, despite all of his obvious vices, meticulously honest. But Jacob decided, early in February of 1849, after having endured a vicious tongue-lashing from Prebensen, that he would endure this kind of treatment no more. Master ship's carpenter or not – it was not worth even one more crossing with this monster of a tyrant! Jacob vowed that he would go to America, away from all the foul-mouthed Prebensens and all the other puffed-up little tyrants of Europe and seek out a new life in that fabled land of promise – America!

Oh, to be sure, Jacob had endured a few milder attacks of the America Fever previously. Even as a schoolboy, he read with fascination stories about wild Indians and galloping buffaloes out on those vast undulating prairies and dense forests in the middle of that broad and fantastic land.

He had bid good-bye just two years ago to the best friend of his boyhood years, Beint Gauslaa, and had received a glowing letter from him about six weeks ago:

This land has exceeded my wildest dreams, Beint wrote, *I now work for a prosperous Yankee farmer near Sheboygan, and I am saving more money in one year than I could in a lifetime in Norway. I am not treated as a mere servant; my Yankee family has nearly adopted me as their son, and I eat each day at their table as an equal. Can you imagine this kind of thing happening on the farm of a rich landowner in Norway? I am learning English quite well, and during the winter months, when there is not much work on the farm, I am able to attend the local district school several days each week. I am the oldest pupil in this school, and the little Yankee children often snicker at my attempts to pronounce words in English.*

There are some young Yankee ladies nearly my age who also attend, but they are very coy and do not want to talk with me very much because I am the only foreigner in the whole school and these young ladies must think I have landed from another planet. The younger children are actually much more open and friendly and are very curious about me. They constantly beg me to tell them about my homeland and my adventures at sea. The schoolmistress is a very prim Yankee lady, no longer very young, and she will tolerate no nonsense from any of her pupils. But she has been very helpful to me. Indeed, I think she must regard me as a special challenge to her teaching competence and she insists on making a proper Yankee out of me.

Did I tell you that I am no longer known as Beint Gauslaa here in America? It is impossible for Yankees to pronounce such a name. Here I have become Ben Johnson, a very easy name for Yankees to remember. In fact, my teacher tells me there was once a famous English poet by that name and she actually found a poem by him in one of her books, but I could not make much sense out of reading it. I have not come far enough in learning English to appreciate such high-brow stuff.

Jacob, you remember how often we spoke together about our dreams of going to America. You must think seriously of coming to join me in this great new land. When you decide to come, please write to me of your plans, and I'll try to give the best advice that I can on making the crossing and getting settled in the new land. . . .

Jacob carried this letter in his pocket continuously ever since receiving it. He had not yet told his family about it, but now that his mind was made up to leave the *Neptune*, he would need to have a serious talk, especially with his father and his older brother, Elias.

When the *Neptune* returned to Arendal, Jacob had a long conversation with his good master, Dietrich Gunderson, who tried to persuade young Jacob to stay aboard long enough to finish his apprenticeship.

"Jacob, in less than one more year you can finish your apprenticeship with me and become a journeyman ship's carpenter. I know many of the master carpenters from Arendal and other ports who would be happy to take you on as a journeyman."

Jacob said nothing. He didn't want to argue with Dietrich.

"As a journeyman you wouldn't have to work for anyone like Captain Prebensen. And if you don't want to go to sea there are good jobs for carpenters right here in our Arendal shipyards. You have too good a future here to throw it away."

Dietrich seemed to be reading Jacob's mind. He could see that Jacob had caught that strange fever for America that had afflicted so many others during these last several years.

After an awkward pause, Dietrich continued, "You shouldn't believe all of those stories that you hear about America. Most of them are not true. Do you know Lars Nygaard who lives only two doors away from my place?"

"Yes, I think you pointed him out to me last time we were in port."

"Then you should know that he and his wife came home to Norway after only three years in America. They left two small children in graves over in America. They died of cholera, and Lars and his wife were lucky to escape death themselves. By selling everything they owned over there they managed to scrape up passage money to return to Norway. Now they are both in bad health, living on the charity of relatives. Lars works as a day laborer when his health allows, and Karin, his wife, works off and on as a seamstress. Not much to show for the small farm and nice orchard they once owned just outside of Arendal!"

"It wouldn't have to be like that," Jacob said.

"That's how it was for the Nygaards. America wasn't good to them. I think many who emigrate come to regret it."

"But many others prosper there."

Dietrich put his hand on Jacob's shoulder for a moment and patted it.

"I know you'll never become wealthy as a master ship's carpenter, Jacob, but it's a good trade. Before you know it you'll be able to afford a cozy little house in Arendal with lace curtains in the windows and a nice young wife waiting for you to come home from each sailing. Isn't that better than chasing some crazy will-o-the-wisp halfway around the world?"

"You're telling me that if I work hard and wait in Norway I'll prosper. I want to go to America to work hard and maybe prosper without waiting."

"Maybe?"

"Yes, maybe," Jacob said. "I know some Norwegians don't find what they're looking for in America. But I also know that many do. In America even poor people can become wealthy landowners in a short time. They would have nothing if they stayed in Norway."

Dietrich could see that Jacob had made up his mind. He stared out at the harbor's entrance for some moments.

Jacob didn't want to seem ungrateful for Dietrich's advice.

"I think in America they will need many fellows like me, just to build all the houses they'll need. Thanks to you and what you have taught me, I'm a good carpenter. Anyway, even a hard first year or two in America couldn't be worse than another year with this tyrant Prebensen. Do you remember the tongue-lashing he gave me when we were preparing to leave Rotterdam just a few days ago?"

"I remember," Dietrich replied pensively.

"The hold cover amidships wouldn't set in place properly. He insisted that I force it in place with a mallet. He wouldn't listen to me. Only a few strokes with a plane and it would have fit snugly. But no, he made me pound it into place and called me an idiot and worse with his vicious curses. I looked at that hatch cover yesterday. The flange board is cracked right down the middle, all because of Prebensen."

"Don't worry about that. I saw it, too. I'll repair it tomorrow. But you must understand Captain Prebensen. Once he makes up his mind to sail nothing else matters. He won't tolerate even the slightest delay. The cracked flange board isn't serious. Anyway, the hatch cover held securely enough."

Dietrich could see that nothing he could say would change Jacob's mind. Finally he offered his hand to Jacob and wished him the best of good fortune. Jacob hoisted his seaman's chest onto his right shoulder and walked down the gangplank, never to set foot aboard the *Neptune* again. He had escaped the tyranny of Prebensen, and his heart was set upon emigrating to America at the earliest opportunity.

When he returned to Skredderstua his older brother Elias was not surprised to hear of his determination to emigrate as soon as possible.

"I've had the same thoughts, Jacob. There's no future for me here. Skredderstue isn't large enough to sustain a whole family -- especially with the poor harvests we've had the last three years. We had to sell two of our cows because of a lack of fodder, and this year Father had to go begging Uncle Christian at Bjorvatn for potatoes -- and last year, too."

"I didn't know it was that bad."

"It was. If Father couldn't earn extra money as a cobbler we would be very poor indeed. As it is, we just scrape through. So far we haven't gone into debt, but how long can that last?"

Jacob was surprised that things were actually that bad for his family. Somehow, he had always assumed that things were going well at Skredderstua. For him, the cottage at Skredderstua had always been the symbol of all that was stable and secure in life, and there were so many good memories. . . .

Jacob's reverie was broken abruptly when Elias said grimly, "Someday I want a real farm, not a rocky little garden patch like Skredderstua. In America, they say, you can easily get a big farm with wonderfully rich soil that will grow just about anything."

"I know what they say," Jacob said. "And I believe it to be true."

"Have you heard that Mother's brother, Gunder Tøvesen from Herefoss, has sold everything at auction and plans to sail very shortly for America?"

Jacob was amazed at this news. Uncle Gunder always seemed so staid, so rigid and bound to tradition. It was hard to imagine him venturing forth on a journey to America.

He asked, "How do Mother and Father react to such news?"

Elias laughed, "At first Mother was very distraught. I think she thought anyone going to America was sure to fall off the edge of the world somewhere in the middle of the Atlantic. But she has come to realize that it may be the best thing for her brother and his family. They've had a hard time of it on that rocky little farm up in the hills."

"I have heard that several times from Mother."

"Not that Uncle Gunder has made the most of his place. He's one of the 'holy ones,' you know. Maybe if he spent a little less time at prayer meetings and lay conventicles he'd have time to take better care of his family."

"So I've heard. I don't know him very well. He's always been too busy with his holy friends to bother with us. When I was about ten I impressed him by reciting all of the Ten Commandments. I didn't have the nerve to tell him that was all I knew of the Catechism."

Elias laughed. "I remember. He thought I was a dunce because I made such a botch of the Creed. You fared better, so you were his favorite nephew in our family."

"When are they leaving for America? Have they booked passage?"

Elias shrugged. "I don't know. Have Mother show you the letter she received last week."

Jacob admitted to no one how nervous he felt when he thought about the long voyage to America, but to his brother he confided:

"It would be better to travel with people I know than arrive there alone. I wonder if they could make room for me."

And so it was that the plans for Jacob's emigration began to take shape. At first his mother was very upset at the thought of losing not only her brother and his family to a strange and distant land, but now also her son, her very own flesh and blood, who would be separated from her by that vast and terrible ocean.

It was Jacob's father, Terje Larsen Skredderstua, who broke the family's deadlock on the whole question of America by declaring:

"If I were a young fellow like Jacob, I would certainly also want to try my fortune in the New World. There are very few opportunities for folks like us to advance beyond these hardscrabble little farms and meager livelihoods that old Norway can afford to give us. Heaven knows that for the last two or three years it has been especially hard for us, and we can not live off the charity of Bjorvatn every year. If Jacob goes, and Elias also goes, perhaps our whole family should follow, once the boys have established themselves in America. I'm now fifty-three years old and in good health. Perhaps there's even a place for me too in that paradise over there."

His wife, Anna Tøvesdatter, was very disturbed with this turn of events. Could they really be serious about leaving their snug little cottage here at Skredderstua? To be sure, it was not a grand palace, but it was cozy enough, wasn't it? Could we really leave all of the neighbors and friends; could we really leave that big cherry tree near the front door that every year blesses us with an abundance of dark sweet cherries? Above all, how could we think of leaving that little grave in Austre Moland churchyard, the grave of our sweetest little child, Anna-Lovisa, who died so suddenly and so sadly eleven years ago? She would be fourteen now. Last Pentecost she would probably have been confirmed at Austre Moland Church. That day had been a sad day for Anna Tøvesdatter. She just could not bring herself to attend the confirmation service that day. It would have been too painful to watch those other girls and boys and try to imagine her Anna-Lovisa as one of them.

Finally, after many tears and much persuasion by her husband and her two older sons, Anna Tøvesdatter agreed that she could not allow the past to obstruct the future. She succumbed, reluctantly, to the ruthless logic of economic and social opportunity.

Gradually a plan was devised: Jacob should go first with his uncle, Gunder Tøvesen, and his party, if they would have him; and then the following year, after Jacob and the others had established themselves in America, the rest of the family would come. Elias begged to go with Jacob, but it was agreed finally that he should help his father and mother with all of the preparations necessary to uproot the whole family. Besides, he would be needed to help with the journey itself when that time came.

They soon were able to reach Gunder Tøvesen with the news that his nephew wanted to join his party, and Gunder was pleased to have a strong young man in his party. Gunder came to Skredderstua on a blustery early March day, and he and Jacob immediately went into Arendal to attempt to book passages on a ship that would sail for America at the earliest possible date.

Jacob suggested they get in touch with his old mentor, Dietrich Gunderson, because no one in Arendal knew more about sailing dates and ship's captains than Dietrich. They found Dietrich at his cottage puttering about in the woodshed. Jacob and Gunder were lucky to find him ashore. The *Neptune* was in port and not scheduled to sail again for about three days.

"So -- you're determined to go?"

"Yes," Jacob said. "We need a ship."

Dietrich took a seat on the long wooden bench by the shed and gestured to them to join him.

"The *Jupiter* and the *Pernilla* leave here in a few weeks, but they're already filled to capacity with emigrants for America. You'd best go to Langesund. In late April and early May there'll be several sailings from there. Your best bet might be the *Juno*, with Captain Carl Helgesen."

"The *Juno* -- Captain Helgesen." Jacob repeated the names aloud to fix them in his memory.

"Yes," Dietrich said. "I've known him for many years. He's a fine fellow. If I got the idea that I ought to go to America, he's the one I'd want to sail with. He usually makes his first crossing about the first of May and will probably stop here in Arendal to load pig iron from the Froland Iron Works for ballast, but you shouldn't wait for that. Go to Langesund to arrange passage as soon as possible."

Jacob looked at Gunder and nodded.

Dietrich said, "You know the coastal sloop from Christiansand to Langesund. It's due tomorrow."

"We'll be on it," Jacob said.

"The *Juno* is a fine seaworthy ship, fully rigged, and Captain Helgesen takes good care of his passengers. They say he even helps them get through the customs and immigration business in New York and gets them started west before they can be exploited by the crooks who prey on the greenhorns."

His words alarmed Gunder. "What crooks?"

"I only know what I've been told. They say there's one vulture, a Dane, who pounces on gullible Scandinavians and picks them clean of any money they've brought with them."

Jacob wondered if Dietrich was saying this to discourage him enough to stay home.

Sensing Jacob and Gunder's fears, Dietrich spoke reassuringly, "I don't want to frighten you. But if it is true about that Danish vulture, such a scoundrel ought to be sent to gallows. That's for sure."

Jacob said, "We'll go to Langesund. Our minds are made up."

"I know," Dietrich responded with a frown of resignation on his brow.

So Gunder and Jacob boarded the coastal sloop that sailed to Langesund the next morning, stopping briefly at each port on the way -- Tvedestrand, Risør, Kragerø -- and they scrambled ashore for an hour or two at each stop to chat with the folks who habitually tarried around the docks. One of them was an old salt in Kragerø who assured them that Captain Helgesen was a good choice. "I sailed two years with him before I retired from the sea. He'll leave here about the first of May and stop at ports between Langesund and Christiansand to load cargo and passengers and in Arendal to load ballast."

Jacob said, "You've sailed to America?"

"Oh yes. Several times."

Jacob remembered Dietrich's warning about the Danish vulture.

"Maybe you could tell us what we can expect on our voyage and when we arrive in New York."

His question unleashed a flood of words from the old sailor as he related his own experiences on the New York docks and told them what he knew about life in the New World and about the experiences of emigrants he had known personally.

When it was time to board the sloop again for the final leg of their journey to Langesund, Gunder said, "Those stories were interesting and a bit frightening."

Jacob could see that Gunder was worried. "Yes," he said, "but I think he might have stretched the truth now and then."

Some hours later the sloop sailed into Langesund harbor and the master of the sloop pointed out to Gunder and Jacob just where the *Juno* was moored and exactly from which pier one could catch a boat out to the moored ship. But it was already late in the day and the two travelers needed first to find a night's lodging. The negotiations with the ship's captain and his bursar could wait until tomorrow morning.

It all went well at Langesund. They worked out the schedule of payment for passage with the bursar and even met briefly with Captain Helgesen who greeted his future passengers warmly. He was interested in hearing that Jacob had been a seaman and even spoke a bit about their mutual friend, Dietrich Gunderson. It had already been arranged that the ship would stop briefly at Arendal harbor, long enough to load the ballasts with iron, and Gunder and his party could board at that time. They were lucky to find room for passage because, Captain Helgesen told them, he had already booked a large party from Telemark; yet there would still be room for Gunder's party, but barely so. Captain Helgesen went on to say that he refused to overcrowd his ship as some captains were known to do.

Gunder and Jacob hastened back to Arendal by the next available packet ship and wasted no time in getting back to Skredderstua with the news of their impending voyage. Gunder hardly had time to eat a hearty meal at his sister's table; he was eager to get back to Herefoss as quickly as possible and calculated that he could make use of the next four hours before nightfall to get to the cottage of one of his 'holy brothers' who lived on the road that led to Herefoss.

It was agreed that in just five weeks Gunder would return to Skredderstua with his whole party, and this would allow a day or two of rest at Skredderstua before going into Arendal to board the *Juno*. And so he trudged off in haste, leaving his sister and her family to contemplate the events of the next several weeks.

On the Way

"They're here! They're here! Uncle Gunder and his whole party just turned off the road and they'll be here very soon!" Klemet shouted excitedly to his mother and sisters in the house.

"Go tell your father and brothers. I believe they're out in the stable," Anna yelled back to Klemet from inside the pantry.

Gunder and his party came with a two-wheeled cart pulled by an ancient nag that plodded along at an agonizingly slow pace. The cart was loaded with chests, but there was a small bench with room enough for two persons. Gunder's wife, Aase Knutsdatter, sat on the right side, and to her left sat another woman with a babe in her arms.

Jacob and Elias ran out from the stable to meet this ragtag parade of rustic travelers that had suddenly descended upon them. Gunder shouted a hearty greeting and bid both Jacob and Elias to come and meet his fellow traveler, Sven Risland. Sven was a dark-bearded man of slight build with a swarthy complexion. He appeared to Jacob to be fortyish, but he was no expert at guessing age.

Along with Sven and Gunder was a retinue of pale-cheeked children that varied in age from seven to fourteen. Jacob and Elias soon discovered that three of these ragamuffins belonged to Gunder and Aase: Anders, the oldest, was fourteen and had been confirmed last Pentecost at the Herefoss Church; Mads was twelve; and Halvor, the youngest, proudly proclaimed to the folks at Skredderstua that he had just celebrated his eighth birthday. There were four others who belonged to the Risland tribe, together with the fifth one who was a mere babe with the mother in the cart. Three of the four older children were girls, so desperately shy that Jacob and Elias could hardly get a look at them. There was one little lad, a skinny little fellow of seven or eight years. He announced loudly to the strange men that his name was Lasse.

Soon the entire party entered the barnyard at Skredderstua. In front of the doorway to the cottage stood Terje Larsen Skredderstua, his wife, Anna Tøvesdatter, and four of their children: Maren, next in age to Jacob, was now in the first bloom of womanhood at eighteen, then there were three younger ones – Kittel, fifteen; Anna-Maria, with the cute button nose and brown eyes, was ten; and shy little mischievous Klemet was only eight. Their father, Terje Larsen Skredderstua, was striding forward to greet each of these pilgrims warmly and shouting out orders to anyone who would listen about unharnessing the poor old mare and getting her into the stable.

By this time Anna greeted her brother Gunder with sisterly solicitude, concerned about the tired travelers who trudged so far:

"You must all be hungry as starved wolves. It's been a warm day for April, and you must all be desperately tired. Come, Maren, and you too, Anna-Maria, we must get food for these good folks, and then we must find places for all to sleep in our little cottage."

After the confusion of unloading the cart and getting everybody ready, a meal was set on the table for the grown-ups. Some of the children would have to sit at an extra small table because there was no room for them at the big table. Anna Tøvesdatter and her two daughters had a healthy meal ready for the travelers, and they all ate greedily after Gunder had intoned a lengthy table blessing.

That night no less than twenty people slept in the little cottage at Skredderstua which was already crowded for its family of eight. Blankets were strewn on the floor in the main hall, and the attic was crowded with children. The three shy daughters of Sven Risland uttered not a single word during the whole evening of spirited conversation. Before retiring, Gunder insisted upon evening prayers and intoned in his uniquely pious nasal voice a special entreaty for the great and fearsome journey they were about to undertake under the divine providence of God.

Awakened and refreshed, in spite of sleeping upon the hard plank flooring, Gunder and his entire party determined they should journey into Arendal early in the day because there were many preparations that could only be made dockside as they anticipated the arrival of their ship into the port. At this point Jacob had to join this group as the solitary outsider to the other two family units. Yet he was happy to have compatriots for the journey.

But now came the most difficult part; he must bid farewell to his parents and siblings, trusting that in about one year they would all be reunited in America. There were, to be sure, other good-byes to near neighbors and boyhood friends, and he told Gunder and his party to proceed into Arendal ahead of him because he had these last minute obligations to fulfill. He needed also to finish packing his flat seaman's chest, taking care to wrap each sharp carpenter's tool into some item of clothing in order to protect it during the long and uncertain voyage ahead.

Then there was the matter of food for the voyage that would be needed to supplement the ship's fare. His mother had packed several boxes with flatbread and cheeses; there were some sun-dried apples, the last of the previous harvest, as well as some dried sweet cherries from the large tree in front of their cottage door. These were carefully packed so that he would have some small amount of fruit, at least for the first part of the journey, to ward off the dreaded scurvy. There were some carrots and a few raw potatoes from the cellar, as well as some salt pork and sausages.

At last the packing was done, the last good-byes were said to friends, neighbors and family, and Elias drove Jacob into Arendal in a wagon that contained all of the earthly goods that Jacob could take with him to the new land. In his pocket he carried some silver and gold coins and some paper currency, loaned to him by his father, enough to pay for his passage and a generous amount besides.

Just before joining the others at the dock, Jacob stopped at a book shop and purchased a guide to learning English that had been published in Copenhagen. This book also gave useful information about emigrating to America. He also purchased a book written by L. J. Fribert, a Danish traveler and writer, that was a handbook for emigrants to America, published in Christiania just two years earlier. With the purchase of these two small books Jacob was at last ready to join the others dockside.

The *Juno* had not yet entered the harbor at Arendal; and, according to the calculations that Captain Helgesen had given to Gunder and Jacob, was overdue by quite a few hours. As the minutes ticked on to hours, with still there was no sign of the *Juno*, Gunder began to get nervously agitated and impatient at this delay. What could have happened between Langesund and Arendal?

In his frustration, Gunder accosted the skipper of the steam tug that was waiting dockside.

"When will the *Juno* come? The ship is overdue by nearly half a day according to the calculations given us by Captain Helgesen."

"My good man," the tug skipper answered, "a sail ship like the *Juno* is dependent upon both the velocity and the direction of the wind. It can't move the same way a horse and cart move on land."

"Is it often that sail ships are this late from their schedule?" Gunder asked.

"Oh yes. There could be last minute unexpected delays in loading the ship and embarking the passengers, in spite of the best estimates that one tries to make ahead of time."

The children in the party began to get more and more restless; and the boys started teasing each other, tussling about in the timeless manner of young boys. The novelty of waiting had now given way to fidgeting and tugging. But the three Risland girls sat utterly motionless like three birds on a perch. Their eyes followed the rambunctious boys, but that was all. They were enveloped in a protective blanket of shyness which insulated them from contact with these lively boys. At times the boys tried to tease and provoke the girls, but they were so utterly passive that they soon gave up on the attempt.

The adults in the party, too, were increasingly impatient and tired of the long wait. Restlessly, they scanned the horizon of the harbor's opening where they knew the ship would appear. There were several flurries of false excitement when they saw the sails of smaller coastal vessels fill the horizon at the harbor's entrance.

At last, in late afternoon, just as the sun began to wane below the silhouette of one of the rocky islands that protected the harbor, they suddenly saw tall square sails and high masts. As the ship neared, they saw its prow and then they saw the full visual panorama of the ship that was destined to be their home for the next few weeks. The skipper of the steam-powered little tugboat that was moored near the dock informed them that this indeed was the *Juno*; he knew the ship well because this was not the first time this ship had made Arendal a port of call before setting forth on her typically long voyages.

"See the way that carved figurehead is mounted at the prow? No other ship in these parts looks like that. It's the *Juno* for sure. I have seen it at least a half a dozen times before, and I can tell by its configuration that it has to be the *Juno*. Now we must fire up our boiler so that we can help the *Juno* maneuver into the dock"

The little tugboat made all sorts of gurgling noises, and the frightened Risland girls shrieked in terror as it blew its loud steam whistle. They had never heard such a piercing and ghastly sound before. Then the tug slowly made its way in the direction of the approaching sail ship.

As Gunder and his party watched from shore, it seemed to take an eternity for the tug and the big ship to maneuver clumsily into the berth at the dock. But finally great ropes secured the ship to the dock, and a small army of workers began first to unload a huge quantity of bricks from the ship's hold, bricks that had come from a kiln near Porsgrunn and were destined for a new building in Arendal. When the unloading of the bricks was completed, the crew members and other dock workers loaded a large quantity of iron pigs from the Froland Ironworks which would be marketed in New York after providing ballast for the ship during its Atlantic crossing.

All went smoothly and according to schedule. The two wives were very apprehensive when it came time to walk up the lowered gangway platform that stood ready to receive them. But sturdy crewmen stood by to help the ladies, and they did the same for the children. At last, after several hours of waiting, it was Jacob's turn to help the hefty sailors with the lifting of those two enormously heavy trunks. This was soon accomplished by these experienced seamen. Jacob's flat-topped sea chest was a featherweight in contrast to those two monsters. Jacob hurriedly scrambled up the gangplank and boarded the ship just in time to see the first big trunk being slid into the steerage hold. The sturdy seamen wasted no time in getting the other trunks down the ladder into the hold where they were securely lashed into place for the voyage.

The ship, Jacob noted, was considerably larger, both in length and in beam, than the *Neptune* which he knew so well. It was not a brig, but a fully rigged square-sailed ship. Instead of a tightly packed cargo hold, filled with lumber destined for Holland, this ship had a large steerage hold for her emigrant passengers. As Jacob clambered down the ladder into the hold, he noted the oppressive darkness and dankness of the air in contrast to the freshness of the air on deck.

Of course Jacob was accustomed to tight crew's quarters, but this passenger hold seemed ridiculously crowded with whimpering children and crying babies and the fetid smells of stale vomit and human sweat. There were two or three small lanterns that tried to penetrate the oppressive darkness of the hold, and Jacob immediately located Gunder and his party. They were busily engaged in trying to settle the children into the narrow bunks which had been assigned to them. Jacob was shown a top-most bunk which was to be his for the journey. It was a narrow prison, to be sure, but he accepted it in good humor, knowing that he had thoughtfully included his battered old hammock in his sea chest, and on warm nights he might be able to escape the oppressive heat of the steerage hold and find some little cranny topside where he could sling his hammock. He had often done this on the *Neptune* on mild summer nights.

He vowed he would do his best to befriend some of the crew members and perhaps this might earn him some special privileges. Unlike most of the other emigrant passengers who were landlubbers, he had some knowledge of the sea and sailing ships. If the occasion demanded, he might even lend a hand to help the crew now and then.

But tonight Jacob was dog-tired. He carefully hoisted himself into his assigned bunk and was sound asleep within minutes.

While Jacob and all the others in the darkened steerage hold slept, the ship cast off her lines from the dock; and, with the help of the steam-powered harbor tug, made her way slowly past the harbor lights and skerries to the open sea. It was a beautiful moonlit night, with a suitable gentle breeze. Gradually the crew unfurled sail after sail from their perches high in the rigging, and the ship gained speed. The swells of the ocean gently rocked the ship and most of the passengers cradled in the steerage hold slept soundly.

For several of the passengers, however, it was the onset of that ghastly green agony of seasickness which would haunt them again and again during the whole voyage. Risland's wife, Anlaug, was one of those so afflicted. Red-eyed, she sat on the bunk's edge with a wide wooden bowl in her lap. Her first night at sea was horrible beyond measure for this gentle woman. She felt ashamed of her affliction, as though somehow it was something that cast an ominous pall over the impending terrors of this long journey by sea.

As she sat in misery throughout that turbulent night, her mind raced back over all of the hesitations and regrets she had from the very beginning about this insane fever for America which had so tragically beset her husband and all the others. Would she prove to be an intolerable burden to the others? Would she die in the middle of this vast satanic ocean and be buried at sea, cast aside like the carcass of a dead animal, with no marker over her head to remind others of the memory of her presence? It was all too horrible to contemplate, and she broke down into a gush of quiet tears, taking care not to awaken any of the others with her private agonies.

At last a few stray sunbeams found their way down the ladder's passageway into the steerage hold. Jacob must have been the first of the sleeping ones to awaken in the entire hold. Nimbly, he made his way down to the hold's deck, taking care not to awaken any of the others. He saw the disconsolate Risland woman and immediately perceived her situation.

"Come," he said to her gently, "you must let me help you up the ladder to the open deck. The fresh air will do you a world of good."

Under the guidance of his strong support she hesitatingly made her way, one unsure step at a time, up the steep wooden ladder, coaxed each step by Jacob's confident urging. As she reached the upper steps, the cool morning air refreshed her lungs and revived her little by little.

Jacob saw the sun, low in the eastern sky, and basked in its long-shadowed morning rays. His bones still ached from the cramped bunk, but he scanned the horizon and saw some hills rising out of the mist directly to the north.

"That's all of old Norway that you'll ever see again, my boy," muttered a salty old seaman as he shuffled past Jacob on his way forward. "So you're headed for America!"

"Yes, indeed," Jacob answered. "Like so many others, I've decided that there is no future for me in old Norway."

" If I was a healthy young fool like you I suppose I might think of emigrating myself. But I was born to the sea. I have an old scold of a wife and three dimple-faced kids in a cottage back in Langesund."

"Well, I have no wife or family, so I'm free to go." Jacob asserted.

"My wife and family would never thrive in America, even if I could find a nice cottage right at ocean's edge in New York for them. No sir. That woman of mine, bless her honest soul, will have no part of this America nonsense. When I come back from a sailing to New York and try to tell the kids about all of the strange and wonderful things I saw there, she shuts me up in a hurry and tells me not to fill the heads of the kids with such nonsense. No siree. When I'm home, I have to watch my P's and Q's, but I'll tell you that it is a wonderful and refreshing sight to see the shores of America, and you'll see for yourself soon enough, if this old tub holds out for another crossing."

With that, he spit a huge cud of tobacco expertly over the starboard side, smiled at Jacob, and hurried his way forward to the ship's bow.

Jacob looked wistfully at the distant shoreline. It was growing more distant with each puff of wind into the fully rigged sails of the *Juno*. He mused to himself for a few silent moments, wondering whether or not he would ever see Norway's shores again. On the other voyages he had made aboard the *Neptune*, there was always the assurance of a return; he had seen Norway's shores disappear and then reappear with some regularity. But today it was different, just as the old seaman had said. This is scheduled to be a one-way voyage. "Good-bye, old Norway! I shall probably never see you again," Jacob caught himself muttering in a half-audible tone of voice.

At this very moment the three Tøvesen boys and the Risland boy emerged on deck, looking a bit pale and peaked from their night's confinement in the steerage hold. Their clothes were rumpled and their hair disheveled; and, above all else, they were hungry – ravenously hungry as only adolescent boys can experience hunger. Apparently the swelling of the sea had not affected them adversely, but as the ship rolled and lurched they stumbled into each other's arms with the exaggerated and good-humored gestures that only boys can make. They rushed up to Jacob and immediately peppered him with a barrage of questions.

"When are we going to get something to eat?"

"What is that land over there – is it England yet?"

"Where can I get a drink of fresh water?"

"Do you suppose the captain would mind if we climbed up the rigging just once?"

And so the questions came, one after another, much faster than Jacob could possibly answer them.

Just then Gunder and Sven Risland appeared on deck.

"Boys, get over there to the ship's galley and help your mother carry the porridge and dish it out so we can all have something to eat up here on the deck!"

The mere mention of food turned the boys into willing servants, and they scrambled to outrace each other to the galley. Aase Knutsdatter had been busy at the galley stove, helping to prepare enough porridge for their whole party. The boys were enlisted to help with the wooden bowls, marked neatly for each member of the party, and young Halvor was given the task of distributing the wooden spoons. On the stove were also several large pots boiling with coffee, and the combined aroma of coffee and porridge helped to overcome the vile stenches that seemed to emit continuously from the hold.

At last the boys got the porridge dishes properly distributed and were ready to dig in when Gunder sternly reprimanded his sons. "Do you think that just because we are out on the ocean and away from the sound of church bells we can be like heathen or animals and just forget about giving thanks to God?"

The boys, shamed by Gunder's admonition, gathered into a tight circle and bowed their heads. Gunder began to intone what must have seemed like an interminable prayer when at long last the "Amen" was finally sounded.

"Shucks, by this time my porridge is half-cold," complained Mads to the other boys. He was fortunate, however, that his father did not hear that complaint, for it would have brought a sharp reprimand, and poor Mads might have had to forfeit his breakfast of porridge altogether.

But Gunder, leader of the party and solicitous of the welfare of all within his care, had just made his way to the port side of the deck where Anlaug Risland stood, pale and languishing by the ship's rail. Gunder tried to coax her to eat a small portion of the porridge, but she refused. Then he urged her to drink a cup of coffee, but this was also refused. Finally, he remembered that his wife had packed a small tin of tea in the provisions box and suggested that a cup of weak tea would perhaps be the best for one in her condition. Yes, she reluctantly agreed, perhaps she could take some tea and a bit of flatbread without butter. She was still nursing her five month old infant and needed desperately, for the baby's sake, to keep up her strength, in spite of this wickedly pitching sea which was churning her stomach apart.

By this time many of the other steerage passengers were mulling about, crowding that portion of the deck amidships to which they were supposed to be confined. Nearly all of the other passengers were from Telemark, Jacob soon learned. They had come by boat from Skien to Langesund, but many of them had traveled by small boats over Norsjøen to Skien from some of the distant upland parishes of Telemark – from Hjartdal and Tuddal, from Sauland and Gransherrad. There were even two families from Austbygdi, north of Tinnsjøen. They presented quite a sight, these people from the inland hills. Most of them had never seen the ocean before. Some of the men wore strangely shaped white and black woolen jackets with shiny silver buttons. Some of the women wore long black woolen dresses, decorated with fancy embroidery in the Telemark style, with tight-fitting jackets and fancy brooches. Others were dressed more plainly in drab homespun, and from their dress and demeanor could not be distinguished from Jacob's own "Arendal party." This is what Gunder's party came to be called by the other passengers and the crew – the "Arendal party."

It was when they came to speaking that Jacob realized that these people indeed were very strange and different. When they talked among themselves, Jacob could hardly understand a word, so thick and heavy was their Telemark dialect. The Telemarkings, on the other hand, complained they could not understand the folks who boarded the ship at Arendal. Gradually, as the two groups became better acquainted with each other, they discovered that by speaking slowly and distinctly they could usually make themselves understood.

Jacob met a hardy fellow by the name of Halvor Traaer who was about his own age and came from Hjartdal. Halvor was a lumberjack; he had cut timber in the mountains and was, he claimed, happiest when he had a sharp axe in hand. Jacob immediately liked this fellow because he was so open and friendly, but he soon discovered that Halvor had one serious flaw; he was passionately fond of strong drink. He had smuggled aboard a large quantity of home-brewed potato alcohol and offered Jacob generous swigs from his flask. Jacob did take a small portion, just to please his newly found comrade, but found the stuff damnably strong. How Halvor could keep on drinking the stuff in such quantity Jacob could not understand, and the more he consumed, the more his personality changed so that he became combative and abusive in his language. He called Jacob all kinds of bad names, especially when Jacob refused to join him on his binge.

Halvor finally became so obnoxious that two stout seamen grabbed the fellow by his arms and legs and carried him forward to the boatswain's locker. There, in a tight cell-like structure, half filled with rope, they heaved poor Halvor head first onto a bed of coiled hemp, and then securely locked him in. From inside the locker came all sorts of vile curses and mad yellings which, fortunately, were muffled in intensity by the thick bulkheads of the locker and the distance of the sturdy boatswain's locker from the rest of the passengers.

Jacob was grateful for the rescue. One of the seamen came back to Jacob after Halvor had been locked away.

"We use the boatswain's locker for this purpose off and on, especially when we have these fellows from upper Telemark and other inland valleys who get out of hand with this home-distilled stuff they insist on bringing aboard. It's happened before and it'll probably happen again when we transport these mountaineers."

"Is this typical of all mountaineers?" Jacob asked.

"Yes, indeed! They're good fellows when they're sober, but when they get drunk the devil gets inside of them. Now, you take your coast-dwelling Norwegian. When he drinks too much, he gets happier than a lark and becomes a first-class clown. When he's sober, he's as somber as a long-faced deacon."

At this point the sailor paused long enough to spit his cud of tobacco into the sea.

"The one thing that you have to watch out for with those mountain boys is their knives. They're very proud of those knives, but when they get drunk, they start to use them on each other. That's why the captain insists upon taking the knives from these fellows as they come on board. He keeps the knives in the captain's cabin and will only return them when they leave the ship. The only knives the passengers are allowed to keep are the kitchen knives the women bring aboard."

"Have you really had any incidents on board where these people used knives on each other?" Jacob asked.

"Well, yes. Captain Helgesen started this policy three years ago when, during his first Atlantic crossing, one drunk fellow from Numedal seriously wounded another passenger, and we thought the poor fellow was going to die. But somehow he managed to pull through. I guess those mountain fellows are so tough they're hard to kill!"

Jacob wasn't really so sure that a drunken mountaineer was any more dangerous than a wildly drunken man from any other place. He had seen, right in Arendal, plenty of hard drinking sailors, and they seemed to get into their fair share of fights with each other. Last year, he suddenly remembered, a man had been killed in a drunken brawl right on the waterfront in Arendal. But Jacob was sorry that his new friend, Halvor Traaer, was so enslaved to alcohol in this manner. Earlier, he had hoped the two of them might team up in the New World and help each other through rough times, but now it seemed to Jacob it would be a risky business to take on a fellow like Halvor.

The days at sea passed slowly and monotonously. There were turbulent days when the sea was rough and the ship was pelted with rain. Those days were especially hard for the passengers in the steerage hold. As the sea grew more turbulent, the beams of the ship began to creak ominously, and some of the passengers wondered if the ship would fall apart. Jacob had to reassure these folks that it was quite normal for ships to creak in heavy weather, and there was no cause for worry because the ship was very sturdily built.

After several days of rough weather, the skies cleared and the sea calmed. There was not the slightest breeze in the air, and the passengers, who first welcomed this calm weather, soon learned that the ship could make no headway without some wind. For eight whole days the ship made no progress at all. During these eight slow days many necessary tasks were performed by the ship's crewmen as well as by the passengers themselves. There was a good deal of cleaning and scrubbing that went on during this time, but there was also a good deal of time for relaxation.

One of the Telemark men brought out his eight-stringed fiddle and soon there was a dance on the deck amidships. Gunder was very unhappy with this development because the "holy ones" were strictly opposed to dancing. The fiddle was the devil's instrument, according to Gunder; and he voiced his objections very loudly, not only to the fiddler and the dancers, but even to the ship's officers. Gunder's objections were met by ridicule on the part of some and silent disdain by others. In the end, Gunder was forced to tolerate these goings-on, but did so under great duress.

It was Captain Helgesen who had the last word. He maintained that these people had the right to their entertainment, even if Gunder and some others did not approve. It was a long voyage and the people could use a little diversion. Defeated in his attempt to stop such goings-on, Gunder resorted to making sure that no persons in his party would participate.

Reluctantly, Jacob was forced to conform to this decision. He really could see no wrong in this innocent pleasure these mountain people were enjoying, and he was even tempted to join in. He noticed several attractive younger women, obviously unmarried, who would have welcomed him as a dancing partner. He could not fail to see some coy glances and subtle smiles from two or three of these girls.

Yet he dared not openly oppose his uncle, so he deliberately sought out a refuge far forward on the ship where he could take the time to study the book on English grammar which he had bought in Arendal shortly before boarding the ship. He soon discovered that the English language seemed hopelessly complicated and inconsistent. There seemed to be no rhyme or reason as to how a word should be pronounced, and the spelling and pronunciation were very confusing. Luckily, he soon found that one of the seamen, Matthias Johansen, had spent time aboard an English ship and could speak English quite fluently.

During idle hours Matthias was willing to sit down with Jacob near the boatswain's locker and go over some of the English sentences in Jacob's book. This was a great help, and Jacob soon learned some of the basic expressions he would need to use in an English-speaking country. Matthias, however, warned him that the way of speaking English in America was somewhat different from that which prevailed in England. All of this was very confusing to Jacob, and he began to wonder if he would ever be able to catch on to this strange and complicated new language.

The first Sunday on board Gunder had attempted to gather his group and any others who would join them for a prayer service on the deck amidships. This was not welcomed by many of the Telemark passengers, and several of the young fellows, including Halvor Traaer, openly heckled Gunder and his small group. Captain Helgesen observed this unpleasant situation and determined that it would not do to have this kind of dissension among his passengers. He called all of the passengers to the deck amidships and addressed them:

"Good people and fellow voyagers, we are here under God's great sky and today is the Lord's day. We are far from the churches where we are accustomed to worship, but we must acknowledge the Lord's presence even here at sea. We have no clergyman aboard to lead us in worship, but we are not heathens. In this situation, I, as your captain, shall assume the duty of reading to you the appointed scripture lessons for this day and I shall ask you to sing together a familiar hymn. After that I shall call upon our good passenger, Gunder Tøvesen from Herefoss, to utter a prayer for our safe passage and the good health of all aboard."

After the captain had spoken, the passengers all meekly took their places and joined in the worship. There was no more heckling, even when Gunder prayed his somewhat lengthy and ardent prayer.

The days stretched into weeks. After eight days of total calm, a breeze suddenly filled the sails of the *Juno*, and she was again able to make good headway toward the New World. The breeze soon gave way to a hefty gale, and the captain was forced to take in some of the sails. The swells of the ocean became gigantic, and the *Juno* found herself in the midst of another storm. The ship bounced on the violent ocean like a little wooden chip. The rain pelted down mercilessly, flooding the deck of the steerage hold.

It was a miserable time for everyone. For poor Anlaug Risland it seemed as though the end of the world had come, and she was sure that within minutes the entire ship would collapse and they would all perish in this terrifying ocean.

She was not the only one afflicted by seasickness. Some of the passengers who had not previously experienced the discomfort of this miserable affliction succumbed, and the steerage hold was groaning with misery. To those afflicted, it seemed that the turbulence would never end, and even those who managed to escape the more severe ravages of sickness were distressed by the constant and violent motion. Many of the passengers began to wonder why they had come on such a journey and would willingly have returned back to their homeland if some magician would have offered them the chance.

It was in the middle of this terrible storm that Anlaug Risland's baby suddenly became violently ill. Her little body convulsed and shivered; and within about two hours of the initial seizure, little Karen Lovisa Risland died in her mother's arms. Anlaug broke into uncontrolled sobs and clutched the poor baby's body to her own in the desperation of her grief. Sven Risland tried to comfort his wife as best he could, but to no avail. The other passengers in steerage were silent and somber in the presence of death and spoke to each other in low tones. Gunder put his hand on the dead child's brow and uttered a prayer, but even this did not calm the distraught mother.

Jacob was sent to inform Captain Helgesen that a death had occurred in the steerage hold. Within minutes, Captain Helgesen returned with Jacob and spoke softly and kindly to both Anlaug and Sven, offering his condolences to this family stricken by the sudden visitation of death. Assessing the mother's hysteria, he took Sven and Gunder aside and spoke to them about the necessity of arranging, within the next few hours, a burial at sea.

"It has, from time to time, been my sad duty to conduct these burials at sea. We have been fortunate on this voyage that we have escaped the visitation of death until this moment. The very young and the elderly are most vulnerable, but I have seen death strike down even the strongest and most vigorous of men and women in the prime of their lives. Two years ago, we suffered an epidemic outbreak of cholera during our Atlantic crossing; and we had to bury twenty-one persons at sea, most of them small children, but several adults as well."

Captain Helgesen went on to explain to Sven and Gunder how the child's body would need to be taken to the boatswain's locker where it would be prepared for burial by being enclosed in a canvas bag which would be sewn shut by the boatswain and weighted with a stone to ensure it would sink properly as it slid from the deck into the sea.

"We have a ritual for burial at sea which is provided to captains of all Norwegian ships by the Church of Norway, but perhaps it will be necessary, because of the storm, to conduct the ritual here in the steerage hold, in the presence of all the other passengers instead of assembling the passengers on the main deck as we would in good weather. The storm shows no sign of abating, and we can't keep the body of a small child for more than a day or two."

Aase Knutsdatter embraced Anlaug and tried to comfort her as best she could, but even Aase's gestures of comfort could not penetrate the uncontrolled grief of poor Anlaug. She began to stammer incoherently to Aase and to the others who were clustered about her and the dead child. Between her sobs she seemed to be saying that all of this was her fault. She should never have allowed Sven to take her and her family on this terrible voyage. It was the work of Satan to tempt them, and now they would need to repent of this horrible disobedience. All who heard her pitied her, recognizing that they too had their private misgivings about taking this fearsome journey and could understand her feelings.

Anlaug resisted fiercely when she was asked to give up the dead body of her child which she clutched in desperation. When Sven attempted to take the child by force, she struck him a quick blow in the face. At this point, Captain Helgesen spoke calmly and authoritatively to Anlaug, suggesting that she could surely embrace the child's body for some more minutes, but that the poor child's soul had now gone to heaven and it was their duty to give the child's body burial, in this case a burial at sea, so that the whole vast ocean could be her grave.

The Captain's words had a calming effect, at least momentarily, upon the poor woman, and after some moments, she handed the child's body into the arms of the captain. But with each pounding of the waves and lurching of the ship, her grief returned, and her sobbing became even more violent and loud after the captain departed with the child's body.

After some discussion with Sven and Gunder, the captain decided that it would be best to conduct the burial service later that day, shortly before sundown. He assembled the steerage passengers and crew members all around him in the crowded steerage hold as he read the solemn words of the burial service. He asked the passengers to join him in singing a beloved old hymn, and he led their singing in a firm and confident voice. Then he turned to Gunder and asked him to utter a prayer on behalf of the family. It was often difficult to hear the words because of the violence of the storm, but every passenger in the steerage hold tried to listen as attentively as possible.

After Gunder's prayer, which Jacob had to admit was very beautiful and appropriate, the captain asked Sven and Gunder to accompany him and several other crew members to the main deck for the actual burial at sea. Crew members had to hold Sven and Gunder securely by their arms to prevent them from slipping on the deck, and the frail little body of Karen Lovisa Risland was given up to the sea.

The storm did not last forever. It seemed that perhaps the offering of the small babe's body to the sea had an effect upon calming the waters. After another day its intensity began to recede, and life aboard the *Juno* began to return more and more to its normal routine. Boredom again began to set in; and as the days wore on, the food supplies began to run low.

Jacob's store of dried apples and cherries had long since disappeared, as well as most of the other special items which his mother had so painstakingly packed for him. The daily fare was now pretty much a matter of porridge, with very little else. The water, stored in large casks, began to grow stale, and the supply began to get dangerously low so that the captain decreed water would have to be strictly rationed. Fresh water could be used no longer for washing or bathing; it had to be reserved for drinking.

On the very day of the captain's decree, Aase Knutsdatter, wife of Gunder Tøvesen, made a horrifying discovery – her little Halvor was infested with head lice. Poor little Halvor had to endure a dousing with turpentine and all the other children had to submit to a rigorous inspection by Aase.

Frustrated by her inability to use fresh water and soap, Aase mumbled and complained bitterly about the unsanitary conditions. She noticed, from the very beginning of the voyage, that many of the other passengers were dirty and slovenly in their personal habits. If her husband Gunder had a passion for piety, Aase's passion was for cleanliness. Relentlessly she kept up her inspection of the children of her party, and even Jacob had to submit to her searching eye. She strictly forbade the children of her party to have close contact with other children in the steerage hold, a very difficult edict to enforce, given the tightness of their quarters and natural conviviality of children with their peers.

At this point the passengers began to question the crew members anxiously about how long it would take to reach their destination, and the crew members tried to reassure the people they were making good progress, but it was still difficult to estimate just how many days it would be before landfall in the New World.

Then early one morning, just as many had despaired of ever seeing land again, the sailors pointed ahead, just off the starboard bow, to a configuration of land, barely discernible in the morning mist.

"We've reached Long Island, and in a few more hours we'll be sailing into New York harbor," Matthias Johansen proudly announced to the first passengers who appeared on deck.

Soon, as the word spread into the steerage hold, every passenger aboard crowded the deck amidships, anxiously peering in the direction of the land on the distant horizon which they could hardly see. The land was flat and low-lying, unlike the mountainous configuration of the land they had left. The passengers of the *Juno* had much for which to be thankful, in spite of the many hardships they had endured; they had crossed the great Atlantic and had now arrived in that fabled Land of Promise called America, and were about to embark upon an adventurous new life in this new land.

Ever Westward

Late in the afternoon the *Juno* finally moored in New York harbor. There were many procedures which needed to be taken care of before the passengers could go ashore; but the captain, thoughtfully, saw to it that a boat came alongside to deliver some much appreciated fresh provisions for crew and passengers – milk, fresh fruits and vegetables, and even some freshly baked bread. The sight of the provisions coming aboard caused much excitement, and there was a scurry as they were distributed and soon greedily devoured by the hungry passengers who had existed chiefly on a monotonous diet of porridge and stale water for the last two weeks.

Like the other passengers, Jacob scanned the horizon to view the lower end of Manhattan in the distance. The ship was yet too far away for Jacob to make out any people ashore, but some of the large red-brick buildings were clearly discernible in the distance. Jacob wondered what mysteries would be revealed when at last they would be able to go ashore into this bustling city which was destined to be their gateway to the New World. After seven and a half weeks at sea, Jacob and all of the rest of the passengers were impatient to step once more on solid land.

The last night aboard ship had been eventful, to say the least. The fiddler struck up a lively tune and soon there was a dance on the main deck amidships. The Telemark passengers were in a merry mood; and as the evening wore on, they became all the merrier, thanks in large part to caches of potato alcohol the mountain people held in reserve for just such an occasion. The merriment became more noisy and raucous as the evening progressed, but all of a sudden the music stopped and the dancing gave way to a drunken brawl. At the center of the action was Jacob's erstwhile friend, Halvor Traaer, and another red-faced fellow from Telemark. It seems the other lad chose as his dancing partner the girl Halvor wanted, and that was all it took to ignite a vicious fight. Soon several seamen separated the two and abruptly escorted the two combatants away from the main deck amidships, Halvor to the boatswain's locker forward and the other fellow to some unknown designation aft.

After some delay, the fiddler tried to start the dance again; but by this time the mood for merriment was gone, and the number of participants dwindled. After about a half an hour, the fiddler finally gave up and carefully packed his fiddle into its homemade case. He seemed resigned to the situation. This was not the first time this sort of thing had happened during his career as a fiddler, and it would probably not be the last.

Meanwhile, Gunder made sure that no one in his party was identified with such goings-on. He assembled his party in their quarters in the hold while the dance was in progress above them on the deck and addressed them in a very serious manner, lecturing them upon how thankful they should each be to God for bringing them safely to this new land of promise, in spite of the tragic death of one in their party, just as God in olden times had brought the children of Israel out of bondage in Egypt into the Land of Promise. It was a difficult time, especially for the children in the party, and even for Jacob, to concentrate on the serious thoughts that Gunder was trying to express to them while just above them the merry-makers were carrying on in their noisy manner.

Finally, after all of his talk about their destiny as God's children, he got down to some specific details:

"I had a good conversation today with Captain Helgesen. He informed me that tomorrow we shall all go ashore and be processed by the American immigration authorities."

At this point Jacob interrupted his uncle, "How'll we get ashore? Will the ship go to one of the docks?"

"No, it's my understanding that we'll all be taken ashore by small boats."

"But what about our luggage, especially those two heavy trunks?"

"The captain assured me that Niels Aslesen, his first mate, will be in charge of our luggage. After we've been processed by the American immigration authorities we'll proceed, as quickly as possible, to the steamship which will take us up the Hudson River to Albany. At Albany, we'll travel by rail to Buffalo."

"I was hoping we'd have a chance to travel by train, at least for a part of our journey." Jacob said enthusiastically.

His uncle continued, "It's more expensive to travel by train to Buffalo; we could take the canal boats, but that would be much slower. It's my understanding that the Telemark party will be traveling by canal boat because most of them do not have enough cash to afford the luxury of the train ride to Buffalo. But I've calculated it's in our best interest to travel as quickly as we can to Wisconsin to allow us time to get settled in our new homes before the winter months set in."

Gunder even had a map he had borrowed from the captain which showed the proposed route they would be taking.

"Here's our destination on this map. It's a territory that has recently been opened up to settlement in the newly constituted state of Wisconsin, and our destination is called the Neenah Settlement, already established by some of our countrymen, including our good friend, Anton Møller from Birkenes, who has written to me of conditions in this new settlement and has encouraged us to join him there."

"My mother has often spoken of the Møller family. They were neighbors of yours in Birkenes, weren't they?"

"Yes, indeed, Jacob. Anton was my best friend in childhood, and your mother knew the family very well. Jacob, it's my understanding you'll join your friend, Beint Gauslaa, at Sheboygan."

"Yes, that's true. But my decision to emigrate was made so quickly that I didn't have time to write a letter to Beint. My arrival in Sheboygan will be a complete surprise to him."

"We'll also disembark at Sheboygan to make our way to the Neenah Settlement, but you're planning to find employment in or near Sheboygan until your family joins you next season, isn't that correct?"

"Yes, that's so. Beint has assured me in previous letters that he'll help me find employment."

Finally, Gunder insisted upon a prayer of thanksgiving. It was a long and, to Jacob, a somewhat tedious prayer. But Jacob did acknowledge that there was much for which they could be thankful. In spite of the death of little Karen Lovisa, the rest of them had all come across the great ocean during the seven and a half week ocean voyage without any serious injury, disease, or mishap. Even Sven Risland's wife, who had suffered so much from sea-sickness, compounded by the death of her child, had recovered from the worst of her afflictions. Yet, in her inner thoughts, she was still plagued by the twin demons of grief and guilt.

The next morning the passengers were loaded into boats to be transported ashore where they would meet the American immigration authorities in order to enter this new Land of Promise. True to his word, Captain Helgesen joined the passengers in the very first boat ashore so that he could personally see to it that each of them was dealt with properly by the authorities; and he also was prepared to send his mate, Niels Aslesen, to accompany the entire group as far as Albany in order to see that they were all well on their way to their new destinations in America.

Once ashore, there was some tedious waiting in line to be interviewed by American authorities. The interviews had to be conducted through interpreters. The interpreter assigned to Jacob and the others in his party was a rather surly Dane who seemed, by his very arrogance, to suggest that Norwegians were an inferior sort of people who really ought not be admitted to this new land, but with reluctance he was forced to approve their entry because he could find nothing wrong with their papers. Anlaug Risland feared that in her weakened condition she might not pass the physical examination. She had lost her usual rosy glow of health and was now sallow and gaunt in appearance, but the examining doctor passed her through the line without so much as a question.

Gunder was disappointed to find out that it would be two days before they could get steamer passage up the Hudson River to Albany, but he was able to get tickets both on the steamer and then on the railroad from Albany to Buffalo. Meanwhile the first mate, Niels Aslesen, found accommodations for Gunder's whole party in a boarding house run by a portly German lady not far from the dock where the steamer was scheduled to leave in two days. Aslesen was able to speak to the German lady in her own language, explaining that these people needed some opportunity to get refreshed and bathed, as well as a fare of good food for the next two days, especially the poor lady who had lost her child during the voyage.

The German lady, Frau Riemenschneider, clucked and chortled in her own language like a mother hen. When she showed Aase a special room with a large tin tub and an abundant supply of soap, hot water, and towels, Aase immediately mustered the children, one by one, into the tub for a thorough scrubbing.

After several hours the scrubbing was all done, and Frau Riemenschneider motioned for everyone to come into her dining room where she had prepared a sumptuous home-cooked meal. Jacob savored the smell of that wonderful meal for years afterwards. She had fried fresh pork chops, and if her guests could have understood her explanations they would know that she was trying to tell them that her husband and son had just butchered two fat hogs, and this was the first meal from that butchering. There were cooked potatoes with delicious gravy, mounds of sauerkraut, pickled beets, and tasty dill pickles. Some of these delicacies none of her guests had ever tasted before. For the children, there were glasses of fresh milk, and for the adults, lager beer. In spite of Gunder's stern opposition to strong drink, he had no objections to this beer. It was always a good Norwegian custom, even in the homes of the "holy ones," to brew beer, especially at Christmas time. But this German lager beer, Gunder admitted, was very special; he had never tasted anything quite like it before.

After the main course, Frau Riemenschneider came into the room with a strawberry torte and coffee for all of the adults. Never in his life had Jacob tasted anything so delicious. Even when the sweet cherries at Skredderstue graced their table at home, his mother was never able to concoct anything to equal Frau Riemenschneider's torte.

After this sumptuous meal, it was time to put all the children to bed. The bedrooms were large and cheerful, with big downy feather ticks on each bed. The children had never seen such luxury and were overwhelmed with curiosity about sleeping in such nice beds. Two of the youngest boys, Halvor and Lasse, suddenly complained of stomachaches. The food had been too rich and delicious for their small stomachs. Aase was embarrassed when the boys heaved up most of their suppers into the slop jar and scolded the boys sharply for their greediness. The boys soon recovered and fell asleep from exhaustion.

On the walls of each of the bedrooms was a crucifix and in the room where Gunder and Aase slept, with their boys, there was a lithograph of the Sacred Heart of Jesus. It was obvious that the Riemenschneiders were Roman Catholics. Gunder had never met anyone before in his whole life who was Roman Catholic. He had always thought of Catholics as utterly beyond hope of salvation because of the corruptions of their church, but he had to admit, privately, in his own thinking, that this fine lady who had taken them in showed a wonderful hospitality befitting a true Christian.

The next morning Frau Riemenschneider had a delicious breakfast waiting for them. Jacob began to wonder what Niels Aslesen had told this remarkable lady that they should be treated in such a pampered fashion. He knew the boarding house was not unreasonably priced, and he had heard tales of terrible boarding houses with bad food and filthy beds. How he wished he might communicate freely with this wonderful lady, but their communication was limited largely to smiles and gestures. Of course, Frau Riemenschneider could understand the few English words and phrases Jacob was able to use, and in this manner he was able to express his "thank you for the good food."

After breakfast, Jacob decided to take a walk about town on his own. He had been confined too long with the two families and their children, and now he wanted to see some of the sights of New York on his own. He wandered about, overwhelmed at the number of fine carriages and beautiful horses that were prancing up and down the streets. There were horse-drawn trolleys on several of the streets, but Jacob did not dare to show his ignorance by attempting to ride them, so he continued to walk. On one corner he paused for a long time, listening to an organ grinder with a little monkey. He had seen a monkey once before in Rotterdam, but he was fascinated with the antics of this little creature. At last he felt obligated to give the organ grinder a small contribution, so he reached into his pocket for a small coin, and he handed it into the tin cup which the monkey held out to him.

Jacob now had only American money. Fortunately, Niels Aslesen assisted everyone in his party to get a fair exchange for their Norwegian money. Several times on his walk Jacob was accosted by men who spotted him as a newcomer and wanted, as nearly as he could make out, to exchange his money. He had been warned against having anything to do with these people because invariably they cheated immigrants.

All too soon the time came to take leave of Frau Riemenschneider's establishment. This had been a most pleasant and refreshing interlude on their long journey, and they were reluctant to leave. When the time came to say good-bye to this good lady, she embraced both Aase and Anlaug with crushing bear hugs, and she patted each of the children, embracing them warmly.

The steamboat *Knickerbocker* was ready for boarding early on the second morning of their stay in New York. They had ample time to walk to the dock, knowing that their luggage had been cared for by Niels Aslesen's watchful eye. They had never seen any vessel quite like the *Knickerbocker*, with its large side-wheels and belching smokestacks. It had three passenger decks; and, as immigrant passengers, they were confined to the lowest deck. Men and women, dressed in their finery, boarded the upper decks; and everyone in Gunder's party looked on with amazed curiosity to see these American aristocrats board the ship. Suddenly ear-piercing steam whistles began to blow, and the *Knickerbocker* left the dock and headed north on its run to Albany.

After passing the Palisades of New Jersey, the countryside became very scenic. There were beautiful estates nestled in the hillsides. The journey to Albany was scheduled to last nine hours, and after several hours the ship passed West Point which was pointed out to all of the passengers as the place where America's military officers were trained. The scenery was lovely, and it was tempting for Jacob and the others to wonder why they needed to journey so much farther westward to find a good home in this new land. Yet the reality was that no immigrant could hope to find cheaply priced land in this well settled region. The people who lived in these parts had already been here for a number of generations, and there would be scant opportunity for a newcomer to find a place here.

The nine hours passed quickly. When they arrived at the dock at Albany, it was but a short distance to a large white wooden building named "Traveler's Inn." It was considerably larger than Frau Riemenschneider's cozy boarding house where they had been the only guests. Niels Aslesen had arranged this accommodation for Gunder's party; meanwhile he excused himself from their party because he needed to get the Telemark passengers who had been their shipmates onto the canal boats which would take them on their slow passage to Buffalo. After tonight Gunder's party would no longer see these Telemark people. Their destination was also Wisconsin, but Jacob learned that they planned to settle in a different part of Wisconsin, in a new settlement west of Madison.

The "Traveler's Inn" was a busy place, and the food could not begin to compare to Frau Riemenschneider's fare. After the children had been settled in bed, Niels Aslesen joined Gunder's party and shared a narrow bed with Jacob for the night. It was destined to be a short night because they needed to get up at four o'clock in order to have a quick breakfast and then make their way to the railway station where the train which would carry them westward was waiting to be boarded. No one in Gunder's party had so much as seen a railway train before, so this would indeed be a special adventure for everyone.

Niels Aslesen was there to help them get aboard the train which stood ready on its track, and he also made sure all their baggage was aboard. Gunder's party was assigned to Car Nine. The seats were numbered, and on each ticket the seat reservation number was printed. Two people could sit side by side on the cushioned seats, and Jacob was assigned to sit with Lasse Risland.

After a considerable wait, the conductor yelled out loudly, "All aboard!" Within seconds they heard the steam engine blow its shrill whistle and the train began to move. This movement was a strange sensation to everyone in the party. Never before had they experienced anything quite like it. The trees began to whirl past the window at dizzying speed; and Jacob understood, from what they had been told by Niels Aslesen, the train covered no less than thirty English miles or more in one hour.

After less than an hour on the moving train, it stopped for about ten minutes at Schenectady. Some passengers left the train and others got on. Jacob and Lasse stepped onto the platform and watched as the engine took on fuel and water. The engine made strange hissing and belching noises, and Jacob had to reassure little Lasse that there was nothing to fear from these terrible noises. After the stop at Schenectady, the train entered the Mohawk Valley, This was a very lovely area of New York State, with mountains on either side of the fertile valley which had many beautiful farms and towns. In some ways the scenery reminded Jacob of Norway, but the houses and barns were distinctly American. Jacob wondered how Wisconsin would compare to this beautiful country. Beint had already written that Jacob should not expect mountains in Wisconsin, only some gently rolling hills.

Later in the day the train made a stop at Syracuse. There was much scurrying of passengers on and off the train, and Jacob and the others in Gunder's party were able to purchase some food from a vendor. During the hours following, they could see many beautiful farms, usually with white wooden houses and red barns. They passed through many small villages, often stopping briefly to take on or discharge passengers.

As evening approached, the train pulled into the station at Rochester, one of the larger cities on their railway journey. They were informed that there would be a stop of one hour here, long enough for everyone to disembark and have a quick meal at one of the nearby restaurants. When they got back on the train, they had only a three hour journey to get to Buffalo, and they arrived in Buffalo about 11:30 p.m. Niels Aslesen had arranged for them to stay at a boarding house near the railway station, operated by an elderly French-Canadian and his wife. The tired children were hustled into bed, and the adults wasted little time in joining them in slumber, tired as they all were from their journey. This boarding house was not nearly as elegant as Frau Riemenschneider's place, nor were the beds as soft. But it was clean, and they all settled in for another brief night of rest because they needed to board their steamship early the next morning.

The *Victoria* was a steamship very similar in design to the *Knickerbocker* upon which they had journeyed from New York to Albany. Like the *Knickerbocker*, the *Victoria* had three decks, and Gunder's party was confined to the lower deck for the next five days, together with more than a hundred other immigrants. Most of the other immigrant passengers were from Germany, but there were several other parties of Scandinavians, as well as a number of Irish immigrants.

Jacob soon discovered, shortly after boarding, that five young men from Valdres were planning to disembark at Manitowoc, the port of call just north of Sheboygan; and he also discovered that there was a party of Swedish immigrants headed for Illinois. Oddly, Jacob found it somewhat easier to understand some of the Swedes than those fellows from Valdres because of their heavy dialect. One of the Swedes was also fluent in German and was able to gain the information that most of the Germans were headed for ports in Wisconsin, including a party of about twenty who were scheduled to disembark at Sheboygan.

The port at Buffalo was very busy with vessels of all kinds, and many tongues were spoken by the multitudes of immigrants that traveled through Buffalo on their way westward. Jacob saw his party's luggage, including those two large curved-topped chests, hoisted aboard by Negro dock workers. Jacob had seen Negroes once before in the port city of Rotterdam, but the rest of Gunder's party had never seen black people. The children stared at these men, bewildered that other human beings could actually have such dark skins. Jacob told the children that in the southern American states black people were held as slaves, that they had been transported from their original homes in Africa to provide labor in the cotton fields of the South. But these fellows, Jacob said, are not slaves. They probably escaped from the South and came to the North in order to be free and were now working as laborers to earn a livelihood here in Buffalo.

All of a sudden, Jacob and the children were startled by the sharp blast of the ship's steam whistle, and a few moments later the gangplank was pulled aboard ship from the dock, the huge ropes that tied the *Victoria* to the dock were unloosened, and the ship began to move out onto the waters of Lake Erie. The water was calm, nearly like a sheet of glass, and the great ship floated smoothly across the water, leaving the port of Buffalo behind within a matter of minutes. Jacob wondered if the surface of Lake Erie was always this smooth. Later, he had an opportunity to talk to a Scandinavian seaman who was one of the crew members on the *Victoria,* and he said the Great Lakes could get very rough if there were storms and high winds. He added that quite a few ships had been lost during storms that could come up suddenly on these lakes.

Jacob found the five young men from Valdres to be jolly fellows, even though he strained to understand their dialect. It turned out that they had time while in Buffalo to take a special trip downstream some miles from Buffalo to see the great falls at Niagara. Jacob was fascinated with hearing about the adventures these good fellows had enjoyed, and regretted that he and the rest of Gunder's party had not had time to take in this most remarkable place. Jacob vowed that someday he would try to return to Buffalo, just to see the falls. One of the Valdres fellows had a cheap lithograph which attempted to depict the grandeur of the falls; but, as he said, one had to visit the place personally in order to experience its real splendor.

The *Victoria* was scheduled to make its first stop in Cleveland late on the first day. The shoreline at Cleveland was, for the most part, low-lying and flat; but there were many signs that this was a thriving town. Quite a few of the elegantly dressed people from the upper decks disembarked at Cleveland, but none of the passengers from the lower deck left the ship. By the time the ship left Cleveland, the sky was dark, but a bright full moon was shining down upon them, and this made navigating the ship nearly as easy as during the daylight hours. Jacob and the others watched the dim lights of Cleveland disappear below the horizon, and then they all decided it was time to lie down on the crude bunks inside their large area, much larger than the steerage hold aboard the *Juno*.

Early the next morning the ship approached the narrow water passage that led past Detroit, having passed some small islands and the narrow passage separating the United States from Canada. A number of passengers disembarked at Detroit, but few passengers came aboard. Among those who did embark were several native American Indians, the first of this race seen on this journey. They are sometimes called "red men," but it seemed to Jacob that they could more properly be called "brown men."

Leaving Detroit, the ship passed through Lake St. Clair and on through an exceedingly narrow passage that led to Sarnia before entering upon the waters of Lake Huron. The next destination of the *Victoria* was Mackinac Island, near the Straits of Mackinac where Lake Huron joins Lake Michigan. Here the ship was scheduled to stop for some hours, and all the passengers were given leave to disembark, but with strict instructions to return within three hours' time. The island contained a military fort, a small village populated by fishermen and traders, and a considerable number of Indians who met the passengers with furs and moccasins and other goods they wished to sell for American dollars.

Most of the immigrant passengers were too cautious with their limited dollars to spend money on trinkets, but one of the Norwegian boys from Valdres bought a pair of moccasins he intended to send back to a young lady in Norway whom he hoped would join him in America the following year and become his wife. Meanwhile the ship took on board hardwood logs to be used as fuel for the steam boiler for the remainder of the journey to Chicago.

When the *Victoria* left Mackinac Island near the end of the fourth day of the journey, she headed for Manitou Island in Lake

Michigan. It was nearly dark when the ship pulled into a crude dock to receive more fuel. Manitou Island, it turned out, was another of the fueling stations along the route taken by steamships on the Great Lakes, and the inhabitants earned a scanty living by cutting timber to feed the hungry burning bellies of a whole fleet of steamships. Because of this practice, in some places one saw many acres of stumps where there were formerly thick hardwood forests. The wood had to be cut well ahead of its use on the ships, so it was piled in great heaps near the docks where it was allowed to dry out sufficiently to be burned as fuel.

The first stop on the fifth day, fairly early in the day, was Manitowoc, on the eastern shore of Wisconsin. One of the crewmen explained to Jacob that ordinarily the ship did not stop at either Manitowoc or Sheboygan, but if there were passengers who wished to disembark at those ports, a brief stop was made. Only the five fellows from Valdres disembarked on this voyage, but Gunder and all the others in his party were excited at their first glimpse of Wisconsin. Many of the buildings at the small port were crudely constructed of logs, but some more substantial buildings of wood and brick had been built recently. Everywhere it seemed there were large stumps where great trees recently stood near the shoreline. The land was low-lying and nearly flat, but in the distance were rolling hills which were heavily wooded.

When the ship left Manitowoc there was a flurry of excitement in Gunder's group because they knew that within several hours they would come to Sheboygan, their final destination on board this ship. About twenty of the German immigrants also were scheduled to disembark at Sheboygan, so there was a considerable flurry of activity as the ship neared the crude dock. Like Manitowoc, Sheboygan was a young settlement, with a few brick and frame buildings intermingled with log structures. The roads were dusty and well-rutted, and the sidewalks on the main streets were made of planks. Most of the original stand of trees had been cut down, and there were stumps nearly everywhere. Many types of vehicles, some horse drawn and others pulled by oxen, made their way along the rutted roads.

Gunder had received from his friend, Anton Møller, the name and address of Carl Sorlien, a Norwegian who lived in Sheboygan and ran a livery stable with a Yankee partner. After Gunder's party disembarked from the *Victoria*, the first order of business was to find Sorlien. According to Møller, Sorlien was helpful to any Scandinavian immigrants who might land in Sheboygan. There were actually very few Norwegian families living in Sheboygan at this time, perhaps ten or twelve at the most; yet Sheboygan did serve as a convenient gateway for Scandinavian immigrants.

Jacob volunteered to run ahead of the rest of the party in an attempt to find Sorlien; the others had to stay close by their baggage which was piled in a heap near the pier.

As Jacob ran in the direction of the main business section of the town, he asked the first person that he met a one-word question, "Sorlien?" Luckily, the person recognized the name and also realized that Jacob could not speak English very well, so he pointed in the direction of the south end of the main business district. Jacob hurried to that location and quickly saw, painted in large letters above a large wooden structure, *Matthew Ames and Carl Sorlien, Livery Stable.*

As he entered the building, he smelled the pungent odor of the horse stable and soon found Carl Sorlien busily forking hay to some of his animals. Sorlien was glad to hear his native language spoken by this young intruder and asked Jacob to help him harness a team of horses to a large wagon. As soon as this was done, the two of them drove to where Gunder's party was patiently waiting.

Sorlien came from Tvedestrand, not so far from Arendal, only four years earlier, and he was anxious to hear the news from Gunder's party. The men loaded the baggage onto the wagon, and then Sorlien directed the Tøvesen family to his own house and deposited the Risland family with his nearest Norwegian neighbor, Elling Strand. In both instances the accommodations were simple, but the hospitality was genuine. Jacob was assigned to a bunk in the livery stable, but invited to take his meals at the Sorlien home which adjoined the livery stable in the rear.

The day that Gunder's party came to Sheboygan was July third. Almost immediately Carl Sorlien told his newly found countrymen: "You must stay here with us at least until July fifth so that you can celebrate your first Fourth of July on American soil right here in Sheboygan. You will need to take that amount of time to rest up from your long journey and make more specific plans about your journey to the Neenah Settlement from here."

Almost forgotten in all of this initial excitement was Jacob's plan to get in touch with Beint Gauslaa at the soonest possible moment, but when Jacob interrupted Sorlien long enough to ask him if he knew Beint, he got an unexpected answer.

"Yes, of course, I know Beint, as you call him. He's now known as Ben Johnson in these parts. But do you know what's happened to your friend, Jacob? He's no longer living in these parts. About a month ago, he and two Yankee boys got a bad case of gold fever and decided to head all the way out to California. I tried to tell him he was crazy, but he wouldn't listen to an old codger like me. I just hope those boys'll make it way out there without getting killed by Indians or bitten by snakes or dead from starvation."

Jacob was utterly stunned by this news. How could Beint leave the good life he described in his letters for something as wild and uncertain as gold in California? Furthermore, he was really depending upon Beint to help him find a place in this new land, and now he had no special friend to help him. Jacob suddenly felt devastated and despondent, and he was tempted to shed tears of self-pity. Was this disappointment an omen of worse things to come? Jacob did not sleep well during his first night in Wisconsin.

The Long Winter

Carl Sorlien proved to be a godsend to Jacob in his confusion and despair. For several weeks after Gunder and his party left for the Neenah Settlement in a wagon pulled by a team of horses they hired from Sorlien, Jacob worked in the livery stable to pay for his room and board with the Sorliens. Carl's wife, Gro, took a maternal interest in Jacob and cooked wholesome meals, and he soon recovered from his long journey.

He soon learned more and more English as he was forced each day to communicate with others in the livery stable. Especially helpful was a Yankee lad who also worked at the livery stable now and then. John Wright was a broad-faced fellow with an excellent sense of humor, and he got on well with Jacob. To be sure, he laughed heartily at Jacob's attempts to use the English language, but then he would always, with great patience, coach Jacob on the correct usage and pronunciation; and Jacob proved to be an apt pupil, grateful for the instruction John was able to provide.

About three weeks later, Carl Sorlien suddenly called Jacob into the front part of the livery stable.

"Jacob, I would like to have you meet a good friend of mine, Mr. Adam Cartwright of Fond du Lac."

"How do you do, Mr. Cartwright."

Carl Sorlien now turned to Jacob, speaking to him in Norwegian so there would be no misunderstanding on Jacob's part.

"Mr. Cartwright is looking for someone with carpentry skills to help his master carpenter with the construction of his new house.

We would like to have you stay on here with us at the livery stable, but when I heard that he was looking for a carpenter I immediately thought of you. It could be a good opportunity for you."

"Yes, I think I would be interested in using my skills as a carpenter, but I'll need to know a bit more about the job."

"Mr. Cartwright has a farm about three miles south of the village of Fond du Lac, which is about forty miles due west of here. In addition to the carpentry help, he may need some help from time to time with the farm work, especially during planting and harvest times.

"I think it will be helpful for me to know more about how farming is done in America, as well as the opportunity to work with American carpenters. Did you tell Mr. Cartwright that I was apprenticed as a ship's carpenter in Norway."

"Yes, he knows about your background. I can assure you that Adam Cartwright is an honest man with a good reputation. He is regarded as one of the best wheat growers in our region, and he is also a blacksmith by trade. He is known as a hard worker, but you can be sure that he will never abuse you or mistreat you in any way."

"Well, I'm not afraid of hard work, but he must understand that my knowledge of English is very limited at this point."

"Yes, but I think this job will give you a good opportunity to learn English much faster than if you continued to stay here with us in our Norwegian household."

"Yes, that's true."

"Your friend, Beint Gauslaa, spoke to me several times how important it was for him to live right with a Yankee family. Within a very short time he was chatting in English nearly as well as the Yankees themselves."

"I think I also should know what kind of wages he intends to pay before I make up my mind one way or another."

Carl Sorlien then turned to Adam Cartwright and they discussed together the terms of Jacob's employment. When Carl explained the terms to Jacob, he agreed that the wages were fair and he was ready to accept the job. It was finally agreed that Jacob would travel the next day with Cartwright. It would take two days by horse and wagon to get to Cartwright's farm, and they would need to spend one night at Greenbush on their journey.

Early on the morning of July twenty-fourth Jacob hoisted his seaman's chest onto Cartwright's wagon, bid farewell to Carl and Gro Sorlien and joined Adam Cartwright on the seat in the front of the wagon. In the back of the wagon was a load of milled black walnut Cartwright had received from a German woodworker in Milwaukee and intended to use in the construction of the main staircase in his new house, as well as some special milled trim pieces for use in other locations. The milled lumber had arrived in Sheboygan by steamship from Milwaukee.

The horses and wagon jostled along over the rough and rutted trail. There were numerous small hills to climb, and then sudden descents into narrow valleys. Everywhere there was a heavy growth of trees, and at times the trail was so narrow that the wagon could barely wedge its way through the tree limbs. They came upon whole fields strewn with stumps with a ripe crop of wheat growing between them, and in several instances there were crews of men, women and children busily cradling the standing wheat, tying the wheat into bundles, and setting the bundles into shocks.

In one of these valleys Adam Cartwright's wagon got stuck in a rut of mud, and the wheels suddenly sank so deeply into the mud that the horses were unable to pull it out. Jacob wondered if there was any possible way the wagon could be moved. Would they have to abandon the wagon and proceed to Greenbush, about ten miles away, on foot? But Adam Cartwright told Jacob to unhitch the horses and lead them off to the side for a well deserved rest; meanwhile he ran off in the direction of the nearest log cabin about a half a mile away.

In about half an hour Adam returned with the owner of the log cabin who was leading a yoke of oxen. Jacob wondered how Adam thought these plodding oxen could possibly pull that wagon out when the horses had failed, but Jacob had to admit that his experiences with oxen were quite limited. At Skredderstua they had always farmed with horses, those sure-footed tan fjord horses so commonly found on Norwegian farms. It had surprised Jacob to see how often the American settlers seemed to rely upon oxen instead of horses, but he assumed it was surely a matter of what the settlers could afford.

When the farmer came with his oxen, it took a bit of skill to hitch them to the wagon. Once they were properly hitched, the farmer prodded them mercilessly with his goad, accompanied with a good deal of yelling. Jacob couldn't quite make out what the farmer was saying to his beasts, but assumed that the language used was not the sort one would use in polite company. The oxen bent into their yoke with utter determination until, miracle of miracles, the wagon wheels began to creak and move; and gradually the heavy wagon was pulled out of the mud hole unto dry ground.

Adam handed the farmer a whole dollar for his effort and for the use of his oxen. Jacob had already learned that a dollar was the usual wage for a full day's work; this was a princely sum for just half an hour's effort on the part of the farmer and his oxen. Perhaps the farmer refused to come for anything less, but Jacob did not think it wise to ask Adam why he paid the farmer so much.

"Jacob, you have now seen for yourself why sometimes oxen are preferred over horses for certain tasks."

"Yes, I am amazed that the oxen could pull our wagon out of that mud hole."

"Our good team of horses seemed only to balk and panic when our wagon got stuck so firmly in this deep mud-hole, but the oxen are perhaps too dumb to panic; they only continued to pull and pull, throwing their steady weight against the yoke until at last the wagon wheels began to move. It is the same way when farmers try to pull out stumps from their fields. The oxen are superior to horses for this task as well. Many of these farmers swear by their oxen and would not trade them for the finest horses in the world."

Jacob strained to understand all of Adam Cartwright's words, but nodded his head that he at least got the gist of what was said.

The next hours passed quickly until at last they came to a small settlement of log buildings. This was Greenbush, and they were scheduled to stay overnight here at Mr. Wade's "Half-Way House," as he called it. The primitive log house was a far cry from Frau Riemenschneider's establishment in New York, or even some of the other inns Jacob recalled from his long journey across half the continent to Wisconsin. But Adam Cartwright knew Mr. Wade quite well, and they greeted each other as old friends. Adam then introduced Jacob to Mr. Wade and they shook hands vigorously. Jacob had some difficulty following the conversation, but he understood that they were talking a good deal about the condition of the road they had just come over, and Adam complained that it had been necessary to hire a farmer with his oxen to pull his wagon out of the mud hole.

Wade responded, "Yes, there are some places where the trail is very bad. I have been trying to get some action on building a plank road all the way from Sheboygan to Fond du Lac."

Adam concurred, "If we ever hope to settle this great state we need to improve our roads so we can move goods and people better."

Changing the subject, Wade spoke in a confident and cheerful voice,

"Did I tell you that I've been making some plans to build an inn across the road to accommodate the ever-increasing stream of travelers that come by this place each week? I've made some sketches that show how I expect the inn will look when it's completed."

Jacob was also invited to look at the sketches and was impressed to see a three-story structure with square pillars in the front, a far cry from the crude log cabin called Half-Way House that was to be their home for the night. Meanwhile, Mrs. Wade prepared a delicious meal of roast pork, complete with potatoes, gravy, applesauce, and apple cider to drink. It didn't quite come up to Frau Riemenschneider's bill of fare, but after the tedious and tiring journey over the primitive road, it tasted very good.

Adam and Jacob were assigned a narrow bed in the loft. When Jacob stretched out on the bed he was startled to hear strange crunching sounds. He was lying on a mattress stuffed with corn husks. This was quite different from the down mattresses upon which he was used to sleeping in Norway, or even the feather or straw ticks that were commonly used in America. But Jacob was dead tired and soon fell asleep on his bed of corn husks.

In the late afternoon of the next day Jacob and Adam Cartwright drove into the yard of the Cartwright farm. Nearly all the buildings, with the exception of two small sheds, were constructed of logs. The house was a modest log cabin, but near this cabin was a large gaping hole in the ground, lined with the rough masonry of freshly laid stones. In fact, the masons had just finished their task several days earlier, and soon it would be the task of the carpenters to erect a framework on this stone foundation. The dimensions of the new house seemed princely in contrast to the cramped little log house in which the Cartwright family was now quartered.

The family consisted of Adam, his wife, Charlotte, and five children. The oldest daughter, Edith, was a grown young lady of eighteen. The next two children were also girls: Hannah, fourteen, and Judith, twelve. Then came the two small Cartwright boys: Adam Jr., nine, and Sylvester, seven.

In addition to Jacob, there were two other hired hands: Frank Maier, a young German immigrant boy of eighteen, and Peter Smith, a red-faced Yankee about thirty-five years old. Peter was the master carpenter and would be Jacob's boss during the construction process. Frank, on the other hand, was expected to be the herdsman for Adam's growing herd of red-brindled cattle that now numbered twelve milking cows, five heifers, a bull, and three small calves. This was considered a large herd, and it was Adam's intention gradually to have an even larger herd. Frank had grown up in his small German farming village caring for cattle; and, in spite of his youth, knew a great deal about cattle. He even assisted in making butter and cheese from the milk produced by Adam's herd.

Frank, Peter and Jacob were assigned sleeping quarters in a small outbuilding quite recently constructed of rough boards.

"This building will eventually be used as a chicken coop, but before we turn it over to the chickens it will be our home during the summer and early autumn, before it gets too cold," Peter explained to Jacob.

And so the three of them – Yankee, German and Norwegian – made a strange trio. Frank had been in America long enough to get on quite well with English, but he spoke with a noticeable

German brogue. Jacob had some difficulty in understanding each of his other companions, but he understood that this situation would force him to learn English more quickly than if he were to be with his own people.

Adam Cartwright owned and farmed a quarter of section of land, one hundred and sixty acres. This seemed to Jacob to be a mighty estate. About half the land had been in natural prairie when Adam purchased it six years earlier. The Cartwrights had come from New York state six years ago and were among the first settlers to take up land in their immediate neighborhood. Now they were beginning to see the little village of Fond du Lac grow at the foot of the big lake called Winnebago after the Indian tribe that once inhabited this area. In addition to being a farmer, Adam Cartwright was also a blacksmith; and one of the earliest log buildings erected on his place was a smithy. Even now, Adam carried on a considerable business at his smithy, servicing the needs of his neighbors by shoeing their horses and oxen as the occasion demanded. He complained that the farm was beginning to demand too much of his time to continue his work at the smithy.

During the last several years Adam had been busy felling tall trees that stood on that portion of his land which was not open prairie. He hauled many of the logs to a sawmill operating in the little town of Fond du Lac, only about three miles from his farm, and the logs were transformed into the boards and structural timbers to be used in building his new house.

"We have lived long enough in that little log cabin," Adam told Jacob, "When one has a gentle lady as a wife and three growing daughters, they long for the luxury of a good house, the kind of house they remember from back East, and so that is the kind of house we shall build."

Then Adam showed Jacob the crude sketches he had made of the house he intended to build. It was to be built like a Greek temple made of wood, with two full stories. Of ample dimension, it would contain no less than five bedrooms on the second floor. Much of the woodwork was to be of black walnut; Adam had a number of these trees on his property. He had the logs sawed at the mill, and some of the boards had been taken to the Milwaukee shop of a clever German immigrant who did the shaping and carving which would enhance the genteel design of the home. The German woodworker had spent most of his time on the trim for the open stairway with its rails and spindles and treads. When completed, the stairway would be the envy of the entire county in its elegance. The millwork done by this German artisan had been carried in the wagon which Adam and Jacob had driven from Sheboygan to Fond du Lac, and it was now carefully stored in one of the log outbuildings.

Before work could begin on framing the house, it was necessary to harvest the crop of wheat. Cartwright possessed one of the few reapers in use at that time, and it made the task of harvesting much easier than if the whole field had to be cut with a cradle. The reaper was pulled through the field by a team of horses. It cut a swath of grain as it went, but a man had to rake each swath from the apron of the reaper, just enough to form a good bundle, and then other hands tied the swath into a bundle and set the bundles into shocks. All hands on the farm were needed for harvesting. Even the girls were pressed into service as they helped to tie the bundles and set them into shocks.

Adam had nearly thirty acres in wheat, a large amount for that time, and his crop of wheat created wealth that was the envy of many of his neighbors.

Adam not only had the advantage of owning a reaper; he also possessed a Chicago-Pitts thresher which could be powered by horses. He had made this substantial investment two years before. Earlier, when his crop was much smaller, it was necessary to use a hand flail to thresh his crop. Jacob was utterly amazed to see how these modern machines could be used to reduce the agonizing and back-breaking labor that had always been associated with the harvesting of grain. When Jacob was assigned, during the threshing days, to bag the golden wheat as it streamed from the machine, he realized that this wheat, which could feed many families with bread for a whole year, was also creating wealth for Adam and his family. It was a kind of gold that he was putting into each bag.

Then he thought once more of his friend, Beint Gauslaa, who had left this land which was capable of producing such a crop of golden wheat on his wild quest for gold in distant California. How do you suppose Beint was doing? Had he arrived in California yet? Had he discovered his first nugget of gold? Perhaps it was only a tiny fleck in the bottom of a pan. Jacob thought he would rather be dealing with this golden crop of wheat than the kind of gold that lured Beint and his companions west to distant California.

At last the harvesting was completed, and much of Adam's crop of wheat was sold for a fair price. Now work could finally begin on framing the new house.

Several additional men were hired for a few days to help Peter and Jacob with the framing. First the rough-sawed joists were laid upon the masonry foundation, enclosing the cavernous cellar and forming the base for the whole superstructure of the house. The house was to be framed in a manner called the "balloon-frame" which Jacob had never heard of. The framing members were called "two by fours," slim by Jacob's reckoning, but set on center every sixteen inches. Peter assured Jacob that this method of framing was not only adequate, but once the house was enclosed with sheathing boards, it was as strong as the old-fashioned mode of framing with heavy timbers. But Jacob remained a bit skeptical; however, he was quite amazed to see how quickly the house took shape by this new method of construction. But it certainly took an enormous number of nails. It was a good thing Adam could use his smithy to forge some of them. Jacob pounded nails so many days, from morning to night, that he thought his right arm was ready to fall off.

Gradually, Jacob caught on to all of the tricks of this new method of building houses; and he realized that the sooner he gained confidence in building in this manner, the sooner his career as a carpenter would be assured. Peter Smith was a good teacher, but upon occasion he could be a bit impatient and short tempered. Jacob, however, with his good humor, was able to get along with Peter very well; and at times Peter actually commended Jacob for his good work. Jacob was very adept at fitting tight places that needed to be planed or shaped with a drawshave, and Peter actually marveled at how clever Jacob could be in these situations. The training Jacob had aboard the *Neptune* with Dietrich Gunderson now stood him in good stead as a carpenter in the New World.

The heat of summer gradually gave way to the cooler temperatures of autumn, and the leaves began to take on their magic color in late September. The house was enclosed and the windows installed. Now Jacob and Peter spent many hours nailing lath to the studs, preparing the walls for their coats of plaster. It was slow and tedious work, and at the end of each day it was hard to see much sign of progress. At last, one day in early October, the lathing was finished, and the next week the plasterers arrived. Jacob was assigned to help these fellows, but soon discovered it was a messy job. After the finishing coat had been applied, Peter and Jacob mounted the window frames and did other finishing touches. One proud day, later in October, Peter called Mrs. Cartwright and her daughters into the new house. He and Jacob had just completed installing the woodwork in the parlor, including the hardwood floor, and Peter wanted the ladies to have the first glimpse of this handsome room. All that remained to finish this room was to hang the wallpaper and bring in the furniture, the carpet and the curtains.

About this time Jacob became aware that Edith Cartwright seemed to be seeking out every possible opportunity to talk with him. Under the pretext of helping Jacob learn English, she would spend hours in his company, chatting with him while he was trying to work without distraction. Jacob, of course, was flattered by all this attention from an attractive young lady, but Peter took a dimmer view of these goings-on. On several occasions he spoke with Jacob privately, warning him not to encourage these attentions from Edith. Peter's main concern seemed to be that her presence was distracting Jacob from doing his best work, but Jacob wondered if Peter might have other motives in giving voice to his warnings. Could it be that Peter, an eligible bachelor, was jealous of this young Norse newcomer? Did Peter have some thoughts of courting Edith? To be sure, he was nearly double her age, but stranger things have happened. Jacob felt uncomfortable. He had not courted Edith's attentions, but he had to admit that he found Edith a charming and attractive young lady and enjoyed her presence. He also noticed that Edith's mother was finding more and more occasions to call her away from his company, assigning petty tasks to draw her away.

Suddenly, one day in late October, Jacob was surprised to learn that Edith was going to leave the next day on a long journey to Fort Atkinson, in southern Wisconsin, to visit her aunt who had been in failing health recently. Jacob also learned that she would not be returning to Fond du Lac in the near future. After several months with her aunt, Edith was scheduled to enroll in the Baptist academy at Beaver Dam in January for the spring term.

On the morning of her departure, Edith made a quick visit to the new house to say good-bye to both Peter and Jacob. She was very nervous as she said her good-bye to Jacob, and he saw tears welling up in her eyes as she darted from the room.

Several months later Peter confided to Jacob that the Cartwrights had sent their daughter away because they didn't want her to become overly fond of any young immigrant foreigner. She should be put into an environment where she could meet proper Yankee young men and not have to settle for a penniless foreigner. Jacob was crushed by this knowledge. Indeed, he had not sought any attention or affection from Edith, but it bothered him that Edith's parents would suspect him of exploiting the vulnerable young Edith. Jacob was thankful she was now no longer around, much as he had enjoyed her companionship just a few short weeks ago.

The mild and pleasant autumn days soon turned raw and cold, and Jacob was preparing to spend his first winter in America. One day in November, a letter came to Jacob from his brother Elias:

14 August, 1849

Dear Brother,

Not much has changed at Skredderstua since you left. Mother and Father are both well and often speak of you and how much they miss you. They both send their greetings and hope all is well with you.

We have had too much rain, so it has been difficult to get the hay crop into our barns. Our grain crop is growing very well, and it will soon be time to harvest. The potato crop looks better than it has for the past three years, but there still are some signs of blight. Father was called up to the manor house at Longum to mend shoes and make some new shoes for the folks up there, so he has been busy. Mother is looking for a letter from you. She received a letter from her brother, Gunder Tøvesen, sent from New York, and she wonders why she doesn't get a letter from you.

Soon the cherry tree will yield its wonderful fruit once more, and Mother will insist upon making some cherry preserve to take with her next spring so you can have a taste once more from old Skredderstua. Maren and Kittel and the others can talk of little else than our plans to go to America next spring. We plan also to sail with Captain Helgesen on the Juno, and we have written him to reserve places for us, but have not heard from him yet. It may be necessary for me to go to Langesund later this autumn to make those arrangements for next spring. It seems that all of Norway is making plans to emigrate to America. At least three of our neighboring families have spoken to us of their intention to emigrate next season. . . .

The letter went on with more details about various members of the family; it was sent in care of Beint Gauslaa because Elias had no other address for Jacob, and Carl Sorlien intercepted the letter in Sheboygan and sent it on to Fond du Lac.

Winter came with unusual fury early in December. By this time Jacob and Peter had moved into a snug cabin on a neighbor's farm, about half a mile from the Cartwright farm, but Frank was living with the Cartwrights because he needed to be on hand day and night to care for the cattle. Progress on the house was slow because there were so many details left in the finishing. One by one the rooms were finished, and Mrs. Cartwright and her daughters were busy measuring for draperies, curtains, bedspreads and carpets. Shipments of new furniture, sent from Milwaukee, arrived in Sheboygan by steamboat, including a new horsehair sofa and several chairs to match for the parlor. Adam sent Jacob with a sleigh and a team of horses to fetch these items from Sheboygan, and Jacob had an opportunity to retrace the trail back through Greenbush, where he stayed once more with the Wade family, to

Sheboygan, where he met Carl Sorlien again. Thanks to a spell of good weather, he was able to load the goods and return to Fond du Lac without any difficulties.

Soon after his return from Fond du Lac, it was Christmastime. The Cartwrights invited Jacob and Peter to a fine Christmas dinner, but Jacob missed his family very much. In spite of Mrs. Cartwright's attempt at providing a festive meal, Jacob missed all the special foods his mother always prepared at Christmastime. Furthermore, the Yankees seemed hardly to celebrate Christmas at all, other than a good Christmas dinner. There was no Christmas tree, no special family celebration of Christmas Eve, no special church service even on Christmas Day. The Cartwrights were Baptists, but seldom attended church services because the nearest church of their denomination was many miles away. Jacob remembered with some nostalgia the great festive worship at Austre Moland, both on Christmas Day and Second Christmas Day, and the many parties during this season back home as neighbors and friends went from house to house during the short days of the Christmas season. But he comforted himself with the thought that next year at this time it would be much better. His family would all be here in Wisconsin, in the Neenah Settlement, and they could have a good Norwegian Christmas together again.

In January Jacob received a very sad letter from Carl Sorlien. Beint Gauslaa was dead! Word had come back to Sheboygan from Beint's two Yankee companions telling of his unfortunate death from fever as they were crossing the Rocky Mountains. Jacob was devastated by this news. He had looked forward so much to a reunion in America, but this was not to be because the gold fever had now claimed Beint as a victim. And now poor Beint, whose life had given so much promise, was destined to lie in an unmarked grave somewhere in the wilds of the American West. It was too sad for Jacob to consider for long. He spoke to Peter about his friend, and even to Adam Cartwright, and they both offered condolences; but nothing could fill the void that Jacob felt in his heart over the loss of his dear friend from childhood.

The winter wore on. Fortunately Peter and Jacob were working almost entirely inside the new house. There were those pesky details of finishing that went on endlessly. It was like a gigantic puzzle to put the staircase together properly, but finally, with a bit of planing and trimming, the stairway with its curved railing stood as the pride of Cartwright's new house. Neighbors were invited in to see this marvel of woodworking and carpentry skill, and Peter and Jacob received many compliments for their fine workmanship.

At last, on March first, the Cartwright family moved into their new home. Some of the rooms were scarcely furnished, and it would be several years before all the furniture and draperies would be completely to Mrs. Cartwright's satisfaction. But it was a great contrast to the humble and crowded log cabin that had been home to the Cartwrights ever since their arrival in these parts. The old log house was destined to become the summer kitchen, and the last major task for Peter and Jacob in the spring was to put clapboard siding over the logs in order to match the appearance of the great new house that stood beside it.

Winter's fury finally gave way to the joys of springtime with its fresh breezes and warm rains. It was time to work the land and plant the crops, and Jacob was pulled from his carpentry tasks to help with these more urgemt tasks of farming. The broad fields of Cartwright's farm were sown to wheat once more. This was Adam Cartwright's main crop and the source of his increasing wealth. Later the hay fields needed to be mowed and the hay crop stored in Adam's log barns as winter fodder for his growing herd of cattle. In June, the summer heat began to swelter and Jacob sweat profusely as he worked in Cartwright's broad fields. At night Jacob was exhausted from this hard labor, but he slept well and ate well during these early summer days.

It came on June twenty-fourth, the letter that Jacob would never forget. It was from Carl Sorlien in Sheboygan, and it was very short. It read simply:

I am most sorry to inform you that, according to a report in a New York newspaper, the Norwegian ship "Juno" sank at sea and all hands and passengers are presumed dead. It is my understanding, dear Jacob, that your family was aboard this unfortunate ship, and I must offer my profound condolences to you.

Jacob read these words, and suddenly his mind went blank and he became faint. It was bad enough to receive word of the death of Beint Gauslaa, but now this! It was by far the worst news Jacob could possibly have received. His father, his mother, Elias, all his other siblings – perished at sea. And here he was, Jacob, all alone in this strange and awesome new land. He was too stunned either to speak or to weep.

The Neenah Settlement

When Gunder Tøvesen and his party left Sheboygan in July of 1849, equipped with a hired team of horses and a wagon, headed for the Neenah Settlement, they were accompanied by a young Norwegian from Sheboygan by the name of Anders Knutson. Knutson was eighteen years of age and had lived in Sheboygan with his parents and siblings for several years, learning to speak English quite fluently. It was fortunate for Gunder that this young man was available because no one else in the party could speak English, and it would be difficult to find the way without being able to communicate during the trek from Sheboygan to the Neenah Settlement.

Furthermore, Knutson's parents, Lars and Anna Knutson, had been profoundly touched by the Haugean religious revival in Norway as young adults, and Anders was brought up in that tradition. As a result, Gunder found in Anders a fellow true believer and spent much time during the long and tedious journey over the rough and rutted trails through the forests discussing spiritual matters and sharing their experiences in the faith. Jacob also had met Anders during his first days in Sheboygan and found him rather indifferent to any overtures to friendship, but Gunder found him a ready companion and kindred spirit, in spite of their differences in age.

Anders was desirous of laying claim to some land for himself, realizing that if he stayed in Sheboygan the best he could expect was work as a day-laborer. He had managed, by scrimping ever since he could earn wages, to save a bit of a nest egg, and now he saw his opportunity to launch forward on his own as he joined Gunder's party.

The road to Fond du Lac was rough but dry during their journey, so they did not experience the difficulties that Adam and Jacob experienced some weeks later after there had been a heavy rain. They also stopped at Greenbush for their first overnight, but there was not room in the Half-Way House for such a large party, so the men and boys slept outside, while the ladies and the girls were accommodated inside. The next day they trudged on to Fond du Lac, and two days later arrived at Webster Stanley's ferry over the Fox River. There were other caravans carrying new settlers into the lands north of the Fox, and Gunder discovered another party of Norwegians. These folks, originally from Telemark, had trudged with their oxen all the way from the Muskego Settlement in Racine County and were now planning to join their relatives in the Neenah Settlement. They had survived the cholera plague in Muskego, even though it had claimed three of their small children, and they decided, as had others, that a location somewhat farther north would likely be healthier than the swamps of Muskego. Gunder's horses could move faster than those pokey oxen, so the Muskego folks were soon left behind.

Anders had been able to get good advice in locating the trails that would lead to Anton Møller's place, just north of the Ball Prairie area which was settled by Yankees; and late in the day Gunder's whole party pulled into Møller's yard.

"Hello! Hello!" Anton shouted excitedly as Gunder's party turned into his place. "We really did not expect to see you quite this soon."

"Hello, old friend," Gunder responded loudly. "Yes, we are really here at last. Our good ship *Juno* made the crossing in seven and a half weeks."

"Then you made better time than we did four years ago. We were nearly nine weeks on the ocean. But now you must tell me who all these folks are that have come with you."

At that very moment Anton's wife, Henrikke Møller, emerged from the log house and greeted everyone enthusiastically:

"Welcome to America, all of you dear people! Welcome to our little Neenah Settlement! You must all be famished and tired from your long journey!"

A round of introductions followed because the Risland family had never met the Møllers before, and the Møllers had only seen the oldest of Gunder and Aase's boys when he was a small child.

"Now at last we can be neighbors again as we were when we were young boys," Anton exclaimed in a loud voice to Gunder. "Our children are all strangers to each other, but I see they will not remain strangers for long."

Indeed, the Møller boys had already begun to chat excitedly with Gunder and Aase's sons and Lasse Risland, but the three Risland girls stood by, aloof from this easy camaraderie.

Gunder now spoke quietly and seriously to Henrikke and Anton:

"You should know that Anlaug and Sven Risland lost their little Karen Lovisa, only five months old, during our crossing. It was the one great sorrow we all had to endure, and I fear that Anlaug is still terribly distraught in her sorrow."

Immediately Henrikke went over to offer her condolences to Anlaug, embracing her warmly. Then she ushered both Anlaug and Aase into the house, chatting excitedly about getting the coffee pot on and some food for everyone.

Aase Knutsdatter could not help but notice how primitive the living was in this supposed new paradise. The log cabin was snug enough, but was crude in comparison to the log homes she had known in Norway, so rudely constructed without any of the fine workmanship that the old Norwegian log houses had.

The Møllers, in fact, had an extra log hut, the first they had constructed in haste when they settled on this land two years ago. Their newer log house, larger and more substantial, had been built just this year and they had moved into it only weeks earlier. Anton suggested to Gunder that he move his family into the old cabin temporarily, and he also suggested that two miles away there was another empty cabin that could probably house the Risland family. He would inquire tomorrow; in the meantime, they could find some way of accommodating the whole party for the night, including young Anders Knutson.

The first Norwegian settlers had come to the Neenah settlement just two years before, in the spring of 1847, from the Muskego settlement in Racine county. Søren Wilson, Knut Luraas and Sven Thompson had all settled on a ridge several miles north and east from Møller's place.

Møller had arrived late in the season in 1847, just in time to get his little cabin together before the winter set in. Now he had a larger log house, a small barn, and several out-buildings; and when Gunder and his party arrived, Anton Møller's first crop of wheat was just beginning to show signs of ripening. It would probably be about two weeks before it would be fully ripe and ready to harvest. The wheat had been sown in a field studded with stumps and surrounded by a zig-zag rail fence made of split cedar logs so the cattle and sheep and hogs would not get in to destroy this precious crop.

"In about two weeks we shall have to cradle and bundle this crop of wheat. If you and Risland and the older boys will all help me, we should be able to finish the job in about two days. I have two cradles, and if we change off using them, we can have an easier time of it."

"Dear Anton," Gunder replied, "We shall be happy to help you with your harvesting. After the long confinements of traveling, it will be good for all of us to work out in the field once more, cutting the grain."

"Right now I am able to take several days to help you locate tracts of land, and then one of you will need to travel to Green Bay to file claims on the land."

This sounded like a reasonable bargain to Gunder, Sven Risland and Anders Knutson; so they settled in for their first night in the Neenah settlement which was destined to become their new home.

The Norwegians were not the only ones who were a part of the great land-taking in the lands north of the Fox. There were many wagon loads of Yankees and Germans, as well as some Irish families who fanned out onto the land that lay ready for the taking. In the same area that the Norwegians called the Neenah Settlement, there were a number of Yankee families who had recently put down roots – the Clarkes and the Joneses and the Rogers families, and the Hopkins family that settled near a big flowing spring.

In the summer of 1848, the Norton family came, all three generations, from McHenry County in northern Illinois. They had trudged behind an oxcart for eleven days. Grandfather Ezra Norton, eighty-seven years old, walked the entire distance, and together with his two teenage granddaughters, had led the four cows and two heifers on the hot and dusty trail. His two sons, Elijah and Lambert, drove the team of oxen and led the way. They had to stop in Fond du Lac for several days, halted by heavy rainfall. The oxcart sank into the ground, and they were forced to leave some of their baggage, including several bulky items of furniture, with some folks in Fond du Lac who promised to look after them until they could be claimed later. Elijah and Lambert had been to these lands north of the Fox the previous year, when they laid claim to several tracts some miles apart. Old Ezra, patriarch of the family, in spite of his eighty-seven years, insisted upon claiming his own eighty acres; and his sons reluctantly carried out his wish for him.

Ezra Norton was born in Connecticut in 1760, the sixth son in a family of nine. In 1777 he enlisted for a six week term in the Connecticut Militia, and he enlisted for several more short terms. He never saw any significant action, but there was one minor skirmish with about a dozen retreating redcoats chased by a whole company of his militia. His greatest moment came when he saw, mounted on his great white horse, General George Washington himself, as he was passing through Connecticut with his staff on his way to New York. Ezra and his fellow militiamen refused to go outside of New England, and when the action of the war shifted to the New York region, they were mustered out from duty.

When he and his fellow militiamen returned to their civilian ways, they had one patriotic duty left; they felt that they were obligated to harry and harass all the Tories out of the land, and they took up this duty with gusto. Some of Ezra's Tory neighbors fled from their homes and sailed for Halifax, carrying with them whatever they could manage to salvage in their haste to leave the land of vengeance which Connecticut had become for them..

Ezra followed the frontier westward, first into New York state, later into the Western Reserve in Ohio, then to McHenry County in Illinois, and now finally to the lands north of the Fox in Wisconsin. After a restless youth, he married later in life and fathered two sons, nearly young enough to be his grandsons. His younger wife had died nearly a decade before, and now he, spry and healthy at eighty-seven, was ready to make a new start on a new frontier.

Elijah, the oldest of the two sons, was fifty in 1848, the year of their migration northward. He was married and had two sons and one daughter. One of his sons and his daughter stayed in Illinois, but his youngest son Peter came with his father and mother to this new place. Peter was twenty-one years old and was beginning to calculate some plans of his own.

Lambert Norton was forty-six in 1848. He had married Emmeline Crawford some twenty years earlier, and they had two daughters, Lydia, eighteen, and Roberta, seventeen. It was a special burden in Lambert Norton's life that he had no son to carry on the proud Norton name. He showered attentions upon his two daughters, secretly hoping they could attract good husbands that in some way could remedy in his life the terrible void that the lack of a male heir caused. Lydia, the older, was the plain one, but generous and kindly by nature. Roberta, the younger, was strikingly beautiful, but she also possessed a fiery and unpredictable nature, sparked with a considerable amount of vanity. In addition, she was quick-witted and capable of manipulating everyone in her family..

Lambert Norton was somewhat apologetic to his wife and daughters that they would need to endure the crudities of frontier life for several years before they would be able to live in the style they deserved. Had they stayed in McHenry County, they could have had more genteel surroundings in a settled environment; but Lambert was not a wealthy man in McHenry County. The Nortons had come too late to claim the best land; and they had to subsist upon a small marginal farm while watching some of their neighbors prosper on their larger estates, living in grand houses. Lambert vowed that he would better his station in life by moving to a new frontier where he could get the best acres. And so he claimed a whole quarter section of good fertile land, some of which was in natural prairie or "oak opening" as it was called, and some heavily forested with a fine stand of virgin hardwoods.

When Norton arrived in 1848, he hired two young Norwegian neighbors to help him fell trees and erect the log house they needed as their first shelter. Although he could hardly communicate with these fellows, he admired their skill with axe and adze, and within several weeks they had put together a reasonably good log house which could serve as the Norton dwelling house for the next several years.

Grandfather Ezra Norton wished to build his own cabin on his own land, but a sudden attack of the pleurisy postponed his ambitions, and he was forced to share quarters with Lambert and his family in a lean-to bedroom which was hastily added to Lambert's log house.

Lambert's quarter section of land included, on its northern edge, a ridge that stood prominently above the surrounding countryside and from which one could have a grand view, especially several miles to the south. It was on this ridge that Lambert established the site for his farmstead and erected his first log buildings; and it was upon this ridge that he intended, as soon as possible, to erect an elegant and spacious house, the grandest in the entire community, and later a barn, the largest and finest among its neighbors. He aspired to become the leading citizen in this new community, and his farmstead should reflect the status he wished to establish here. This was not McHenry County where he was forced to look up to all those others who had more wealth and status; this was the new Winnebago County, carved out of lands recently ceded by the Indians, and he intended to be a man of substance and influence in this new place.

1848 and 1849 had been years of great influx into the Neenah Settlement, both by the Yankees and the Norwegians; and farther to the west, on the low-lying flat lands near the Wolf River, a number of German families had begun to settle. Quite a number of the

Norwegian families came north from the Muskego Settlement where some of them had settled as early as 1839, and among these were the three Baklistulen brothers, Johannes, Kittel and Halvor, together with their elderly father, Anund. They had ventured forth from their little mountain farm in Hjartdal parish in Telemark, among the earliest to emigrate from that region. In Muskego they bought their land during the dry season and tried to farm a low-lying piece of land which was subject to flooding during rainy seasons and often overrun by mosquitoes and snakes. They had been attracted to this level flat land because they remembered all too well the struggles that their ancestors and their mountain neighbors had on those few little rocky fields on the steep mountain slopes of Hjartdal.

The three brothers survived the terrible cholera epidemic that swept through the Muskego settlement, but the oldest brother, Johannes, lost his wife in childbirth and the mother of the three brothers also died in Muskego, but their father survived. The brothers vowed, as did a number of their neighbors, that they would sell their flat, marshy acres and go north, far enough north, they thought, to escape those dreadful plagues that visited Muskego. So they looked for land that had sufficient elevation to escape flooding, yet they also wanted to find adjacent tracts of marsh land where it would be easy to harvest a crop of hay within reasonable distance from their new homesteads. They also found, several miles to the north, a large wooded swamp, and they purchased small tracts in order to have access to the cedar and tamarack trees for fence rails and firewood.

The Baklistulen brothers and others who came from the Muskego settlement had the advantage over the newest immigrants of speaking English quite fluently. At the outset, they were able to communicate readily with their Yankee neighbors. The more recent Norwegian immigrants who came to the Neenah Settlement directly from Norway, as in the case of the Tøvesens and Rislands, came to depend upon their English-speaking countrymen in many ways.

Most of the Norwegian settlers were content with small tracts of land, often only forty or sixty acres. Only the Baklistulen brothers and one or two other Norwegian settlers chose to acquire as much as an entire quarter section. As Lambert Norton looked about to observe his Norwegian neighbors, he immediately recognized that the Baklistulen brothers had ambitions comparable to his own. In fact, after learning that Johannes and Kittel had each claimed a quarter of a section, Lambert decided to buy an additional eighty acres that adjoined his land to the west. He now had title to two hundred and forty acres, but the new eighty acre tract was heavily forested and it would take a good deal of time and labor to bring it into cultivation. He now had the satisfaction of owning the largest tract of land in the entire settlement. Lambert had to borrow money to buy that additional eighty acres; his ambition somehow outstripped his supply of ready cash. But he remembered all too vividly from McHenry County that those who claimed the largest tracts of land earliest were the ones who ultimately prospered the most, even if they had to take a chance at the beginning by going into debt.

True to his word, Anton Møller spent two days with Gunder Tøvesen, Sven Risland and Anders Knutson tramping over unclaimed lands, seeking out surveyor's markings and assessing the fertility of the soils. Finally, at the end of the second day, all three of the newcomers had located lands upon which they wished to settle. Gunder and Sven selected eighty acre tracts that adjoined, while Anders found sixty acres about a mile and a half west of the others. It was now determined that Anders would make the trek to the land office in Green Bay to file the claims on behalf of the other two as well as himself; and, upon his return, Gunder and Sven were to assist him in erecting a small cabin on his land. Anders was obligated to return to Sheboygan with the horses and wagon which had been leased from Carl Sorlien. He intended to spend the winter with his parents and return to his newly acquired land in the spring.

Gunder and Sven now faced the first and most essential task of erecting the first cabins in preparation for the winter. They decided to assist each other and enlisted the boys as their helpers. One by one the trees were felled and the logs prepared with both axe and adze. The boys assisted by cutting brush and smaller trees, as they were able. The two families decided to locate their farmsteads close to each other since they had adjoining land. After the cabins were completed and the families moved into their new homes, they erected a small log shelter for animals and fenced in with rails an area to contain the animals which they had yet to acquire. One day, after the barn had been erected on Sven's land, Gunder came leading a cow he had acquired from a neighbor who lived several miles away. The children would need milk during the winter, and they could all use a taste of butter and cheese now and then. This cow would have to suffice for now for both families.

Gunder's wife, Aase Knutsdatter, insisted that the men should dig a well which could serve both farmsteads before winter set in. Fortunately, not far from Sven Risland's cabin, there was a soggy spot, not exactly a spring; but it seemed to be a good place to sink a well. The two men worked for several days, digging a deep hole and shoring up the sides with rocks and timbers. After getting down about fifteen feet, it was evident they had uncovered a good flowing underground spring, a source of water sufficient for both families.

After the well was completed, Aase insisted upon one more improvement: the interior of her cabin should be whitewashed. She had seen, in the cabins of some of her new neighbors, how pleasant and cozy the inside of a log cabin could be, if only it were covered with whitewash. When the job was done, Aase was ecstatic. Now with a good supply of water and a freshly white-washed house, her passion for order and cleanliness had been satisfied.

Anlaug Risland, on the other hand, was so grateful finally to have arrived in her new home that she was nearly indifferent to any of the concerns which obsessed Aase. Each morning she would sigh with relief that the long hideous journey was over, yet her mind was still plagued by those haunting restless demons of grief and guilt over the death of her dear little Karen Lovisa. She had nightmarish visions of the body of her little babe sinking into the depths of that satanic ocean. No amount of money could ever bribe her to cross that terrible ocean again. It was good to be here in this place, even though it was so far from her place of birth. She soon learned that she had a number of Norwegian neighbors, and this was a source of some comfort to her. Although her new home seemed a far cry from the fabled paradise which drove her husband and others to come here, she found comfort in the fact that her entire family, except for Karen Lovisa, had endured and survived that terrible ocean crossing. Now they could get on with their lives. Sven and little Lasse seemed happy, and even the girls found pleasure in collecting the colorful autumn leaves and exploring the woodlands near their homestead.

On a Sunday early in October, Gunder gathered together both his family and the Risland family for a special day of thanksgiving. He read a sermon from the *huspostill,* the book of sermons intended for use by the laity when it was impossible to hold a service in a church, and this was followed by the singing of several old hymns, and concluded with a long prayer in which Gunder gave thanks to God for bringing them all to this new place of great promise and opportunity. Again and again he identified their deliverance with that of the children of Israel from the bondage which they endured in Egypt and the parting of the water across the Red Sea before they could enter the Land of Promise.

With only one cow to furnish milk for the two families and no oxen, it was apparent that both Gunder and Sven would need to find some kind of employment during the coming winter months in order to earn money to make a good start in the spring. They discovered that Søren Wilson, one of three earliest settlers in the Neenah Settlement, needed some extra hands to cut down trees on his property and was willing to pay Sven and Gunder the handsome sum of one dollar per day to each man. Gunder was particularly pleased to work for Søren Wilson because he was also one of the Haugean persuasion, having been profoundly touched by this religious revival before he emigrated to America.

In mid-October of 1849, a lonely figure trudged past where Sven and Gunder were cutting trees on Søren Wilson's farm. He motioned to Sven and Gunder, asking them the directions to Søren Wilson's cabin. Clean-shaven, except for a fringe of whiskers, the man seemed to hobble hesitatingly in his manner of walking. His posture was somewhat hunched over; and in spite of the lateness of the season, he was sweating profusely. He wore a heavy coat; perhaps he had decided it would be better to endure the heat of the garment on this unusually warm day in mid-October than to have the extra burden of carrying it. He already had a small valise to carry.

Sven and Gunder were astonished to be addressed by this complete stranger in Norwegian. In this land of many tongues, how did he know to address them in their own language? But they did not question him about this. Recognizing his weariness, they were pleased to point out to him that Søren Wilson's cabin was only a short distance away, just beyond the small clump of trees where they were working.

When evening approached, Sven and Gunder stopped briefly at the Wilson cabin before setting out for their own places. Søren met them at the cabin door and invited them to step in, if only for a moment.

"Risland and Tøvesen, I want you to meet my very best friend and my true mentor in the Christian faith, the Reverend Elling Eielsen from Muskego. He has finally come here to share with us the true Word of the Lord. God be praised for this man and his presence with us. Many of us believe that he is the true successor of our father in the faith, Hans Nielsen Hauge himself."

Sven and Gunder were somewhat surprised to learn that this stranger who had asked directions of them less than an hour before was none other than Elling Eielsen. To be sure, ever since their arrival in America they had heard the name of Eielsen spoken with high praise among the true believers. The Knutsons in Sheboygan had been the first to mention his name and to extoll his virtues as a true prophet of God. But they also discovered that many of their other countrymen did not praise Eielsen so highly, especially some of those who came to the Neenah Settlement from Muskego. They claimed that Eielsen was a sharp-tongued dissident and a cause of division among the Norwegian settlers wherever he went. His claims to the title of "reverend," they said, were spurious, and the other Norwegian clergy did not recognize his so-called ordination as valid. Yet his followers were passionately loyal and proud to call themselves *Ellinganer*. No one was more passionate in his loyalty to Elling Eielsen than Søren Wilson.

It was arranged that Eielsen would preach at Søren Wilson's place the next day at eleven o'clock in the morning, and he would also baptize any unbaptized infants or small children at that time. Sven and Gunder were instructed to get in contact with all their neighbors and invite them to hear Elling Eielsen.

Gunder was disappointed that quite a few of his neighbors expressed either indifference or downright opposition to the visit of Elling Eielsen, in spite of the fact that he had heard some of these same people deplore the fact that no regular Norwegian religious services had yet been held in the newly-founded Neenah Settlement other than the private readings of the *huspostill* in their homes. He was most disappointed, however, with the negative response he received from his long-time good friend, Anton Møller:

"Gunder, you know I came first to the Muskego Settlement before we came north to the Neenah Settlement, and I must tell you that many people in Muskego felt that Elling Eielsen's presence there was disturbing and disruptive."

"But Søren Wilson declares that Eielsen is the true heir to Hans Nielsen Hauge, our father in the true faith. Sven Risland and I conversed with him personally at Wilson's place yesterday."

"I am sorry, my dear friend Gunder, but I don't think that we need the kind of disruption that Elling will bring here into our new Neenah Settlement, and I do not wish to give support to his visit here. Most of the others who came here from Muskego will agree with me."

"I am very sorry that you feel this way about Eielsen because I believe he is a true prophet of God, anointed by God to bring us the true faith here in this new land."

"This man may be a prophet of God, as you say, but there are true prophets and false prophets. Why does this man sow division and dissent wherever he goes?"

And so the two old friends found themselves in profound disagreement over the visit of Elling Eielsen. To be sure, they still remained friends, but a barrier now existed between them that would be difficult to resolve.

Quite a number of people gathered at Søren Wilson's place the next morning, many of whom Gunder and Sven had never met. Undoubtedly some of them came out of curiosity, but others likely came because of a genuine hunger to hear God's Word. Elling Eielsen spoke to the assemblage at Søren Wilson's place with the passion and fire of an Old Testament prophet, denouncing in no uncertain terms every manifestation of sin and evil that one could imagine. He began his sermon by denouncing emphatically the sins of drinking, dancing and playing cards. Repent and be converted to the true faith and put aside all of these corrupting frivolities, he proclaimed to his hearers. Embrace the true faith as Jesus and the Apostles proclaimed and as Martin Luther and Hans Nielsen Hauge preached, not the false faith of mere formal religion, but the true conversion of the heart to Jesus Christ.

Then he launched into a vigorous attack upon the false religion of the official Church of Norway with its dead formalism and the priests of that Church who were mere hirelings in God's vineyard, living in wanton luxury, while their parishioners were starved spiritually. These false priests, he said, have now begun to assert their presence even here among the Norwegian immigrants in America; and Elling seemed to imply that it was his duty to expose their falseness and lead the Norwegian people into the true paths of righteousness and faith as revealed in the Scriptures and expounded in Luther's Small Catechism.

Gunder agreed whole-heartedly with everything Eielsen proclaimed. He knew only too well about the fat priests who simply lorded it over their people. Why, when he went to that false priest at Herefoss to get his dismissal papers from the parish before he emigrated, he was given a humiliating lecture by that miserable usurper who called himself a priest of God. Now, thank God, we don't have to deal with that kind of priest any more in this new land. We now have a genuine spiritual leader like Elling Eielsen to lead us into the paths of true righteousness. His reluctant countrymen who were indifferent or hostile to Elling were dead wrong, thought Gunder. This man has been sent by God to minister to us. Next to Søren Wilson, Elling Eielsen had no more ardent supporter in the Neenah Settlement than Gunder Tøvesen.

A Sudden Surprise

The days after June 24, 1850, were the worst days Jacob ever experienced in his whole life. Dark despair crowded out all semblance of rational thought, and Jacob even entertained thoughts of suicide. What really was the use of living anymore? Only some inexplicable will to live stayed his hand from self-destruction.

He remembered the tragic suicide of one of the neighbors near Skredderstua just three years ago. The man, a father of five young children and husband of a hard-working wife, became despondent over his mounting debts; and one day he hanged himself from a beam in his horse stable. Jacob's father had been one of those assigned to cut the lifeless body down. The man's body could not be given Christian burial; it could be buried in the cemetery at Austre Moland, but his father and several other neighbors had to carry the body to the cemetery at night, lift the crude coffin over the fence, and bury the poor man under cover of darkness, with no words of blessing or comfort for the poor widow and her children. It was horrible, and Jacob wondered at the time whether it was necessary, by church law, to treat suicides in such a heartless manner.

What stayed his hand more than anything else was the conviction he had always held that a person who committed suicide took the coward's way out, and Jacob never wanted to be shown as a coward.

But living those days after that terrible letter was much harder than dying would have been. Jacob nurtured the wish that a lightning bolt would strike out of the sky and kill him. Other equally dark thoughts haunted his mind as he tried to cope with his overwhelming and all-compassing grief.

The only relief came in the form of work – hard and exhausting physical labor – so at night he could tumble into bed and sleep from sheer exhaustion. But even in his dreams there were disturbing recurrences. He dreamt often of his family, and each of them was vividly present in his dreams just as they had been over a year ago when he last saw them and had to say goodbye.

Fortunately for Jacob his fellow-worker, Peter Smith, was a perceptive fellow who seemed unusually understanding and helpful during this terrible time. Perhaps it was because Peter had lost his own father a little over one year earlier and could understand Jacob's grief in the light of his own. It was Peter who prescribed the work therapy for Jacob, and the two men tackled their newest project on Adam Cartwright's place with almost demonic energy. This project was to erect a barn of somewhat modest proportions which could be used first to house Adam's small herd of milking cows but later transformed into a horse barn when his herd would grow too large to be housed in this building. The building was not going to be of log construction; there was now a good source for rough-sawn boards from the local sawmill, and the barn would be constructed first with massive posts and beams, and then covered with newly sawn boards from logs Adam was able to supply to the sawmill from his own land.

Jacob found, in the midst of their daily labors, that he often stopped to tell Peter some particularly fond memory he had about various members of his family. He thought about his mother's fondness for the sweet cherries from her favorite tree that grew just outside the door to their cottage at Skredderstua. He thought about his father, busy at the cobbler's bench, working on a new pair of shoes for someone, or perhaps patching an old pair, all the while singing to himself familiar old songs. He thought about his brother Elias, yielding the scythe more skillfully than anyone he knew as he cut the hay crop on their small fields at Skredderstua. He thought of his sister Maren, of her beautiful features and her gentle manners. He thought about mischievous little Klemet, always up to some new trick. Then there were Kittel and Anna-Maria – certainly they had both grown since he last saw them over a year ago, and how he wished to see them once again.

These moments of memory brought a kind of sweetness and a terrible bitterness at the same time. He even thought of Captain Helgesen and Niels Aslesen and other crew members of the *Juno* he came to know during his crossing a year ago. What really could have happened to the *Juno*? She was surely a seaworthy ship, was she not? Of course, those storms in the Atlantic could be ferocious and dangerous.

Jacob remembered during his own crossing, at the time of the most severe storm, the thought had momentarily entered his head that perhaps the ship would not make it. But then, as an experienced seamen, he knew that a good ship like the *Juno* was made to take terrible punishment from the ocean storms, and it was difficult to sink a good ship like the *Juno* that had such a competent captain and crew.

Day after day Jacob plodded along on the job with Peter. He took some satisfaction in seeing the framework of the barn take shape and even recovered a bit of his natural good spirits on the day that all of the neighbors came for the barn-raising. Both Jacob and Peter climbed high aloft the timbers to pound the pegs into place as the timbers were held precariously in their places before being fastened together.

Mrs. Cartwright and her helpers put before the barn raisers a wonderful meal after their task was done, and Jacob did not lack an appetite on that occasion. But in the midst of the conviviality, the black thoughts hit again. He even caught himself wishing that he would plunge down by accident from his high perch during the barn-raising, but then that stubborn will to live took over, and Jacob was ashamed that he entertained such thoughts, if even for a fleeting moment.

Two days after the barn-raising, on July seventh, Carl Sorlien suddenly came riding into the Cartwright farmyard on a sorrel mare. When Jacob spotted him, he saw that Carl seemed to radiate a kind of enthusiasm he had never before seen in him. He ran up to Jacob, almost unable to restrain his excitement.

"Jacob, my dear boy, I have great news for you. The report of the sinking of the *Juno* was a false report! Your family landed in Sheboygan just two days ago, surprising us all."

Jacob at first merely stared at Carl Sorlien in sheer disbelief.

"They insisted upon coming here as rapidly as they possibly could, and they should be arriving here in another hour or so."

At last Jacob was able to mutter a response: "Can this really be true? You have seen them and they are coming this way?"

Jacob could hardly get the words out, overcome as he was by conflicting emotions.

"I rode ahead to break the news to you so that you could have some time to recover from the shock before greeting them," Carl said to Jacob quite deliberately and calmly.

Jacob now had to sit down on the grass in order to recover his composure.

"Poor boy! What agony and grief I must have caused you by that letter I sent to you with the false information which had been published in the New York newspaper. I don't know how they could have been so mistaken!"

Carl was not one to show his emotions freely, but on this occasion he was overcome with solicitude for Jacob. But Jacob still had difficulty believing what Carl was telling him, wondering if somehow this could all be some cruel hoax.

Just now Peter came to join Jacob where he was seated on the ground; he had also heard Carl's excited proclamations to Jacob, but the words were in Norwegian. Peter could only guess, by his tone of voice, that Carl must be sharing some good news.

Carl turned to Peter and explained in English just what had happened, and Peter immediately ran to the back door of the elegant new farmhouse and shouted out the news to Mrs. Cartwright and the others in the house. Suddenly everyone was excited, and there was a good deal of scurrying in every direction. When Mrs. Cartwright heard that Jacob's family was due to arrive in a short while, her housewife's concern for hospitality took charge.

"Those poor people who have had to journey so far! We must get some good food together for them." And at once she began to scurry about in her summer kitchen, building a fire in the stove so that Jacob's long-lost family could have a good healthy home-cooked meal as their special welcome on this happy day of reunion with their son..

Adam Cartwright was away on an errand in Fond du Lac, so he missed all the initial excitement, but about twenty minutes after Carl brought the good news Adam drove into the farmyard with his horsecart loaded with supplies. It took Adam a few minutes to understand what all the excitement was about; he heard only excited and incoherent shouts, first from Peter, then from Carl, and even from Jacob himself. Suddenly the message broke through, and Adam broke into an unrestrained shout of joy. He had been terribly worried about Jacob. He had grown quite fond of the lad, and now he was fully as excited as any of the others.

About two hours after Carl Sorlien arrived at the Cartwright farm, the horses and wagon could be seen approaching. Carl had given to Elias and Terje, on a hastily scribbled sheet of paper, a sketch that showed exactly the location of Adam Cartwright's farm, and now, thanks to that simple map, they found their destination.

Jacob's mother could hardly restrain her excitement upon seeing her son once more; but Nordic stoicism took over, and she did not dare to exhibit openly the intensity of her feelings, certainly not in front of strange folks. Even Terje had similar feelings, especially after he learned that poor Jacob had been under the delusion they had all perished at sea. How the poor boy must have suffered when he heard those terrible false reports!

Elias drove the team of horses they had rented from Carl Sorlien with his experienced skill in handling horses. When they approached the roadway which led to the Cartwright farm, Jacob bolted out from the rest and ran to meet the wagonload which carried his own precious family.

"Mother! Father! Elias!" he stammered out excitedly in a loud voice. "I never thought this moment would come! I never thought I would see any of you ever again!"

There were shouts of recognition, and Terje felt tears streaming down his cheek as he saw, for the first time in over a year, his dear son. It was a precious moment, destined to be etched forever in the memory of each and every one in the family. Even little Klemet was caught up in the significance of this moment. To Jacob it seemed a miracle, a sort of resurrection; and he beheld each member of his family with a sense of grateful wonder, hardly believing this actually could be true.

Soon the loaded wagon arrived in the Cartwright farmyard, and there were the inevitable introductions. Jacob and Carl had to serve as interpreters, but the joy of the occasion clearly transcended the limitations of human language.

Terje looked with wonder at the Cartwright farmhouse. It was grander than the manor house at Longum; and he soon learned that his son Jacob, together with his friend Peter, had been the builders of this magnificent house. Could it really be true that they had indeed arrived in Paradise where ordinary people could aspire to live in such stately dwellings?

Jacob savored this remarkable reunion with each member of his family. He was surprised at how grown-up both Kittel and Anna-Maria had become, and even little Klemet had changed. He was no longer just a mischievous little elf-child.

Then there were the inquiries about how the crossing went. Did Niels Aslesen take you all the way to Albany as he did with Gunder's party a year ago? Did you stay with Frau Riemenschneider in New York? Which steamship did you take on the Hudson, and which ship on the Great Lakes? How did you like the train ride from Albany to Buffalo, or did you take the canal boats?

Mrs. Cartwright mustered her kitchen crew, and tables were set up outside because it was such a lovely summer day. Soon her delicious welcoming meal was ready to serve. Jacob's mother could hardly believe that they, poor common folks that they were, could be welcomed as guests by these fine aristocratic Yankee folks. What a truly remarkable place this new land must be. She wished that she could talk directly to Mrs. Cartwright to express her gratitude. After the meal was over, she had her opportunity when Jacob stood by to translate into English directly to Mrs. Cartwright what she wished to say.

As evening drew near, Mrs. Cartwright calculated the plans for accommodating her guests overnight. There were two large empty bedrooms upstairs, and the males could be accommodated in one and the females in the other. The younger ones could sleep on the floor because there were not beds enough for everyone, but there were extra quilts and corn husk ticks to provide some comfort even for those on the floor.

The next morning the men gathered to have a serious conversation about plans for Jacob and his family. Adam knew he would now lose his good workman, but he was happy that Jacob was now reunited with his family. Peter was sad to lose his capable helper and partner, Jacob; but it was inevitable that Jacob now must join his own family. Adam insisted that the family must stay at least two more days to recover from the rigors of their long journey, and Jacob concurred with this thought. But Jacob, Elias and Terje were also anxious to get on to the Neenah Settlement as soon as possible. They needed to claim their land and get settled in their new home before the long winter would set in.

Adam spoke directly to Terje, using Jacob as his interpreter, and Jacob did his best to translate Adam's words for his father.

"You need, first of all, to purchase either a four-wheeled wagon or a large two-wheeled cart. And you will find it is more advantageous for you to purchase a yoke of oxen than a team of horses during this time when you first will settle on your land."

This bit of advice was somewhat of a surprise to Terje.

"I don't understand. We have always used horses. Why would it be advantageous to use oxen?"

Adam turned directly to Jacob.

"Tell your father about our experience that time when you first came with me when we had to get the oxen to pull our wagon out of the mud hole. Then also tell him that the biggest task that you'll have will be to remove the tree stumps from the fields you'll be able to clear."

Jacob then spoke for some moments with his father. Adam saw Terje slowly shake his head in response to what he was hearing.

Finally Jacob turned back to Adam.

"Father says it's hard to believe that oxen can really do those tasks better than horses. He's always been particularly fond of horses and has prided himself on his knowledge about horses. But he says he'll accept your advice. Obviously you know better the conditions that we have in this new land. He also asks if you know where we can purchase a yoke of oxen.

"Tell your father that my neighbor, John Campbell, has a good yoke of oxen he will sell at a reasonable price. You can also tell your father that I have an extra ox cart which he can purchase from me very reasonably."

And so later on that very day Terje became the owner of a yoke of oxen and a cart, and he was able to pay for both oxen and cart in gold and silver coins. This was his first purchase in equipping himself and his family for the task of getting settled and established in America. As he paid for the oxen, he mused to himself that the day would surely come when these oxen will have done their good work of clearing the land, and then they could be replaced by a team of horses. Neither Terje nor his sons had experience working with oxen, but they were ready to learn.

Jacob was anxious to hear all of the news about what had happened to his family since he had seen them last. He was told about the purchase of Skredderstua by Consul Lund for 850 specie dollars, and also the sale of the livestock and other items they needed to dispose of before emigrating on the first day of May. He heard news about their neighbors and some of his childhood friends, and there were a few pangs of homesickness as they talked so much about Skredderstua.

In the morning, Jacob, Elias and their father had much to discuss. There were supplies they needed to purchase to make the journey to the Neenah Settlement and sustain their family after arriving there. Terje was advised to fill the bottom of his cart with rough-sawn planks which could be very useful in constructing the first cabin they would need to build after they located the land upon which they wished to settle. Adam insisted upon giving the family a supply of wheat from his abundance, suggesting that some of this supply should be kept for seed because as soon as they were able to clear a few acres, they could plant wheat as their first crop, even if it meant scratching around the stumps left after the trees were cut down. Terje bought a plow from Adam that could be used to break the sod and cut through the roots of the roughly cleared areas to prepare for the first plantings.

Finally, Terje bought two young heifers from Adam's herd. These heifers had already been bred and were due to have their first calves in about two months, just in time to provide the family with a source of milk during the coming winter. It would be the task of Maren and Anna-Maria to lead these two heifers when they made their journey north from Fond du Lac to the Neenah Settlement.

On the morning of their departure the cart was loaded with the original baggage which the family brought from Norway, Jacob's carpenter's chest and other belongings and the items which Terje had just purchased during his stay in Fond du Lac. The cart was so full there was no space for anyone to ride.

Just as they were about to leave, Peter Smith came with a half-grown puppy on a leash and gave it to Klemet.

"It is a good thing to have a dog when you live in a little log cabin in the woods. He will warn you when strangers approach and will help watch your cattle. Besides, he will be a good pet for Klemet."

Klemet did not understand Peter's explanation, which Jacob had to translate, but he was overjoyed at the prospect of caring for this delightful pet. At Jacob's prompting Klemet learned to say his first English words to Peter:

"Thank you! Thank you! Thank you!"

And Peter, in response, shook Klemet's hand warmly.

"You are welcome! You are most welcome!"

At last the oxen began to pull the cart, and it creaked forward at an agonizingly slow pace. It would take a day and a half to get to Webster Stanley's ferry across the Fox River, and probably nearly that to get to the Neenah Settlement beyond that point.

With the exception of a sudden thundershower when they were encamped on the second night, all went well for the travelers. Anna Tøvesdatter was horribly frightened by the lightning and thunder. She had never experienced a storm of such ferocity in her home-land, and she began to wonder what other terrors they would experience in this strange new land. Jacob was not frightened by the thunderstorm, but realized that their progress was likely to be much slower on the morning of the third day because of the mud they would have to trudge through on the trail which led to the Neenah Settlement.

Fortunately, they did not have many more miles to go. They passed log cabins and partially cleared fields. The air at times was filled with smoke from the fires that had been set to burn the brush and tree branches from the endless task of clearing the land. Nearly all of the cabins they passed were occupied by Yankees, and Jacob was the only one in their party who could speak to these people to ask directions or simply exchange greetings.

At last they came to a cabin where the family could speak Norwegian. What a relief this was to Anna and Terje and the whole family. They discovered that this family, some folks by the name of Naess from Hjartdal in Telemark, lived on the extreme south edge of the Neenah Settlement in an area called Ball Prairie. All of their neighbors were Yankees, they said, but about two miles to the north and west, many of the folks were Norwegians. They also discovered that it was not far to Gunder Tøvesen's place because he, too, lived on the south edge of the Neenah Settlement, but farther west. Anna and Terje were reluctant to leave because it seemed so good to be with folks again who could talk Norwegian, even if it was a bit difficult to understand their dialect; but when they heard that they were probably less than two English miles from Gunder's place, they were ready to hasten on.

It was about three o'clock in the afternoon, or so it seemed (Terje's clock was still packed securely in the big trunk) when they arrived at Gunder Tøvesen's place. Gunder and Sven Risland and Gunder's two older boys were not at home when Terje's family drove the oxen and the cart into the farmyard. The men had been hired by their Yankee neighbor, Lambert Norton, to cut down trees, and the boys went along to help carry the branches and clear away underbrush. The men were each given one dollar a day for their work, and Mr. Norton agreed to give each of the boys twenty-five cents per day for their help.

Aase Knutsdatter was overjoyed to see her husband's sister and her whole family.

"Welcome, welcome, to our new home in the woods of Wisconsin! The last time we saw you, dear Anna, you were hostess to my whole family and also the Rislands when we were on our way to Arendal."

"It's so good to see you again, dear Aase. You look so healthy and well. America must agree with you!" Anna responded.

"How long ago that day we were at Skredderstua seems now. Hello, Jacob, and you too Terje, and Elias," and Aase then proceeded to greet each member of the family warmly.

"You must all be tired and hungry as wolves. Halvor, run over to Anlaug Risland and tell her that Terje and Anna and their whole family have arrived."

She turned then to Anna and Terje once more, explaining:

"Our men will not be home until nearly dark, but we can help you unload and unpack some of your things for surely you will be staying with us for some days."

Terje then assured Aase the things on the cart would not need to be unpacked immediately. There would be time enough for that later.

"Gunder spoke of you just this morning at breakfast," Aase continued, "wondering if it would not be soon when you would be coming to our little Neenah Settlement. It's so good to see you all again, and now in this new place we can truly be neighbors and not separated by such a great distance as we were in Norway. Now, you must tell us all about your voyage and all the news from home."

Aase chatted on and on, hardly allowing her guests time to get in a word. When Halvor returned with Anlaug Risland, there was another round of greetings, and then Aase and Anlaug excused themselves for a while and went into Aase's cabin to put on the coffee pot and prepare a little lunch. It was too early for supper, but surely a little lunch would help these tired and hungry folks to recover from their journey.

There were other tasks as well. The oxen needed to be unyoked and a place found for the oxen and the heifers. Klemet's little dog could not stop barking from all the excitement, but when he saw the big ugly black dog that belonged to Lasse Risland, poor little "Max," as Klemet called him, suddenly became quite frightened and docile. Klemet and Lasse and Halvor soon became a threesome and went galloping off on their boyish adventures. Both Lasse and Halvor now considered themselves "Americans," and they had a good deal to show this newcomer, Klemet Skredderstua, who just came off the boat from the Old Country.

Aase soon had it all figured out how the guests were to be accommodated. Maren and Anna-Maria were to stay with the Risland girls. They had plenty of room in their loft for two extra. Anna and Terje would stay in the cabin on the trundle bed that rolled out from under the bed she and Gunder shared. Jacob, Elias, Kittel and Klemet could be with their boys in the loft. Surely it would be big enough and sturdy enough to hold them all, wouldn't it?

No coffee ever tasted as good as the coffee Aase served her guests on that beautiful July afternoon, and with the coffee were some slices of her good wheat bread with some wild plum jam.

"Yes, Anna, we have some of these nice wild plum trees on our property. Of course, they don't really compare to that wonderful cherry tree you left behind at Skredderstua, but these plums do make a good jam."

During the course of the conversation, Anna became a bit confused when Aase began to refer to taking the oxen and heifers into the *barn*. Whatever could Aase mean? How could the oxen and heifers be taken into the *children*? Perhaps Aase was confused, what with all of this excitement of a whole family descending upon her all at once. Certainly the animals belonged in a *fjøs* or a *stall*, but for some strange reason Aase continued to refer to that building as *barn*. She would have to ask Jacob about this. She began to notice other changes in the way people spoke Norwegian here in America. They would suddenly use words she had never heard, and seemed to think nothing of it, as though everyone ought to understand what was meant.

As the sun grew low in the western sky, Gunder, Sven and the two boys returned, tired and sweaty, from their day's work on the land of the rich Yankee, Lambert Norton. They were surprised to see the cart in their yard, and the extra animals tied in the barn.

"Yes, they have arrived," Gunder thought to himself, and then he spied them, the whole family from Skredderstua, as he opened the door into his house. There was another round of greetings, and Gunder had many questions to ask of his sister and her family. When did they arrive in New York? Did they have a good crossing? They came on the *Juno*, didn't they? Was Helgesen still the captain? And then the questions turned more and more to Norway and the latest news they had from there.

In the meantime, Aase, with help from Anlaug Risland, set before her guests a good meal. She apologized that all she could come up with for meat was salt pork, but she had good potatoes and fresh garden peas. Then there was something called *tomatoes* which were red and served in slices. Anna had never seen or tasted these before, and she began to wonder how many more strange new foods she would find. Let's see: just today she had tasted for the first time *wild plum jam* and *tomatoes*. How many more surprises would there be tomorrow?

Gunder did not quite approve Aase's plan for the sleeping arrangements. That loft was certainly not big enough for his three boys plus one boy and three men, or nearly a man in the case of Kittel. Would it not be better to let the men sleep in the summer kitchen? The fire in the stove had been out for about an hour, and Jacob, Elias and Kittel would be more comfortable out there. Besides, the loft might not be able to bear the weight if so many were to sleep in it. Jacob and his brothers were satisfied with the new arrangement, and soon everyone settled down for the night's rest.

When they were at breakfast the next morning, the men began to talk about the important task they needed to undertake as soon as possible – to locate and claim the piece of land destined to be their home in the New World. Gunder suggested that they look at a tract of land immediately to the south of the quarter-section owned by Lambert Norton. It was gently rolling, with good drainage on the upper forty, but on the lower forty it might be well to dig a drainage ditch in the future. Certainly that lower forty could be purchased from the land office more reasonably than the upper forty. The land was well forested, but with occasional smaller oak openings. The trees stood straight and tall, mostly oaks, but also hickory trees and a few maple trees; and in one corner of the land there were a few isolated pine trees among the hardwoods.

Terje and his sons walked with Gunder, Sven and the boys as they went to work that morning for Lambert Norton. On the way, Gunder showed them the land that he had described.

"As you can see, this fine piece of land is only about one and a half American miles from my place," Gunder confided to Terje.

Terje was still somewhat confused about American distances and measurements. Already Jacob had told him a number of times that he should never confuse an American mile with a Norwegian mile.

Terje and his two sons walked over the land carefully, taking great pains to observe every characteristic of the soil, the trees and the drainage. At last they arrived at a consensus. This was indeed beautiful land and a great contrast to the miserably uneven and rocky soil of Skredderstua. Eighty acres of this land seemed like a grand estate to Terje and his sons.

"Do you really think we need to claim any more than this upper tract?" Terje asked his sons.

He had already been told the upper tract consisted of forty acres, and when Jacob explained to his father the size of this tract in Norwegian terms, Terje realized that these forty acres contained more land than most of the larger farms in the Austre Moland parish.

But Jacob and Elias persuaded their father that he should also claim the lower forty, even if he didn't clear or drain that land in the near future.

"You have four sons," they said, "and someday they will need more land."

This was the telling argument for Terje. In his mind he actually thought that a tract this large could eventually be divided into four farms -- one for each son in the family.

And so Terje agreed finally that he would be willing also to claim and purchase the lower forty acres. They located the surveyor's stakes and walked the entire perimeter of the land one more time before they decided to return to Gunder's place.

Now they would need to file a claim, and it would be best if Jacob could travel to Green Bay to the land office as soon as possible to ensure that their claim was valid and they could purchase the land. They were not sure what the price would be, but Terje still had more than half of the money intact which he had received from the sale of Skredderstua to Consul Lund, and this had all been converted into American dollars in New York. Terje would have to send some of that money with Jacob to Green Bay, hoping that Jacob would not need to spend most of it just to purchase the land. There were so many other needs that had to be met as they anticipated settling into their new home.

It took Jacob more than a week to make the trip to Green Bay and back. He was lucky to catch a river boat for part of the journey beyond the great rapids in the Fox, but most of the way he had to walk. At the land office he discovered that he, acting on his father's behalf, could get a clear title on the land from the eastern speculator who had purchased vast tracts of these western lands, and he was asked to pay $150 for the upper forty and $50 for the lower forty acres. Upon his return, he was happy to report to his father that there was still a considerable portion of his money left, even after paying for the land.

Terje Larsen Skredderstua now had in his hands a document that declared in English, a language which he did not understand, that he was the sole owner of eighty acres of land in Section 26, whatever that meant, and that there were no prior claims or encumbrances on this land. Terje bristled with pride at the very thought of his ownership. Never in his life did he think he would own so much land, and such beautiful land it was. It needed only labor to turn it into a good farm; but he had four sons, and he was not too old himself to do his share of the labor.

That night, after Jacob's return, Terje gathered his whole family together and announced that tomorrow they would leave Gunder's place and establish a temporary shelter on their own land and get busy with the task of establishing their new home.

Jacob suggested that they should build a cabin of modest proportions in which they could survive the long winter. In the meantime they should cut the logs for their larger log house this autumn, allowing them time to cure out during the autumn and winter, and then dress them all properly next spring. Jacob said he had seen too many log cabins hastily thrown together using green logs, and as the logs began to dry out they would crack and buckle and cause no end of problems. If they were going to build a log house, it should be done properly, just as their ancestors had done for generations in Norway. The first cabin they would build immediately would, of course, have to be constructed of green logs; but after wintering in it for one season the building could be turned into their summer kitchen. It should therefore be located very close to the intended site of their more permanent and larger house.

A Visitor From the South

As the weeks went by, the heat of summer gave way to the occasional frosts of autumn, and the hardwoods in the forest were ablaze with color. It was a time of unusual beauty, but also a time of furious activity for Terje and his whole family. There were so many tasks before they would be ready for winter.

The cabin had been built; it measured only twelve by fourteen feet. The logs were chinked with smaller pieces of wood wedged in and then covered with a mixture of sand and slaked lime.

Most of the first settlers lived on dirt floors in their cabins, but Anna was not happy about the prospect of living like so many heathens or Hottentots, as she put it. One day Jacob and Elias hauled some smaller straight logs into a pile near the house, dug a pit in the ground, and began the tedious task of using the long saw, one man standing above and one below, sawing these logs in half lengthwise. It was an odious and time-consuming task, and from time to time they were able to recruit Kittel to relieve one or the other of them. But they were determined that their mother should not have to spend her first winter in America on a dirt floor.

When enough of the logs, twelve feet in length, had been sawed in this manner, Jacob fitted them together, flat side up, so that as they were laid, side by side, the result was a reasonably flat floor. Jacob had seen this method used in some log cabins and it was called a puncheon floor. Usually it was crudely done with axe and adze, but Jacob decided that if the building was going to continue in use as a summer kitchen for some years to come, it needed an adequate floor. After the rough sawing, Jacob used a drawshave and plane to make a smoother surface.

On a trip into Winnebago Rapids for supplies, Jacob stopped at a blacksmith shop and purchased some long iron spikes to fasten the logs to the supporting timbers underneath. Anna Tøvesdatter was pleased with the special effort her sons made to give her this fine floor.

If they could have carried more planks on their load from Fond du Lac, perhaps those could have been used for the floor, but they already had used their small supply of planks to construct the loft at one end of the cabin. The loft was the sleeping place for the four sons. Anna and Terje slept in a bed that Jacob fashioned from small logs, using a network of ropes to hold the mattress-tick above the floor. He fashioned a second bed for his two sisters, Maren and Anna-Maria. The second bed was much lower than the first and a bit shorter, so when it was not in use it could be pushed under the higher one.

Terje was able to purchase, in Winnebago Rapids, an iron stove and three small windows, and when these were installed, the cabin was ready to provide a snug haven from the cold storms of winter.

They also built a shelter for the animals. In fact, this was the first structure they built when they began their encampment upon the land. At that time the weather was so mild that the family camped underneath a large canvas for several weeks; but when the animal shelter was hastily finished, its first inhabitants were the human animals, and the poor oxen and heifers were tethered outside, night and day, fair weather and foul. When the family finally was able to move into the completed cabin, it was a day of rejoicing for all, including the oxen and the heifers, because they now inherited the building that was rightfully theirs from the beginning.

It was just in time because Dagros presented them with a little bull calf early in September, and about two weeks later Red-Nose had her little heifer calf. The two new mothers were pleased to have a new home for their babies. Now the family could begin to milk these heifers who had come into the fullness of their bovine maturity, and Elias already calculated that the little bull calf could be gelded and turned into an ox as he grew and matured, and the little heifer calf added to the herd in several years as a milking cow. Maren and Anna-Maria had taken on the special tasks of caring for the new calves, milking the cows, churning the butter, and making cheese now and then.

Elias was often relieved of duties with the building projects in order to take his scythe wherever he could find grass to make a supply of hay for the animals, enough to last the whole winter long. Gradually the haystack next to the animal shed grew larger and higher, until both Terje and Elias agreed they probably had enough to feed twice the number of animals they had.

There were many things which they had to buy or borrow from neighbors, especially food for the winter. Terje bought two hogs from Sven Risland, and on one late September day the hogs were butchered and most of the meat was salted down in two large crocks which Terje had purchased on a trip into Winnebago Rapids.

Aase Knutsdatter was very generous to her sister-in-law and family in providing many extra items for the larder, including some of her wild plum jam. Shortly after their arrival, Maren and Anna-Maria discovered a patch of blackberries on their land; and, in spite of the scratches they had to endure, they picked many buckets full of these tasty berries. They also discovered an abundance of nuts, especially hickory nuts, which they had never seen before. They had to learn from some of their neighbors how to crack them open with a hammer in order to get at the delicious nutmeats inside, but the girls soon became experts at this task.

On one late September day Jacob set out on foot in search of standing pine trees. He had already cut down the five larger pine trees on his father's land; and he determined that the new and larger cabin should be constructed of straight pine logs, not of oak or hickory logs which were full of knots and hard to work smooth. Gunder had told him that just a few miles north there were many more pine trees; and Jacob resolved that, if at all possible, he would secure the logs before the heavy weather of winter set in.

Jacob walked for several miles due north from his father's land, and he met several Norwegian settlers whom he had not known – Helge Traaer, Halvor Romme, and Johannes Funer. These folks had all come from Telemark and had settled within the past two years. They told Jacob he could probably find good stands of pine just a few miles north of the Rat River, on land being settled by some German families. Halvor Romme offered to accompany Jacob. He had a small boat hidden in the tall grass which they could use to cross the Rat River so they would not need to ford it. In fact, most of Halvor's land was on the north side of the river.

Together they walked about two miles in a northwesterly direction until they came to the cabin of one of the German settlers. This man, Friedrich Winckler, knew some English, so Jacob was able to communicate with him. Winckler told Jacob he did not have any suitable standing pine on his own land; but his neighbor, Heinrich Meyer, about one mile to the west, had quite a number of tall pine trees and Jacob could probably work out a deal to cut some of those trees. In fact, Meyer was anxious to clear the land as soon as possible and would probably welcome Jacob's help in that task. Winckler offered to accompany Jacob and Halvor because Meyer knew no English. Winckler would be able to explain the whole situation to him in German.

Jacob was able to purchase the standing pine trees at a reasonable cost; and a few days later he returned to Meyer's place with his father and his two brothers, Elias and Kittel. They spent two days camping out in Meyer's woods, cutting the tall pine trees for the log house. After the trees were cut and trimmed, they were piled near Meyer's cabin where they could stay until winter when Jacob and his brothers would return with the oxen and sleigh to transport them home. During the winter months Jacob could work the pine logs into square timbers to construct the kind of log house he wanted to build.

One day, in the middle of the family's busy preparations for winter, a strange man walked up to their door and greeted them in Norwegian. He was one of the neighbors they had not yet had an opportunity to meet, a fairly young man by the name of Ole Olson Strømme. He said he came from Vraadal in Telemark, and that he and his mother and step-father had settled here last year, having moved from Muskego.

Strømme was making the rounds of as many Norwegian families as he could to tell them that a Norwegian minister was due to arrive in the Neenah Settlement any day now, and a service would be held October twenty-fifth in Ole Saersland's barn because it was the largest structure in the whole settlement. Folks should plan to spend the whole day at Saersland's place, so they had better pack a lunch. So many new Norwegian families had arrived just this year that it was hard to keep up with them all. The minister was named Preus, and he was coming from "Kaskeland" to hold this service for the people of the Neenah Settlement. If there were children to be baptized or young ones to be catechized or any marriages to be performed, Preus had written that he was prepared to stay some days in the settlement to take care of those needs.

When Strømme spoke about marriages, his face reddened into a blush, and it came out that he himself was the first to be married. His bride-to-be had recently arrived from Norway; and when they heard that a Norwegian minister was scheduled to visit the settlement, they decided to wait for him to perform their wedding properly rather than go to a justice of the peace, as some of the others had done in the absence of a minister. Ole Strømme was a talkative fellow, and Terje and the whole family enjoyed his visit. It was good to know they had such a nice neighbor just a couple miles away, and they looked forward to times when they could afford to be more sociable and get acquainted with some of their countrymen who were settling here.

The Rev. Adolph Carl Preus was born in Trondhjem in 1814 and educated at the theological faculty of the Royal Frederick University at Christiania. He had received his *candidatis* in 1841, taught school for several years before he was ordained in 1848, and served as *kapellan* for two years at Gjerpen in Telemark before deciding to come to America.

He came to this country as the successor to the first regularly educated and ordained minister of the Church of Norway, the Rev. Johannes Dietrichson, who served the congregations in the Koshkonong settlement in Dane and Jefferson counties, the largest concentration of Norwegians in Wisconsin at that time. The congregations in Koshkonong had been established in 1844, and already they had constructed their first church buildings. Unlike Dietrichson, who was, in the minds of many, pompous and over-bearing, Preus was a gentle and mild-mannered person with a kindly and sympathetic smile for everyone. He had not been in Koshkonong very long before he came to the Neenah Settlement and visited several other outlying settlements to serve his country-men who had so recently arrived.

Many of the Norwegian immigrants had great difficulties pro-nouncing American names, especially the many names derived from the Indian tongues. They had no difficulty with names like Muskego or Neenah, but Koshkonong was a tongue twister, and most of the Norwegians called that place "Kaskeland," so word now spread that the minister from "Kaskeland" was coming. Most were pleased with this news.

Among those who were less than pleased was Anna's own brother, Gunder Tøvesen. To Gunder the arrival of Preus meant that the Neenah Settlement would come under the oppressive hand of the officials of the state church. Their long arm of authority would reach even here; and as they stood so officiously in their cassocks and ruffs, they stood ready to enslave the people into the false ways of their dead orthodoxy. Gunder, and those others who thought as he did, hated every vestige of the establishment represented by the official clergy of the Church of Norway. In Norway the truly converted believers were forced by law to stay within the bounds of that corrupt institution, but here in America they need not pay heed to these beguiling serpents of falsehood.

Both Anna and Terje were surprised at the vehemence of Gunder's response to the anticipated visit of the Rev. Adolph Carl Preus. What they did not realize at first, and came to know later, was that Gunder, like several others in the Neenah Settlement, had come under the spell of that itinerant preacher among the Norwegians, Elling Eielsen. Eielsen had visited the Neenah Settlement in the autumn of 1849, several months after Gunder and his party arrived. He attempted to gather a following, and was successful in gleaning a minority of the settlers into his flock, including both the Tøvesen and Risland families.

Elling Eielsen had been a lay preacher, first in the earliest settlements in Illinois and later in Wisconsin, While in Illinois he managed to get himself ordained by a pastor of the Franckean Synod; and, as a result, he and his followers sometimes were called Franckeans. His ordination was not recognized as valid by the clergy who came to this country from the Church of Norway. To Eielsen's way of thinking, the refusal of the other clergy to recognize him only proved that they were false prophets, intent upon leading the true people of God astray; and he railed against them with greater vehemence. Eielsen organized no official congregations and kept no records of his pastoral acts, such as baptisms or marriages. To do so, he felt, would be to give in to the stifling formalism of the Church of Norway which had snuffed out true Christianity from the people entrusted to its care. He would have none of it.

But Anna and Terje were not influenced by Eielsen's way of thinking. This difference with Gunder and his family, as time went on, caused considerable strains in their relationships.

On the appointed day in October, wagonloads of people descended upon the Saersland farm from every direction. Terje and Anna and their family had to travel about four miles in a northeasterly direction to get there. Many of the people who gathered at Saersland's farm were strangers to Terje and Anna, and most of them spoke the Telemark dialect which was difficult for Terje and Anna to understand. The Telemarkings, on the other hand, claimed that the Sørlendings, which is what they called the people who came from the south coastal regions of Norway, spoke more like Danes than true Norwegians. But on this festive day of coming together, all those differences were forgotten.

The Rev. Adolph Carl Preus was there to greet all who came, replete in his cassock and ruff; and there were many who broke into tears of joy, just to see a minister dressed like that once more, bringing back memories, both sweet and sad, of old Norway. Ole Saersland and some of his neighbors had hauled in some large logs upon which people could sit, and there was a table at one end of the barn which could serve as an altar.

The older people, and that included Terje and Anna, were invited to sit inside the barn, near the front. Pregnant women were also given seats, but the others had to scramble for the remaining seats as best they could. Many folks had to stand outside for the entire service. Most of those attending had brought with them the hymnals which had been packed so carefully with other belongings when they emigrated to this country. They usually carried the hymnals carefully wrapped in white handkerchiefs. Preus had wisely selected hymns that were likely to be well known to the worshippers.

A wizened little man by the name of John Helgeson presided as *klokker*, announcing the hymns and leading the singing in a strong, shrill voice as the service got under way. There was no bell to call the worshippers together as there would have been in their parishes in Norway, and everyone present missed the ringing of the bells. After the first hymn, the liturgy they had heard from childhood was heard for the first time in the Neenah Settlement. Tears came to the eyes of many as they sang for the first time in many months or years the melody of the old *Kyrie;* and Preus chanted both the collect and epistle of the day, as was customary in the Church of Norway. After another hymn came the sermon, the first sermon that many had heard for several years.

Jacob had some difficulty hearing the sermon because he was among the many who had to stand outside, but he heard enough to recognize that Preus was using many of the same thoughts he had heard previously in Gunder's prayers – thoughts about how the immigrants who came to this land were like those ancient Israelites who had been led to a Land of Promise. But, as the pastor emphasized, the way to this Land of Promise was not always easy. He spoke sincerely and sympathetically of the sufferings which many of them had to endure – the loneliness of life in the primitive log cabins, the absence of their loved ones who were left back in Norway, the absence of their churches with the ordered life which began with baptism and continued through confirmation and the vows of marriage, the times when they could kneel at the Lord's altar to receive Holy Communion, and then on to the time of departure from this life and the committal of the dead to consecrated ground.

All of those certainties and assurances of their Mother Church in Norway they had left behind when they crossed the great Atlantic and came to this new and promising place. But today, he said, their old Church had come to them again, even though there was no special church building such as they had known in their home parishes; today Ole Saersland's barn became for all of them as holy as the most beautiful and sacred of any of the churches they had left behind in Norway.

As nearly as Jacob could tell, this was pretty much the gist of the sermon. The pastor spoke with great earnestness and sincerity, and there were many who had tears in their eyes as he spoke. It was so good to come together in this fashion because it also invoked many tender memories of the life they had left behind.

At the end of his sermon Pastor Preus announced that after they had lunch, there would be a special meeting to organize a congregation in the Neenah Settlement so an orderly and proper ministry could be conducted. He also announced that in two days, on October twenty-seventh, they should gather again here at Ole Saersland's barn to celebrate Holy Communion, and at that time he would also officiate at any baptisms or acknowledge those children who had been baptized at home by lay persons. At the conclusion of the service three children were brought forth: Halvor Halvorson Uvaas and Karen Anderson had been baptized at home by John Helgeson, and Maria Augusta Boiesen had not yet been baptized, but she was baptized at this service because her parents would not be able to come on October twenty-seventh.

After the service was over there was a great buzz of activity as many of those who had not previously met had an opportunity to get to know one another. Most of the settlers, it turned out, had come from various parishes in Telemark, especially from Hjartdal, Tuddal, and Sauland. But there were several families from Austbygdi and Gransherrad, as well as from Heddal. Jacob also met several people from Numedal and Toten, and there was even a Danish man by the name of Anders Jørgensen. There were several other families of Sørlendings, including Anton Møller and his wife Henrikke and their five sons.

On this beautiful October day Anna Tøvesdatter and Henrikke Møller had a long conversation sitting together on a log. The maples in Ole Saersland's woods were aglow with brilliant colors, and there was still a deep red hue on the sumac bushes that grew on the forest's edge.

It was reassuring to Anna that there were good neighbors like Henrikke Møller with whom she could share her inmost thoughts. Anna had met Henrikke just once before, at her brother Gunder's cabin when they first arrived in the Neenah Settlement some months earlier. Since that time there had been little time to converse with neighbors.

"It's a pity that my brother, Gunder Tøvesen, and his whole family cannot be here to enjoy this day with us. I cannot understand why he can be so opposed to this visit by Adolph Preus." Anna confided to Henrikke.

"Nor I, dear Anna." Henrikke answered. "But Gunder has been influenced by Elling Eielsen and his followers. Anton told me how painful it was for him to have to tell Gunder that he could not support Elling's visit here last year."

"I think your husband spoke to my Terje about this when we first came here, and it saddened me then that Gunder and Anton should have their differences."

"When we first came to Muskego, before we settled here in the Neenah Settlement, Claus Clausen, the pastor at Muskego was so kind to us. Perhaps I failed to tell you that we lost a little babe just a few months after our arrival there."

"No. How old was this child?"

"Our poor little daughter was only eight days old when she died. When she was born I was so happy that at last I had a daughter."

"You poor dear! I lost our little Anna-Lovisa when she was barely three years old."

"So we have both had our sorrows. Perhaps it is harder to lose a child as you did after she had been with you for three whole years. It was certainly hard enough for me during those first months at Muskego; but, as I said, Claus Clausen was so kind and helpful to us. Yet Elling and his followers could only find fault with everything that Clausen stood for."

"So, you left a little grave at Muskego, just as I had to leave a grave at Austre Moland."

"Yes, and it was not easy to leave that grave, but I realized then and I realize it more now that we really had no opportunity to get ahead in Muskego. The good land had all been taken, and so we joined some of the other Muskego folks and came here."

"Are you happy that you have come here?"

"On a beautiful autumn day like today, one can easily be happy. Anton and the boys seem to be happy with their new life here, and Anton is optimistic about the future we have here for our family."

"But it must have been hard for you to leave Norway. You were not used to farm life, were you?"

"No. My father was a merchant in Arendal. We had a very nice home with many fine furnishings, and my father loved music, insisting that each of his children should learn to play musical instruments. We had a beautiful pianoforte, and I took many lessons when I was a young girl."

"You must miss that life living out here in these crude log cabins."

"Yes, of course, I miss especially my piano. But my poor father first had terrible business reverses and lost his merchant business; and then, when I was only fourteen, my dear mother died. My brothers went to sea as sailors, and my poor father lives now with his youngest sister in Arendal."

"Even so, it must have been hard for you to leave your father, knowing that you'll likely never see him again."

"Yes, indeed it was. But Anton had his heart set upon emigrating to America, so here we are. I do get letters from my father quite frequently, but he is in poor health and I am afraid that one of these days I shall get a letter telling me he has died."

It was a bit easier for me to leave because both of my parents died some years ago. I have only my older brother and his family back at Flaa in Birkenes."

"My Anton has promised me that as soon as we can afford it, he will buy me either a piano or a melodeon. He also has a keen ear for music and would like our sons to grow up with music in their home. But right now, like all the others here, we are hard pressed for cash, and so this dream for a musical household must be put off until better times."

It certainly was a great pity, Anna mused to herself after her conversation with Henrikke, that Gunder and his family were of a such a mind-set that kept them from sharing this wonderful day. She loved her brother dearly, but she could not understand his prejudices against both church and clergy. Certainly Adolph Preus was a fine man, literally sent by God, to Anna's way of thinking, to help all of these folks in this new settlement; and she was pleased to have this opportunity to share this day with so many of her new neighbors.

They had all been so busy getting settled on their new land there was scarcely any time to socialize with neighbors. Terje and Anna were greeted cheerfully by Ole Strømme, and he summoned to his side the young lady who tomorrow would become his bride, a beautiful girl by the name of Yli Haugen. She was very shy, deeply self-conscious, especially in the presence of older folks like Terje and Anna.

Jacob noticed that his sister Maren was conversing with Johannes Baklistulen. Johannes was some years older than Jacob and was one of the early settlers in the Neenah Settlement who had come from Muskego. He came with his parents to this new land over a decade ago and was well versed in the English language. His brothers Halvor and Kittel were also present, and he introduced them to Maren as well. When Jacob sauntered over in the direction of his sister, she summoned him to join her and introduced him to the three brothers.

Jacob could not help but notice that Johannes was paying special attention to his sister, and he was a bit taken aback at this sudden turn of events. It was evident that Johannes Baklistulen was courting his sister, and Jacob almost subconsciously resented this intrusion upon his family. It seemed to him that he ought to step in to protect Maren and ward off Johannes or any other suitor who might have some notion of taking her away from his family.

At the afternoon meeting, Pastor Preus explained that there were now only three properly ordained Norwegian clergymen in America. Claus Clausen was at Rock Prairie, Wisconsin. He had been ordained by a German Lutheran clergyman and even though he had not had a full and complete university training in theology as a pastor of the Church of Norway would normally have, he had been properly trained in Denmark as a teacher of religion, His ordination was recognized as valid by Pastor Dietrichson; and he continued to serve, first at Muskego and now at Rock Prairie. Preus explained that he himself had only recently arrived in America, taking up his work as pastor at Koshkonong as the successor to Johannes Dietrichson who had returned to Norway. The third pastor was Hans Andreas Stub who came to Muskego in 1848. Perhaps some of those who came to the Neenah Settlement from Muskego knew both Clausen and Stub. Pastor Stub, he explained, might have come here to the Neenah Settlement himself, but he had been in ill health lately, and so it was decided that he, Adolph Preus, would be the first pastor to visit this new northern settlement. Preus explained that he hoped and expected that within the next year or two several more clergymen would arrive from Norway to take up work among the many Norwegians who were settling in Wisconsin and even beyond Wisconsin into other adjacent states.

It was important to organize a congregation in order that arrangements could be made for pastoral service, meager and sporadic as that might have to be for the next several years. He spelled out some of the requirements to be a properly organized congregation. John Helgeson, who had been trained as a teacher in Norway, was appointed secretary and instructed to write down the articles as they were presented by Pastor Preus.

The first article stated simply that this was to be known as the Norwegian Lutheran Church of the Neenah Settlement in Winnebago County in the State of Wisconsin. Then there were several articles which stated the adherence of the congregation to the Bible as the Word of God and adherence to the Lutheran

Confessions, especially to Luther's Catechisms and the Unaltered Augsburg Confession, as well as the ancient creeds, Apostolic, Nicene and Athanasian. The rituals of the congregation were to adhere to the Altar Book of 1585 of the Churches of Norway and Denmark.

Next, said Pastor Preus, it would be necessary to select three men as deacons who will be responsible for the spiritual oversight of the congregation, especially during the long periods of time when no pastor would be available. After some discussion, the names of Jens Anderson, Ole Peterson, and Johannes Baklistulen were placed in nomination. After these names had been suggested, there was an awkward silence because no one dared to suggest any others. So it was concluded that these three men should function as the first deacons of the congregation.

The next item was to select a precentor or *klokker* who could lead the singing of the congregation and function in the pastor's absence for emergency baptisms and burials of the dead. John Helgeson was unanimously selected for this position. It was also to be his responsibility to provide bread and wine for communion and see to it that there was water for baptisms.

Now came a difficult part for Pastor Preus to explain. In Norway, the state supported the church by tax revenues; but in this land, all of the churches were independent from the state, and so it would be necessary for each member of the congregation to subscribe money for the necessary funds to support the congregation.

There were several questions from people who had difficulty grasping this obvious fact. Ole Naess wondered if there would not be funds available from the Church of Norway which could sustain the congregations that were organized for Norwegians here in America. It took a bit of explaining to dispel any notion that money would be forthcoming from Norway, at least not in any significant amount. It would be necessary, Preus said, to appoint three men to collect dues from members of the congregation in order that the work of the congregation could go on.

Then there were questions about how much would be needed and how the money would be spent and how much each member would be expected to subscribe. For some, this was a rude awakening to some harsh realities. They hardly had enough to exist from day to day; how could they be expected to contribute money for this purpose? For a moment, it seemed to Jacob, the whole idea of organizing a congregation would have to be dropped because there was so much confusion about how much money would be needed and how the money should be raised.

It would cost about eighteen dollars for each pastoral visit, explained Pastor Preus, and some additional money should be raised, anticipating the day when the congregation could build its own house of worship. The congregations at Muskego and Koshkonong already had church buildings, constructed of logs. It was premature, Preus thought, for a church building here in the Neenah Settlement, but in several years they would need to confront that issue.

Ole Naess again spoke about the expenses, wondering if the congregation could get along on only one visit a year from a pastor. At eighteen dollars per year, that wouldn't be too expensive, he calculated. But others spoke against Ole's suggestion of only one visit per year. It had been so good, they said, to have Pastor Preus here; we should have several visits each year. More families are coming to our settlement each year. There are children who will need to be baptized and catechized and confirmed. There are some young fellows, like Ole Strømme, here, who would like to be properly married by a parson instead of by a justice of peace. There was a murmur of repressed laughter at that suggestion. Finally, it was agreed that Pastor Preus should try to arrange for three or four visits each year, either by himself or one of his colleagues.

After all this discussion, it was finally resolved that a committee of three collectors of dues should have the responsibility to solicit the congregation for necessary funds. Anders Jørgensen, Ole Halvorson Uvaas, and John Nelson Bjørndalen were nominated for this responsibility and duly elected.

There remained one final task of organization. After John Helgeson had completed writing the articles, each person desiring to become a member of the congregation should attach his signature to the document. The men, as heads of their household, were instructed to sign. Widows or unmarried women could also affix their signatures. Jacob was somewhat surprised when Maren stepped forward to sign her name. All in all, there were eighty-six signatures affixed to the articles of the congregation. In a few instances, the men were unable to sign their names, and so they made an "x" and John Helgeson signed for them.

Pastor Preus announced that each family should read devoutly the *huspostill* on all the Sundays when they could not assemble for worship, and teach their children the catechism and the great hymns of the church. Tomorrow, he announced, he would officiate at the wedding of Ole Strømme and Yli Haugen; and in the afternoon at two o'clock he would be at the cemetery, where three small children had already been buried, to read the rite of Christian committal and attempt to give comfort to those who mourned the loss of these loved ones.

On the morning of October twenty-seventh, there was a special service of Holy Baptism at Ole Saersland's barn. Nineteen children were baptized at this service, or, to be more exact, ten were baptized and nine others were blessed because they had been baptized earlier by laymen. Although most of the baptized were infants, there were several older children.

On the afternoon of October twenty-seventh, many of those who had gathered two days earlier were back at Ole Saersland's barn for the service of Holy Communion. Most of those assembled had not had an opportunity to partake of Holy Communion for several years, and the mood was very somber. One hundred and thirty people registered with Pastor Preus for Holy Communion, and each one received a warm handshake after affixing a signature to a record book. The service followed the order they had known from Norway, and the table in Ole Saersland's barn was a high altar for those who worshipped there on that day. The solemnity of the occasion was punctuated by overcast clouds and sporadic showers.

On the way back from this service, Terje turned to his wife and his two older sons and said, "Now we are a real *bygd* (parish), and someday we shall have a church with a steeple and bell just like Austre Moland!"

Logs for the Schoolhouse

George and Matilda Knott came directly to the Neenah Settlement from Vermont in the summer of 1849. They settled upon the tract of land that originally was claimed by Ezra Norton, but he relinquished his claim to the Knotts because of his advancing age and some persisting health problems that forced him to live as a semi-invalid with his son, Lambert. It was a difficult decision for Ezra to sign over his claim to another; but he took some consolation in the fact that this new family that wanted to buy his land came from New England, just as he had.

The Knotts brought with them George's father, Matthew Knott, a veteran of the War of 1812 and a widower. George Knott had attended a classical academy in Vermont for three years where he studied Latin, history, English literature, and mathematics. He might have continued his studies had it not been necessary for him to return to his father's little Vermont farm to take over much of the work because his father had broken his leg and the break was slow to heal.

Of all the Yankee settlers in the Neenah Settlement, George Knott had the most formal education and the greatest passion for learning. He had an agile mind and could memorize long passages of poetry with ease. His favorite poets were Shakespeare and Milton, but he also was quite fond of some of the more recent New England poets and could recite many of their poems with great feeling.

Matilda Knott had attended a female seminary in Vermont for several years and began to teach school at fifteen years of age in a remote small village in Vermont. After four years of teaching, she married George Knott and within a year gave birth to a son, Matthew Knott II, named for his grandfather. Matthew II was now six years old and had two younger siblings, Ralph, four, and Margaret, three. The Knotts decided to come west because their tiny rock-bound Vermont farm seemed incapable of providing them with a decent livelihood. They were related to the Clarkes on George's mother's side of the family and located in the Neenah Settlement because of that connection.

During the summer and autumn of 1849, the Knotts were busy establishing themselves in their new home, getting some of the land cleared and building their first log structures. In the winter, Matilda Knott gathered some neighborhood children into her small cabin, together with her own children, conducting a kind of school. Ten children attended this makeshift school off and on during those winter months. Most of them were children of their Yankee neighbors; but two of the Landsverk children were included because they lived so close by, and Torger and Anna Landsverk thought it would be good for their children to have this chance to learn English. The Landsverk children could not speak English when they came to Matilda Knott's school, but within a few weeks they were chatting with their comrades and learning to read English from the primary reader Matilda Knott used to teach them.

In the autumn of 1850 Matilda Knott continued to teach these children; but now there were twelve in her crowded cabin. There were others who wanted to attend, but Matilda had to tell those families that she did not have room to accommodate any more than the twelve children already enrolled. During the winter months George Knott often joined his wife in teaching the children. They were a captive audience for George's penchant for reciting poetry, and poor little Aslaug Landsverk was mightily puzzled and confused over "*Quips and cranks and wanton wiles; Nods and becks and wreathed smiles.*"

Clearly something needed to be done about providing more space for a school, and more permanent arrangements needed to be made for properly organizing a school district and hiring a full-time teacher. Matilda had been donating her time to this effort with little thought of compensation, but several of the families whose children were involved made gifts of food and produce to the Knotts. Torger Landsverk provided them with a butchered hog and Frank Jones gave a whole large sack of flour. But Matilda Knott told her neighbors that she could not carry on in this fashion after this year. She was, after all, a busy wife and mother and many household tasks had to be neglected because of her teaching. They would have to try to find another teacher next year.

Matilda's decision prompted a sudden informal gathering of some of the Yankee neighbors early in November at Lambert Norton's log home.

"Something ought to be done about all these foreigners that are flooding into our county every day. They ought not be allowed to come into this country if they can't speak our language and conform to our customs!"

Samuel Hopkins spoke these words emphatically at the beginning of the gathering. Several others in the group nodded their heads in agreement with Hopkins, and this encouraged him to speak further on this subject.

"These Norwegians who have managed somehow to get legal claims to so much of the land here in our township are really getting to be a problem. Most of them can't speak a word of English, and those who can, speak with such a horrible accent that you can't understand what they are trying to say. How can we possibly have a decent form of government with all these foreigners taking up so much of the land all around us? I don't see how these people could ever really become civilized to the point where they can function as good citizens in our new community."

At this point, Carrie Hopkins looked around at the others in the room, as if daring them to disagree with her husband. She chimed in to reinforce her husband's sentiments:

"Those people seem to me to be scarcely human. The other night we were awakened by three drunken Norwegian fellows who made so much noise that they could be heard a mile away, yelling and carrying on like so many wild Indians filled with firewater.

And have you seen how some of them live in such filth? Their children are clad in rags and are dirty from head to toe, and they keep on having babies, one after another. In ten years we will all be overrun by them."

Others joined the Hopkins couple in giving vent to their misgivings about all of these new immigrant families crowding in upon their Yankee world. Some had read similar sentiments in newspapers identified with the Know-Nothing movement.

At this point, however, Lambert Norton broke into the conversation with some opinions which countered those previously expressed.

"I've found these Norwegians I've employed to be among my best workmen. They're not a lazy lot, that's for sure. One Norwegian can probably outwork two or three of our young Yankee dandies when it comes to felling trees and clearing the land. If it were not for these fellows, most of my land would still be in heavy forest. To be sure, one sometimes has a bit of difficulty communicating with them, but somehow we manage to make ourselves understood."

Samuel and Carrie Hopkins glared at him, but Lambert continued to speak.

"Another thing about them is that they seem to be almost naively honest. If you have agreed to pay them a certain amount, they will hesitate to accept a penny more, even though you offer it freely to them."

At this point, Emmeline Norton also ventured her opinions.

"I stopped by one of their cabins the other day, on that farm just a mile west of our place, and the lady invited me into her house for a cup of coffee. The log cabin was very modest and crudely furnished, but everything was clean and neat. Of course, we had great difficulty in communicating, but the Norwegian woman seemed to appreciate my coming, and she even gave me some delicious butter which she had just churned shortly before I came into her house. She had the most darling little yellow-haired and blue-eyed child I have seen who presented me with a small container of nuts she had gathered in the woods. Although these people have come from a strange land and speak a strange language, they will in time make good citizens. It is up to us to lead them and help them and educate them to American ways. This frontier country is large enough to contain many kinds of people, and it will need the hard labor of many to make it the kind of place that we'll want to have in the future. I say that if these people are willing to work so hard, we ought to help them become good Americans, even though that will take time."

Someone ventured the thought that at least these Norwegians were not Roman Catholics, like the Irish who were crowding into many places these days.

"Well," Samuel Hopkins answered, "they may not be Roman Catholics; but Will Richards visited that religious meeting those Norwegians had last week, and he said they carried on in a pretty strange manner, something like the Catholics, mumbling and chanting in a strange tongue here in this good Protestant land. And their preacher was all doffed up with a long gown just like a priest. It looks pretty suspicious to me, and I wouldn't doubt but they're in cahoots with the Catholics in some way or another, even though they deny it and want to be called Protestants."

Clearly the opinions in this Yankee gathering were quite divided upon the subject of the ever-increasing number of immigrant neighbors who were encroaching more and more upon their community.

At last George Knott hit upon a topic to which they could all give their assent – the community desperately needed a schoolhouse and a school teacher. It would not do to have all of these children, whether Yankee or Norwegian or Irish, growing up in ignorance.

"And besides," George Knott said, "if we have a schoolhouse right here in the middle of our community, it will give these immigrant children an opportunity to learn how to speak English properly, and in a few years these Norwegian folks will be just like us."

This was the telling argument for all who were gathered that day at Lambert Norton's place. If the community was going to have a future, it would need to get a school started, and the sooner the better.

George Knott offered a small piece of land on the corner of his farm as a suitable site for a schoolhouse; and the rest agreed that it would be a good site because it was centrally situated, especially for the Yankee settlers, at a good crossroads location.

Lambert Norton, who still had acres of tall hardwood trees to clear from his land, offered to donate the standing timber for logs if volunteers could be found to cut the logs and haul them to the school site. George Knott was elected chairman of the temporary school board, with Lambert Norton and Elijah Clarke as the other two members, and they were instructed to try to get volunteers to cut the logs for the new schoolhouse.

At this point Samuel Hopkins suggested, in a rather surly tone of voice, that if the Norwegians were such good workers and wanted their children to be educated, why not ask them to cut the logs and do most of the work, under Yankee supervision, of course. The others agreed that their Norwegian neighbors should be asked to join them in this enterprise.

They next needed to address the problem of finding a suitable teacher for their school. Elijah Clarke suggested that Mr. Mary, the Methodist preacher who had recently held the first meeting in Clarke's cabin for the handful of Methodists in the community, had a younger sister who was unmarried and wished to join her brother and his family in this part of Wisconsin. She was living in Jefferson County in the southern part of the state, but there were no teaching positions available to her there.

Mr. Clarke also had some information, given to him by Mr. Mary, about the salary expectations. He also had spoken to one of the county officers about how tax assessments should be made to each property owner within the school district they were in the process of organizing and reported his conversation to the others.

Torger Landsverk was assigned by the three members of the school board to recruit some of the Norwegians to cut the logs and help erect the schoolhouse on George Knott's property. He was well acquainted with the Knott family because his own children had been enrolled in Matilda Knott's little log cabin school, and he spoke enough English to communicate quite well with his Yankee neighbors. So Torger went from farm to farm to enlist helpers for this task. Wherever he went he found a ready response and willingness to help with this important task. He encountered only one reservation. Some of his neighbors thought that the school ought to be available from time to time, when it would not be used for English school, as a parochial school for Norwegian families where their children could be properly instructed in reading and writing the Norwegian language and in the catechism and Bible history. At the recent organizational meeting of the congregation, there had been some discussion about organizing such a school for the growing number of children in the parish.

Torger Landsverk reported this request to the three members of the school board. At first there was a considerable reluctance to consider this unusual request. But after some discussion, Lambert Norton, perhaps with an eye to gaining some favor in the eyes of his Norwegian neighbors, suggested that under the circumstances it was a reasonable request, provided it did not interfere with the proper scheduling of regular schooling in English. With some misgiving and reluctance, the other two board members finally agreed, and Torger Landsverk returned to his Norwegian neighbors with the good news that a way had been found to use the building for both purposes.

A day late in November was appointed to begin cutting the logs in Lambert Norton's woods for the new schoolhouse. Fifteen Norwegians showed up on the first day with their axes, adzes, and saws. Jacob was one of the group. Torger Landsverk acted as captain of the work party, but Lambert Norton was on hand during the morning hours to help Torger determine which trees should be chosen. They labored from early morning to dusk and during that one day were able to fell and trim enough trees to build the schoolhouse. They all needed to return the next day with horses or oxen to snake the logs out of Lambert Norton's woods and get them to the building site, which was about a half a mile away. Once at the site, they needed to dress the logs properly with the adze and notch them. On the third day, they actually began construction of the building; and within a week the Neenah Settlement had its first schoolhouse.

Jacob Larsen was unhappy that the job had to be done in such haste with green logs, but he was told by Torger Landsverk that this building would probably need to be used only for a few years, perhaps only four or five, until the district could be more properly organized and sawed lumber would be more available to construct a better building. Jacob was also unhappy that the school would have only a dirt floor, but again he was told that many of the children, even from Yankee homes, were still living on dirt floors. There would be time enough to provide a proper wooden floor when a more substantial building could be built.

Quite a few of the Norwegian families in the Neenah Settlement lived too far away from the new schoolhouse to send their children to it. Some of the Norwegian families who lived several miles west of the school decided that they also should have a school, and within a year another log school was erected on Helge Mathison's property. Nearly all of the families in this west district were Norwegian except for a cluster of seven Irish families who had settled in their midst. Both the Knott School and the West School began without regular teachers.

Matilda Knott continued to teach her group in the new log schoolhouse during several weeks of the winter and several more weeks during the spring months of 1851. Her enrollment grew from twelve to twenty-one, with most of the increase coming from Norwegian families. Klemet Larsen and his sister Anna-Maria were sent to this school, and even their older sister Maren occasionally attended as a visitor. Each morning George Knott began the day by reading stories to the children and reciting long passages of poetry.

During two weeks in March when Matilda Knott was not teaching, John Helgesen came to the Knott School where he conducted classes in Norwegian and drilled the Norwegian children in their catechism lessons and Bible history. After his session at the Knott School he held another at the newly erected log building of the West School. In the fall of 1851, Josephine Mary, the sister of the Methodist preacher, came to the Neenah Settlement to take over the Knott School as its first regular and full-time teacher.

The Demons Return

The first winter for the family from Skredderstua dragged on and on. It was a more severe winter than they ever had experienced in their homeland, and the little stove in the log cabin glowed red-hot just to keep the folks warm when they stood within a few feet of it. Most of the time the cabin was quite snug and warm; but in the mornings, when the fire had gone out, the whole cabin could get dangerously cold, with frost on the log walls. Anna Tøvesdatter suffered much during those cold winter mornings, in spite of the fact that she wore all the heavy garments that she had, just to keep from freezing.

During the coldest part of the winter Jacob and Elias took turns getting up in the middle of the night to refuel the little stove, and this proved to be a better plan. All too slowly the warming of spring came; and soon the snow began to thaw, producing a sea of mud that both man and beast had to endure.

On some of the winter days Jacob, Elias and Kittel kept themselves busy by dressing the logs they had cut in September on Heinrich Meyer's place and had recently hauled back to their farm by oxen and sleigh. These logs were to be used for the new and larger log house. They were shaped square by Jacob's careful skill. After the adze had done its work, Jacob used a draw shave to make the surfaces even more smooth, using the shavings and chips for kindling in their little stove. When the men were not working on the logs for their new house, they were in the woods which bordered on the natural oak openings, cutting more trees in order to clear land for their first wheat crop.

In February, Jacob and Elias had to yoke the oxen to their crudely made sleigh and go to Winnebago Rapids in order to buy more flour and other supplies because their food stores were running dangerously low. To buy these supplies, it was necessary to spend more of the cash left from the sale of Skredderstua.

In order to replenish their funds, Jacob, Elias and Kittel all volunteered to work for Lambert Norton who was willing to pay each of them a dollar a day for cutting trees on his property. Norton soon discovered that he had hired three excellent workmen. Even Kittel, who had not had much experience felling trees, soon became adept with his axe, thanks to the helpful coaching of his two elder brothers.

In addition to their daily wage, they were provided with a warm noon dinner at the Norton cabin, and this gave them an opportunity to get to know Emmeline Norton and her two daughters, Lydia and Roberta. Jacob struggled with his best English as he tried to communicate with the Norton girls, and they often giggled at his attempts. Elias and Kittel only listened because they knew very little English, but little by little they began to catch on to words and phrases. After they returned to the woods, they often asked Jacob to explain some words and phrases they had just heard, and then they would practice repeating them to each other.

During one of the noon interludes in the Norton house, Roberta asked Jacob to accompany her into a small bedroom adjacent to the main living area of their cabin. This room was occupied by Roberta's aging and ailing grandfather, Ezra Norton, who was now completely bedridden. Roberta had to shout into his ear because the old man was very deaf. As she tried to explain who Jacob was, the old man stared out of his red-rimmed eyes at Jacob and began to speak in a surprisingly loud and clear voice:

"So you've come from a far land to become an American. You seem to be a likely looking lad, just the sort of fellow this country needs. I was once a young fellow like you, straight and strong, and I took up my musket and bayonet way back in 'seventy-seven when my militia was called up, and we chased them damned red-coats right out of the land. That we did, young man, so you and your like can have a chance to build up this new country."

At this point the old man began to cough, and Roberta cautioned him, "Grandfather, you'd better not speak for a while; just lie back and rest for a few minutes."

But the old man soon recovered from his coughing spell and was intent upon speaking some more to Jacob.

"And do you know what else – when I was about your age I saw, in Connecticut, none other than General George Washington himself, mounted on his white horse, riding right through our town on his way from Boston to New York. I'll never forget that moment as long as I live. He was the father of our country, you know – a great man – and I saw him with my very own eyes. . . ."

Now old Ezra Norton began to cough some more and tears came to his reddened eyes. Roberta gave him a spoon of cough medicine and he eased back on to his pillow.

Jacob took Ezra Norton's feeble hand in his own, thanking him for the visit and asking him now to rest. This was a moment etched forever in Jacob's mind because somehow it linked him personally to the beginnings of this great republic.

And so the days went on through most of the month of March. Jacob was a bit concerned that the building of a more permanent house would be delayed because of all of the time spent working for Norton, but it couldn't be helped. They needed the money and sacrifices had to be made.

On one blustery March forenoon, Aase Knutsdatter surprised Anna Tøvesdatter as she knocked on the cabin door. Anna could see that Aase was distraught and anxious. She had hardly come through the door and unbuttoned her coat when she exclaimed:

"Anna, I'm very concerned about Anlaug Risland, and I am at my wits end knowing what to do. I honestly believe that she is losing her mind."

"How can that be, Aase? The last time I saw her which was, let's see, about two and a half months ago, she seemed quite normal and even good-humored as she talked about the antics of her Lasse and your Halvor and some of their adventures."

Anna spoke as she was pouring a cup of coffee for Aase and motioned for her to sit at the table.

"Yes, Anna, but that was some time ago; and during the confinement of this winter, things have not gone well in the Risland cabin. Anlaug blames Sven bitterly for the death of their little child and keeps bringing it up again and again.

"What a burden that must be for poor Sven. He certainly did not wish for the death of that child." Anna responded.

"Her mind is more and more obsessed with the loss of that child, especially over the fact that the poor child has no grave except the ocean. I know that you lost a little one some years ago, and I thought that maybe if you could talk to Anlaug you might be able to comfort her or relieve her mind in some way that I cannot seem to do."

"Of course I shall try to talk to her, if you think it would do any good." Anna suggested tentatively.

"I feel so utterly helpless. I try to reason with her, but she will not listen. She only cries, and sometimes she shrieks and carries on like one possessed by the devil. At other times she gets so morose and silent I can't get a word out of her. I am so worried about her and her whole family. The girls are frightened by it all, and poor Sven has to bear the brunt of much of her anger, it seems."

"How terrible it must be for everyone in the family." Anna added sympathetically.

"She blames Sven for disobeying God by coming to this terrible and heathen place. If they had stayed in Norway, she keeps saying, her little Karen Lovisa would still be alive. She also blames Gunder for persuading Sven to come to America, and so it goes on and on. Her eyes take on a wild and glassy look when she gets these spells, and I'm at my wit's end to know what to do. She even claims she wishes she were dead so she could go and comfort that poor baby who got tossed into the sea"

It was good for Aase to talk to Anna about her concerns, and she stayed for nearly two hours. Anna finally agreed that within the week she would try to come to visit Aase, and then she would also try to talk to Anlaug.

As spring came, Terje and his sons had long discussions on what plans should be made for crops and where the wheat should be planted and which area should be reserved for pasture for the cattle and oxen. It would be necessary, as soon as possible, to hitch the oxen to the plow Terje had purchased from Adam Cartwright and begin to turn over furrows between the tree stumps. It would not be easy work because the plow would probably snag on buried tree roots, and then they would have to get in with shovel and axe and grub-hoe to get the land prepared for its first seeding of wheat.

In spite of the possible difficulties, Elias was almost like a child in his gleeful anticipation of getting their first crop planted. Each day he would walk carefully through the stump-strewn area that was to become their first wheat field, assessing whether it was time to sink in the plow for its first furrows in this wonderfully virgin and fertile land that had waited so many millennia for this very moment.

At last the day came when the oxen were hitched to the plow and the first tentative furrows began to appear, revealing the rich dark brown soil. To be sure, there were those pesky tree roots that stopped the plow every so often, especially when Elias tried to skim as close to the standing stumps as possible.

There were a number of round granite rocks, dark gray in color, that needed to be carried off the field. Jacob and Kittel carried them to the building site, with some occasional help from Klemet. In fact, Jacob coveted these stones for the foundation of the house, and the pile grew larger and larger as the plowed field expanded in size. However, some rocks were too large to be moved, boulder-sized monsters that seemed to be permanently lodged deeply in the soil. It was necessary to work around these monsters, at least for the time being.

After the plowing, Elias went over the field a second time with a make-shift harrow that he and Jacob had devised out of some misshapen hickory logs. The logs with their sharp points were dragged over the plowed land to further pulverize the soil and prepare it to receive its first planting of seed.

Then the day finally came when Elias stepped out on to the field with a wooden bucket tied around his neck so that his arms were free. The bucket was filled with wheat that Adam Cartwright had given to Terje; and Elias, with his right hand filled with the golden wheat, scattered the seed as evenly as he could upon the dark brown soil. He had planted grain many times at Skredderstua, usually rye or barley, but this wonderful wheat had a special feel in his hands.

After the wheat was sown, Elias, Jacob, Kittel and their father, Terje Larsen, all went out onto the land with home-made wooden rakes that Jacob had contrived and gently covered the wheat with a thin layer of soil. Now, God willing, they had only to wait until the sunshine and rains could do their good work, and the wheat could be harvested in several months.

In addition to the wheat field, a considerable area was worked up and planted as a garden, including a sizable area for potatoes. Anna and her daughters had carefully gathered seeds from some of their garden crops at Skredderstua that last summer before they emigrated, and these seeds were now sown in American soil with the hope that, like the human immigrants, they too could be successfully transplanted. Anna also obtained from Aase some seeds for plants they were never able to grow in Norway, and one day Johannes Baklistulen paid a call on the family and brought with him several packets of seeds – beans, peas, carrots – plus some roots which he carried in a bucket, roots of rhubarb and asparagus, as well as a good number of strawberry plants. Soon the vegetable garden was carefully hoed and planted with the hope that it could help to sustain its hungry family, not only during the summer months, but on into the autumn and winter as well.

Once the crops were planted, Jacob could turn his attention to building. First, he discovered that a sawmill was in operation in Winneconne; so he hauled several of the shorter pine logs as well as several hardwood logs to this saw-mill in order to have a good supply of planks and boards needed in constructing the house.

It was several weeks before the sawmill could accommodate Jacob because of a backlog of other work, but Jacob was able to get an estimate from the owner that his logs would be sawed in less than three weeks. He also needed to get other supplies, many of which were available in Winneconne because steamboats were now able to transport cargo along area waterways. So Jacob was able to purchase nails and other hardware items, slaked lime for masonry, and windows, as well as some other millwork now being produced in standard dimensions at a reasonable cost at a mill in Oshkosh. Now it was necessary to dig the cellar of the house by hand. Jacob purchased two extra shovels so the task could proceed a bit faster, and Terje and Kittel joined Jacob and Elias in this task. Within four days they dug out a cellar of sufficient depth, and now the foundation stones were carefully lowered into place, the heavier stones at the bottom of the cellar. The slaked lime was mixed with sand to provide a mortar mix suitable for building the cellar wall, which would also provide a substantial foundation for the building. The wall was about eighteen to twenty inches thick and firmly bonded with mortar.

At the top of the masonry wall a squared timber was embedded into the mortar to provide a suitable surface upon which the rest of the structure could rest. It was important that these timbers should be absolutely level; Jacob fussed and tapped them into place, measuring them and re-measuring them with a level again and again. Finally, after nearly a half day spent at this task, Jacob nodded his approval to the others, and the cellar was left for several days so that the mortar could set and dry. The cellar's outer dimensions were sixteen feet by twenty-eight feet, and this seemed palatial to Anna and her daughters as they compared it to the little cabin in which they were living.

Next, Jacob laid down the first carefully notched logs on the two lengths of the foundation. These logs had been painstakingly prepared to hold the cross joists which were mortised snugly into place to support the main floor. By this time it was necessary to make a second trip to Winneconne because the sawed logs were ready at the mill. These logs would provide the planks for the subfloor as well as thinner selected pine boards which would be used for the finished floor.

Once the sawed lumber arrived, Jacob insisted that the subfloor should be laid diagonally to give greater stability to the structure. Terje and Elias wondered why this was necessary because it would be much simpler and quicker simply to lay the planks across the joists in a perpendicular fashion. But they gave in to Jacob's wish because he told them this was the way it had been done for Adam Cartwright's fine house in Fond du Lac which they had both admired so much.

After the subfloor was completed, the main task of erecting the house proceeded. Each log was carefully hoisted into place, a process that required all four men, especially for the longer logs. Jacob had carefully squared each log with the adze, and had used the draw shave on the inner surface so that it would be smooth on the interior. On the exterior, many of the adze marks were still visible. The logs were carefully shaped so that no mortar would be needed to provide a tight fit, just as had been done for generations in the carefully built log buildings in Norway.

As each log was lifted into place to make sure of its fit, Jacob stood by with his adze and plane and draw shave to adjust any portion of the log that did not fit snugly. Once Jacob determined that the log fit properly, it was lifted off again, and the top surface of the under-log was smeared with pitch. Then the log was lifted back in place and securely spiked at the end where the notches had been carefully done in Norwegian fashion. And so log by log, Jacob built up the walls, providing the appropriate openings for doors and windows.

Within a week, he had come to the point where the joist beams for the second story could be installed. Then another floor was put in, and the walls were extended higher. On the gable ends there was room for windows of full height, but on the long side of the house there would be half-light windows because the roof line was low. Soon it was time to put in the roof beams.

On the day the roof beams were completed, Jacob went into the little pine grove, where a few little pine seedlings were growing, and cut a little tree which he mounted at the peak of the roof beam on the east side of the house. Maren and Anna-Maria prepared a special lunch for the men, and a table was brought outside for a little family celebration on this important day. Terje sang some old Norwegian songs he remembered from his days when he was a soldier in the old fortress at Christiansand, and even Anna Tøvesdatter was in a giddy and merry mood. Their house was going to be the finest in the whole neighborhood, thanks to that clever son of hers, as well as his good helpers.

Unfortunately, the merriment was abruptly interrupted by the sudden appearance of Gunder Tøvesen who arrived breathless and agitated.

"A terrible thing has happened!" he shouted while trying to catch his breath. "Anlaug Risland is dead, by her own hand."

Suddenly the mood of the whole family changed, first to surprise and shock, and then to profound sorrow that such a thing could happen right here in the Neenah Settlement to someone so close to them.

Anna gasped and exclained, "That poor family already has had to endure so much!"

"Late this morning Sven Risland came running over to our place. The poor man was nearly beside himself. He had just discovered that Anlaug had hanged herself in their cattle shed. He had not had occasion to go inside the shed since early in the day, so no one had seen Anlaug since mid-morning. The girls were visiting some friends about a mile away and Lasse was at our place with our Halvor, so Sven had been alone, cutting trees and trying to clear land in the far corner of his farm."

Terje had vivid memories of his own about dealing with the suicide of one of his near neighbors in Norway.

"It is terrible for everyone concerned, with suicides," he uttered ponderously.

"Anlaug may have been dead for some time before we discovered her body dangling in that place. What a horrible thing to have happened. No one could have predicted she would do such a terrible thing. Of course, she has been very depressed, as you know, and has spoken to my Aase much about those demons that have afflicted her mind, but no one expected it to go this far."

Gunder sat down by the table and his sister poured him a cup of coffee.

"Sven and I had the gruesome task of cutting down the body and carrying Anlaug's lifeless form into the Risland cabin. Sven was beside himself, blaming himself for what had happened. Right now Aase is trying as best she can to look after the whole Risland family. The girls have been summoned home and Lasse can only stand beside his father in shock. Aase insisted that the Rislands should stay with us. It is entirely too much to expect them to want to enter that cabin where the mother's body is laid out on the bed."

"No, of course not." Anna Tøvesdatter spoke solemnly to her brother, "I spoke to poor Anlaug several times, trying to get her to tell me about her afflictions, but it did not seem to help to try to reason with her. I tried to quote some passages of Scripture to her in order to comfort her about the death of her little daughter, and I even tried to share with her my own experiences of grief when our little Anna-Lovisa was buried in the churchyard at Austre Moland. But that seemed to make things even worse. She would go on to rant and rave about that poor child's body being cast into the ocean."

"Yes," Gunder said, "she seemed to have an obsession about her child's body in the ocean. Aase told me she would rave on and on about that."

Anna continued, "At times, I thought maybe I had helped her a bit by talking with her, but at other times, it only seemed to be worse. I've never felt so helpless in all my life, and now this. What's going to happen to poor Sven and those girls and little Lasse?"

After some more discussion it was decided that Jacob should make a coffin for poor Anlaug out of some of the boards which were intended for the finished floor in the new house. They could always get some more boards. Now they would all need to pull together to help this unfortunate family as best they could. Terje suggested they should summon John Helgesen to assist with the burial of Anlaug, and the sooner she could be buried, the better for all concerned.

In spite of Gunder's negative feelings about the newly organized congregation, he did not object to calling John Helgesen. This was an hour of deepest need, and they were fortunate that a site had already been established for a burial ground. There had already been three deaths in Neenah Settlement; two were small infants and one a child of six who died suddenly of some unknown malady. Anlaug Risland would be the first person of adult years buried in the settlement's cemetery.

John Helgesen was solicitous when Terje called him from the field where he was laboring. When Terje asked him about the problem of burying in consecrated ground a person who had committed suicide, Helgesen only furrowed his brow and responded in his own deliberate fashion:

"Yes, I know in Norway there were those customs and regulations about these matters. But we are in Norway no more; our conditions here are quite different from those that we had in our settled parishes in Norway. I think the only thing I can do under the circumstances is to read the brief order for committal of the dead I have used in the past, and when Pastor Preus returns for his next visit to our parish, I shall have to consult him on this matter. In the meantime we must think of that poor family and try to be of as much help and comfort as we can."

It was decided the burial would take place the next morning at about ten o'clock. In the meantime, John Helgesen would see to it that a grave was dug, and Terje would make arrangements with the family. Meanwhile, word of the tragedy spread around the community. Many of the Norwegian settlers and even a few Yankee families came to the burial site the next day, some out of curiosity, but most out of profound sympathy for the family which was visited so tragically by death.

The Roof is On

The beams stood bare and exposed to the elements for several days because of Anlaug Risland's death. Anna insisted that the Risland girls should stay at her place, and the men gladly gave up their sleeping quarters in the loft of the cabin in order to provide space for the girls. The weather was mild, and the men did not mind sleeping outside, under a canvas awning.

The oldest Risland girl, Berit, had just turned fourteen, and her two younger sisters, Gro and Tone, were now twelve and eleven. It was a very difficult time for these girls who were utterly bewildered by the sudden tragedy which struck them. They were by nature shy and withdrawn, but Anna Tøvesdatter and her two daughters, Maren and Anna-Maria, decided they should try as hard as they could to provide a new life for them.

Maren was particularly friendly to the girls, and they soon began to look up to her as a special kind of older sister. The last months with their mother in her distracted condition had not been easy for the girls. They had been emotionally scarred by it all, but Maren treated them as she might have cared for some unfortunate wild creatures who had been wounded and needed special care to come back to health. It was in Maren's nature to be just this kind of caring and thoughtful person, and when Jacob saw how his sister treated the girls, he admired her greatly. Anna, too, had many of the same qualities and became a kind of surrogate mother to these mother-starved creatures. Gradually the girls began to open up a bit as they gained confidence in all the members of the family that had taken them in. They were especially shy around the menfolks, and it took much longer for them to adjust to the presence of so many active men in one household.

The wheat crop was beginning to ripen, and in just a week or so Elias would have to sharpen his scythe and cut the first swaths of this beautiful golden crop. Then everyone in the household would be busy in one way or another with the task of harvesting. Elias also was taking more and more time away from building the house because he was busy cutting grass for hay wherever he could find it. He often had Klemet as his helper. After the grass was cut, Klemet would rake it into the oxcart; and when the cart was filled with the new-mown grass, he and Elias would drive it to the farmyard and spread it out on the short grass near the cattle shed to dry. In this manner, a fairly large stack of hay was gradually accumulated next to the cattle shed.

In the meantime, Jacob and Kittel and their father continued to work on the roof of their house, first nailing on the roof boards, which were spaced apart to accommodate the cedar shakes which would soon be nailed upon them. While Jacob and Kittel were working on the roof, Terje was busy splitting cedar shakes with a riving knife and mallet. Jacob had obtained some fairly large dry cedar logs from Johannes Baklistulen, and he sawed them into shingle length chunks. Terje soon became adept at splitting the shakes, and his pile of shakes grew larger each day. Jacob insisted that his father should not work on the roof. It could be too dangerous for an older man, he thought, fearing he might lose his footing.

Before the shingles could be put on the roof, it was necessary to build the chimney. Jacob made a special trip to Winneconne where he was able to purchase the bricks as well as two additional stoves and the necessary stove pipes. One of the new stoves had an oven and would be used in the kitchen. The other stove was similar to the one they already had in their present log cabin. One of the small stoves would be installed in the parents' bedroom downstairs, and the other would be put upstairs. Thus, the chimney would need to service three stoves. Jacob had not had a great deal of experience laying bricks, but he had carefully observed the masons and bricklayers when he worked on Adam Cartwright's house, and he was confident that he could build one small chimney. He also asked the man at the brickyard a few questions about properly lining a chimney, and received some good advice from him.

Once the chimney was completed, it was time to shingle the roof, but now it was necessary once more to delay for some days because Elias determined it was time to begin cutting the wheat crop. Jacob and Kittel were also needed for this task, and each man had his own scythe equipped with a cradle, so the cutting of the crop could be done as quickly as possible. It would not do to delay very long because if the wheat became over-ripe, it would begin to hull out, and much of the crop could be lost.

Terje and his daughters and the Risland girls all helped with tying the grain into bundles and setting the bundles into shocks where the grain could cure. Only Anna was exempt from the field work; she had to prepare all the food for the hungry crew and, from time to time, had to bring cold water out to the field for the hot and thirsty workers.

It was not a large field; it contained perhaps three and a half acres, but if one discounted the space taken up by stumps and other obstacles, the area was considerably less. But it was a good crop. The wheat had grown tall, so there was a good deal of straw in each bundle. The heads of wheat were full and the individual kernels of wheat were round and firm. Adam Cartwright's seed was excellent, of a much higher quality than some used by several of the neighbors.

When Lambert Norton saw the fine crop his neighbors had on land that nearly bordered his own, he marveled that there could be such a difference between his own mediocre crop and their fine crop. At first he was somewhat petulant and jealous, but he soon swallowed his pride and inquired of Jacob just what kind of wheat they were growing. When Jacob told him about the seed they had obtained from Adam Cartwright of Fond du Lac, Norton immediately knew the reason for the disparity. Adam's reputation as a wheat farmer was known far and wide, and Norton begged Jacob and Elias to sell him a quantity of their wheat for seed for next year's crop.

No sooner had the last shock of wheat been set up, when Ole Strømme appeared to inform the family from Skredderstua that Adolph Preus was expected once more to make a visit to the Neenah Settlement. Preus had written to John Helgesen, apologizing for the long delay in his return since his last visit in March, but he expected to get to the Neenah Settlement in just three more days, and a service was scheduled again at Ole Saersland's barn in four days. Ole said he was glad folks had at least that much notice because this was such a busy season for everyone, and each family would need to plan their work so they could take time off for the service.

Terje was especially glad to hear that Preus was returning at this time. He thought especially of poor Sven Risland, and he wanted to arrange an opportunity for Preus to talk with Sven. He also wanted to talk to Preus himself about how suicides should be handled in a church cemetery here in this country. He was glad that poor Sven and his family did not have to bury Anlaug under cover of darkness with no words of comfort whatsoever. At least many friends and neighbors here in the Neenah Settlement, even a few Yankee families, tried to extend their condolences to Sven and his family, and Terje thought that this was the Christian thing to do rather than to have to lift the coffin over the cemetery fence under cover of darkness.

In spite of the fact that Preus came at the busiest time of the year, a large crowd gathered at Ole Saersland's barn. It was a hot day, and Preus sweat profusely, but insisted upon wearing both cassock and ruff for the occasion. The ruff began to wilt badly, and his wife would need to launder and starch and iron it again once he returned to "Kaskeland."

Preus was apologetic to the people of the Neenah Settlement for not coming earlier. He explained that there were just too many demands from more and more settlements of Norwegian immigrants. He spoke at some length about some of the communities west of Madison he had visited and said he hoped that one or two Norwegian ministers would soon arrive so that more regular visits could be made to the many settlements that were springing up in so many places.

There were more children to be baptized and more young boys and girls to be catechized. When he asked about the deaths in the congregation, he was told of the suicide of Anlaug Risland, who, although she was among the followers of Elling Eielsen, her family had been ministered to by John Helgesen and buried in the settlement's only cemetery. Preus was solicitous and asked many questions about Anlaug's condition and about Sven and his family. When after the service Terje stood in line to talk privately to Preus, he finally had his opportunity to ask a real Norwegian minister those questions that had been bothering him about the proper burial of one who had committed suicide. Preus spoke to Terje gently:

"My good man from Austre Moland, I know that in Norway there are old customs, but I have always thought that the custom you speak of can be very cruel to those who are left behind. In the case of this poor woman, we cannot possibly judge what drove her to do what she did. Perhaps if I had been here to speak to her, or if some other pastor had spoken to her, it could have helped to relieve her burdened mind. But we must now think about her poor family. You think I should speak to Sven, her husband. He was not here for our service, you say, because both he and your brother-in-law are followers of Elling. But if you can persuade him to speak with me, I will gladly try to bring him what words of comfort I can. Perhaps if I could come to your home tomorrow, especially to speak to the three young girls who now live with you, the father and the little brother could also be invited."

And so it was arranged that Adolph Preus would come to the house of Terje Larsen Skredderstua for dinner and an early afternoon visit. When Anna Tøvesdatter heard this news, she was overcome with housewifely anxiety about how she should entertain such an honored guest. In all of her life she had never entertained a pastor in her home, and she was both honored and burdened by this unique opportunity. It was Maren who approached the whole matter with greater calm than her mother, and as soon as she heard that Preus was coming, she began in her mind to plan all the details of serving the dinner.

Terje made a special visit to Gunder Tøvesen's house late that afternoon. Gunder, of course, had not come to the service, but when Terje explained how solicitous Preus had been about Sven and his family, Gunder agreed that Sven should meet the pastor. It was clear to Gunder that this American pastor was not the same kind of officious bore that so many of his colleagues were in Norway. Perhaps this man could actually help Sven and his family, and he would not stand in the way.

The next morning Anna and Maren decided that since it was such a nice day it would be better to eat outside, setting their table under the shade of the large oak tree. It would be very pleasant there, and it would also give the pastor a good view of the beautiful new house they were building. It was so much finer than the usual log cabin built by the settlers, whether they were Norwegian or Yankee. Anna and Maren had decided to kill several chickens for the occasion, and they did their best to prepare a delicious meal for their distinguished guest. When Preus arrived at their home, he immediately expressed his admiration for the fine house which was under construction.

"This proves to me," he said so that all could hear, "that our good Norwegian farm families can not only survive in this country, but can thrive and succeed, sometimes as well as or even better than their Yankee neighbors."

He went on to compliment Terje and Anna on their fine and clever son Jacob who had the skill to build such a fine house, and all the other members of the family for being such good helpers in this project. It was a warm day, and Preus asked Anna and Terje for permission to remove his coat. On a warm day, he suggested, it is appropriate to sit in one's shirt sleeves.

Just as they were exchanging pleasantries, Gunder Tøvesen appeared, accompanied by Sven Risland and his son, Lasse. Anna had not expected her brother and quickly began to make calculations about whether she had dishes enough to set another place and food enough to serve one extra person. Terje made the necessary introductions, and shortly after Gunder had met the pastor, he begged to be excused. In his mind, this occasion was intended to help Sven and Lasse, and he would only be an interloper if he stayed. Much as she loved her brother, Anna was somewhat relieved when he decided to leave. She and Maren had figured very closely, and now there would be food enough for all to have generous portions.

Sven was shy in the presence of this pastor whom he had never met. Preus attempted to put him at ease when they first met, but Sven was so quiet and withdrawn that it was difficult to read his mood. Had he merely come under duress at the begging of Terje and Gunder, or would he be able to speak to the pastor and hear with profit what the pastor had to say to him?

Preus was sensitive enough to gauge the situation, so he decided during the meal to speak of lighter things, discussing some of his experiences while traveling from place to place. He complimented Anna on her delicious meal. Often, he explained, while traveling it was difficult to get good food at hotels and inns and public places, but when God's good people entertain their pastor, they spoil him with these delicious meals. But, he said, with apparent sincerity, of all of the meals served to him in America, this one today served under the oak tree would have to rank as one of the very best. There were, of course, some good ladies in his parish at Koshkonong who were also very good cooks. He wanted Anna to know this, just in case she would be tempted to too much pride.

After the pleasantries of the meal, he took Sven aside and strolled with him out of sight of the rest. Terje and his family were not sure just what the two men talked about; they could only surmise. But they spoke together for nearly two hours. When they returned, the others could see a difference in Sven's whole bearing. He appeared as one relieved of a tremendous burden and even managed a smile or two for his host and hostess.

Preus, too, looked somewhat relieved that the intensity of their long conversation was over. He spoke confidentially to Terje just before he bid the family farewell:

"I'm not so sure I've helped him as much as I wish I could. I tried to bring him whatever comfort I could, and I think I helped him to get away from blaming himself for what happened. Guilt is a tremendous burden to bear, and I hope I've helped to lift that burden for this man today."

When Adolph Preus left after expressing his thanks to the whole family for their hospitality, Terje spoke quietly and sincerely to Anna: "That man is truly sent to us by God. How gently he deals with people, and how fortunate we were to have him as our guest today."

The next morning Jacob and Kittel returned to the task of shingling the roof of their house. The first row was the hardest because the shingles had to be cut shorter than the others in order to fit. The twenty-eight foot length of the house seemed endless as they nailed shingle after shingle and row upon row. At the end of the first day of shingling, they could see they made progress; but there was a good deal more to be done before the job would be finished.

In the meantime Elias and Terje and Klemet were busy pitching bundles of wheat carefully into the oxcart and transporting them to a stack near the threshing floor they had prepared near the stable. The ground was firm, and if the rain held off, they could soon begin beating the grain with their flails and putting the golden wheat into sacks. If the rains came, they could cover the stack with their large canvas, and most of the wheat would stay dry.

In the midst of bringing the grain to the stack, Elias noticed some ominously dark clouds on the western horizon. Elias sent Klemet to summon Jacob and Kittel to the field, as well as his sisters and the Risland girls. They would have to rush to save as much of the crop as they could. If the dark clouds brought a violent thunderstorm, much of the grain would shell out in the shock; at least they could save most of what was already in the stack. They had stacked about two-thirds of the shocks in the field; and, with some luck, they could probably get most of the rest under cover. When Jacob and Kittel came, they suggested that instead of taking the time to stack the remaining grain, they take the cattle out of the stable and put the grain into the stable as quickly as possible. Elias might wish at this moment for a team of horses that could move much faster than those pokey oxen, but there was no point in wasting time wishing.

By working frantically, they managed to get all except five shocks under cover before the rain began to pelt down upon them with great force. Many of the bundles had been unloaded in haste into the stable, and tumbled in every direction, but at least they were safe from the soaking rain. The canvas was tied securely around the unfinished stack, and the workers ran for cover.

Dagros and Red-Nose and their calves had to endure the fury of the rain storm and the thunder, but they probably welcomed the cool shower bath as a relief from the intense heat they had suffered during the past few days. Elias lamented that those last five shocks could not be saved, but was grateful they were able to save nearly all of their crop. They learned the next day that several of their neighbors had not been so fortunate. Beautiful wheat fields were suddenly flattened and much of the crop shelled out under the pelting power of the heavy downpour.

The unfinished roof left the new house open to the elements, and water from the rain soaked much of the interior. Fortunately, the finished floor had not yet been installed, nor the trim around the doors and windows, but it would take some days for the building to dry out. Much of the area around the new house turned into a sea of mud, and Jacob and Kittel had to spend two days just cleaning up after the storm. Gusts of wind had picked up some of the building materials, including many of the shingle shakes Terje had so painstakingly prepared for the roof.

After several days of gentle breezes from the south and bright sunshine, things began to dry out and return to normal. On the third day, sooner than they had anticipated, Jacob and Kittel returned to the roof, and two days later they nailed the final row of shingles into place. At last the house was completely enclosed; now the smooth pine boards could be laid down for the floors, and the windows and doors could be trimmed with the millwork Jacob had prudently stored in a corner of the stable.

Soon word began to circulate throughout the Neenah Settlement that Jacob had built the finest log building in the whole community. Visitors came to inspect the house, and Jacob often had to explain just how he constructed the building. Some of the Norwegian settlers remarked that the house resembled some of the fine old log buildings they had known in Norway that had stood, in some cases, for centuries.

It was not just another log house, soon to be abandoned when the family gained enough wealth to afford a better home. Jacob calculated that someday he would cover the exterior of the building with clapboards and the interior walls with plaster. Jacob was still not totally convinced that the "balloon frame" method he first saw used on Adam Cartwright's fine house in Fond du Lac was the best method of building a house. He calculated that the thicker walls of this log home would shut out the winter's cold and the summer's heat more effectively than those houses made by the "balloon frame" method. It would take a while longer before the house would be finished to his full satisfaction, but in the meantime the family would have a tight and cozy home. Now Jacob could only anticipate the day when he could tell his mother that she could move into this fine new house, much finer than any house in which she had ever lived, including the old cottage at Skredderstua with the sweet cherry tree at its front doorstep.

Maren's Secret

The wheat was threshed by using a flail. Elias had threshed in this manner at Skredderstua, but this was a larger crop than he had ever harvested before. Terje and Kittel were his helpers during most of the operation because they wanted Jacob to concentrate upon finishing the house. Jacob told his father and brothers about the harvest machinery he had used on Adam Cartwright's farm near Fond du Lac, but they all seemed to dismiss as absurd the possibility of their ever using such contraptions to take some of the hardest physical labor out of harvesting crops of grain. They were resigned to doing things the old-fashioned way and hardly expected that this would change in their own lifetimes.

The five soggy shocks that had to be left in the field on the day of the great rainstorm eventually dried out, but much of their wheat had been lost. Elias wanted to thresh out first the bundles that were so hastily thrown into the cattle shed, in order to reclaim the use of that building for the cattle. After the wheat had been flailed on the make-shift threshing floor, the grain had to be winnowed to separate the lighter chaff and dirt from the golden wheat.

After a good deal of hard work, they put the sacks of wheat into the oxcart Jacob had repaired so that no wheat could leak out of the cart if the sacks should break open as it jogged over the rough and rutted roads on its way to market. They planned to take it to Winnebago Rapids where there was a flour mill, and they had some of the wheat ground into flour for their own use. Elias and

Terje made two trips to Winnebago Rapids to carry their crop to market, and each time they returned with some supplies, but mostly with the cash they received for their first crop. To be sure, they saved a sufficient amount of the wheat for seed for next year's crop and the additional amount which had been requested by Lambert Norton, plus some extra seed which could be sold to other neighbors.

When the marketing was completed, Terje and Anna thought the family should have a special party to celebrate their first successful harvest in America. Terje was almost giddy with joy on this occasion and suddenly produced a bottle of brandy which he had purchased on his last trip into town.

"I think we should drink a toast to our successful first harvest," he explained to his astonished family.

He was never known to be particularly addicted to alcohol; but usually at Christmas time in Norway, especially when he was able to make extra money as a shoemaker, Terje often bought a bottle. He always gave it to Anna so she could ration it carefully for use on festive occasions. But this was unusual. Never before had he purchased a bottle at the end of a harvest season. Anna took the bottle and carefully poured a small amount into cups for each adult, and Terje proposed a proper toast for the occasion. He also reminded the family that within a short time there would certainly be another occasion when it would be appropriate to drink a toast, the day when they could finally move into their fine new home!

At this point Maren suddenly surprised her family by standing in her place at the table and announcing:

"You may yet have a third occasion to make a toast very soon, dear Father! Johannes Baklistulen has asked me to marry him, and I have given him my tentative consent, depending, of course, upon your approval."

Maren had carried this secret for about a week. She wanted to wait until after all the turmoil of the harvest was over to tell her family the exciting news. Certainly Jacob and other members of the family had some knowledge that Johannes was courting Maren ever since that day when the congregation was organized last October. Johannes found a number of occasions to visit the family since that time, but he gave no indication that his intentions were to make Maren his wife so soon.

Terje and Anna were a bit taken aback by Maren's sudden announcement and looked at each other questioningly, trying to read each other's thoughts. Jacob, sensing the awkwardness of this moment, broke the silence by speaking:

"Dear Maren, you have really surprised us all with this wonderful news. Have you made any plans for a wedding? We must certainly invite Johannes to our house very soon to discuss this matter with him. But, Maren, we will be so sorry to lose you as a daily member of our household."

"Oh Jacob," Maren responded light-heartedly, "Don't be so serious. You can't expect me to stay here forever and become an old maid, can you? Besides, I won't be that far away from all of you."

Nodding to Maren, Jacob continued:

"You have been so helpful, especially with your care of the Risland girls and all of the other wonderful things you have been able to do during this time when our family has had to work so hard getting settled in America. How is Mother going to manage without you? And, for that matter, how will all of the rest of us manage?

"Oh, Mother will manage just fine, you can be sure of that. Just look at all of the good help that she has!" Maren answered.

"Of course, you will not be far away from us, as you have just said, but I must confess that I am a bit sad to think of losing you within our household at the same time that I am happy for you and your future."

"Yes, Jacob, I think I shall have a fine future as the wife of Johannes Baklistulen."

"Certainly Johannes is a fine man and a leader in the community, and I have no doubt that he will make an excellent husband for you. Father, Mother, Brothers, and Sisters, I raise my cup to toast the engagement of my lovely sister, Maren Terjesdatter, to Johannes Baklistulen!"

Jacob's toast broke the awkwardness of the moment, and the rest of the family joined him in toasting the engagement. By this time Terje regained his composure; and after he put down his cup and the others in the family sat down again in their chairs, he remained standing and addressed his family.

"This is indeed a most significant and momentous occasion; and, my dear Maren, I wish you the greatest happiness in life. You are very dear to me; and, as Jacob has already said, you have been most helpful to our entire family during our adjustment to life here in the New World. We have shared some sad and discouraging times together, but we have been fortunate that most of our times together in the last several years have been happy and hopeful times."

"Thank you very much, Father. Your kind words mean a great deal to me," Maren said with great feeling.

At this point, Terje choked up a bit and lifted his hand to his face to wipe away a stray tear that blurred his vision. He felt a bit overcome; and while he shared the joyous spirit of the occasion, he was a little miffed that Johannes had not come to him personally to ask the hand of his daughter before an announcement was made. But he would not, for all the world, betray to his daughter his feelings on this matter. Better to let it pass. He would have his opportunity to speak to Johannes soon enough.

The three Risland girls had been silent onlookers to this family drama. They had already become an integral part of this household, and Maren had been their chief mentor and guide in the painful adjustments which they had to make after the terrible tragedy which had so upset their lives. The news of Maren's engagement suddenly brought these girls face to face with another chasm of uncertainty, and their faces betrayed their anxiety.

Maren suddenly became aware of the situation and immediately went to the girls who were seated apart from the others. She embraced each of them and spoke to them very quietly and earnestly. Jacob and the others could not hear what she was telling the girls, but it was evident that her conversation was having a calming and reassuring effect. Within a few moments she had them giggling and light-hearted as she worked the magic of her good humor upon them.

When Maren returned to the table, Terje spoke once more to his family, this time relaxed and seated in his chair:

"I have given some thought, even before today, to the fact that we can not always stay together as a family the way we are now. It is natural that each of you, in good time, should choose a spouse and establish your own families. When that time comes for each of you, you will very likely launch forth on your own and leave your old parents here with only the memories of these good times together that we are now enjoying."

"Oh, Terje, this is not the time for such heavy thoughts!" Anna interrupted.

Terje continued, seeming to ignore his wife's comment: "Elias and Jacob, you are the oldest, and it is likely that you will be the next ones to leave us. Perhaps you should be thinking even now about what your future should be what that time comes. Kittel, you are not so far behind, but we hope to have you here for quite some time yet, and Anna-Maria and Klemet are much too young to have thoughts like these, but their time will also come. Your mother and I will grow old here in this place. It is a good place; that we have discovered. And now we shall soon move into a fine new house, thanks especially to Jacob's skill, with the assistance of the rest of you. We have had a fine crop of wheat this year, largely because of Elias's skill and labor, but with the help of the rest of you. While it is sad for me to think of Maren leaving us, we can be consoled that she will not be far away, and I hope when the time comes for each of the rest of you to leave home, that you will not be far from us."

Elias and Jacob realized these words were addressed primarily to them. Certainly Jacob had begun to think more and more about launching forth on his own. He had heard just yesterday that good jobs were available for carpenters in Appleton where the new university building was about to be built, and he had given some thought to that possibility. It would be an opportunity to earn good wages.

Elias, too, had thoughts of his own which he had not yet discussed with anyone else. He knew that less than a mile away, just to the south and east a bit, a tract of eighty acres had not yet been claimed; and he was thinking very seriously of staking a claim on this land. It was good fertile soil that bordered on a creek, but it would need some drainage and was heavily wooded. He had walked over the land several times, and it was really very close by. Now that his parents and the rest of his family were settled, he should be thinking of his own future. Since his father had brought up the subject, it would be a good time to discuss this matter with him.

In the days following Maren's announcement, Anna Tøvesdatter had opportunities to speak to her daughter about many things. She confidentially informed Maren that Terje had been a bit disappointed that Johannes had not spoken to him before news of the engagement came out. Maren told her mother that she was responsible for this because Johannes had wanted to speak to Terje, but she had insisted that she should be the one to talk to her family first. When Anna conveyed this to Terje, he was much relieved and insisted that Johannes should be invited at once to join the family at a special dinner in order to welcome him into the family in a proper manner.

Johannes Baklistulen lived about two and a half miles east and north from Terje's farm. Between their farms most of the land was occupied by Yankee families, except for Torger Landsverk's farm which was located right in the middle of the Yankee settlement.

Johannes and his two brothers, Halvor and Kittel, had come to the Neenah Settlement from Muskego in 1847, among the first of the settlers to arrive. To be more accurate, they came to claim their tracts of land in 1847, but returned to Muskego for the winter, and came back the following spring to settle upon the land. Johannes was the oldest of the three brothers. They had emigrated, together with their parents, in 1839 from the Hjartdal parish in Telemark.

While in Muskego, Johannes had married Tone Olavsdatter, but within a year after their marriage, she died in childbirth, and the child also died. This was a terrible blow to Johannes, but the move to the Neenah Settlement helped him to readjust his life and focus his energies upon new opportunities.

In Norway, Johannes and his brothers grew up on a mountain farm where the chief income was derived from cutting timber in the heavy forests, and so they grew up as lumberjacks.

For the past several winters, he and his brothers had worked in a lumber camp in the northwoods pineries of Wisconsin bordering upon the Wolf River, and this had been an important source of income. As a result of their work in the pineries, the Oshkosh lumber man who operated a series of camps offered the Baklistulen brothers the opportunity to try their luck at running their own camp, and they were busy trying to recruit men from the Norwegian settlers in the Neenah Settlement to work for them. In fact, Johannes had already offered jobs to Elias, Jacob and Kittel for the coming winter. Elias and Kittel were intent upon accepting these jobs, but Jacob had some other plans. As a skilled carpenter, he felt that he could earn better wages, perhaps on the job at the Lawrence Institute building in Appleton.

Because Johannes had come to America so early, he learned English well and could speak it fluently, with hardly a trace of an accent. This was quite unusual, and it gave him an advantage in dealing with his Yankee neighbors. It also gave him a position of leadership in the Norwegian community.

The day that Johannes Baklistulen was invited to join the family for dinner under the oak tree was a festive occasion. Again, Anna and Maren prepared three chickens and their garden provided many of the other items on the menu. There were some toasts of welcome, and Terje's bottle of brandy was nearly empty after the toasts were completed. Perhaps he would need to get a new bottle, or perhaps several, considering the possibility of a wedding in the near future.

Among other topics discussed that day was the possible date for the wedding. Both Maren and Johannes felt they should wait until Pastor Preus returned again to the Neenah Settlement. This would likely be late in October, according to their best information. They could, of course, be married by a local justice of the peace, or perhaps by a Yankee preacher in Winnebago Rapids or Oshkosh; but they both preferred that Adolph Preus conduct their wedding, and the family concurred in this decision. Anna quickly calculated that perhaps the good pastor would once again be their guest and return to their completed house, this time under much happier circumstances than his last visit.

Maren and Johannes discussed their wedding plans in greater detail. Maren wished her sister, Anna-Maria, to be her bridesmaid; but she also suggested that the three Risland girls carry flowers for her wedding. She wanted to include them in some fashion, and there would likely be some forest flowers or even some clusters of colorful leaves which could serve as decorations. Johannes wished to have his brother Halvor as his best man. The wedding would take place here at Terje's farm. If the weather was unusually mild, it could be under the oak tree, but if the weather was not so mild, the main room in the house would be large enough for the occasion.

After Johannes left, Jacob took his father aside to discuss an idea that had occurred to him as he heard the wedding plans being made.

"I think we should get a price on clapboard siding and other exterior trim for our house. I thought this could wait for several years, but it would be nice if we could finish the exterior of the house in time for Maren's wedding. It would be a nice way to make the wedding a special celebration for her. I think the sawmill in Winneconne should have siding available for us at a fairly reasonable cost, and the good profit we have had from our wheat crop ought to be able to cover most of the cost."

At first Terje was a bit reluctant to commit so much money for what he regarded as mere decoration. He also questioned Jacob about the clapboard siding. In Norway, most of the houses used vertical boards, just as they had on the house at Skredderstua. But Jacob informed him that in America it was the fashion to use these horizontal clapboards. They could be painted white and the trim of the house a different color. The result could be very pleasing.

For a few dollars, they could probably have a house that would be the envy of their Yankee neighbors who were all still living in hastily built log cabins. Jacob could not resist this last thought, even though he knew it was a bit inappropriate to think about provoking envy.

At last Terje gave his consent for Jacob to get a price on the clapboard siding and the paint that would be necessary. Terje also suggested that the interior log walls should be either white-washed or painted before the wedding. At this point Jacob had already completed laying the pine boards for the finished flooring, but they needed to be painted, and there was some work to be completed on the window and door trim before the interior of the house would be ready.

The very next day Jacob set out on foot for Winneconne where he spoke to the owner of the sawmill about prices on clapboard siding and other lumber which would be needed to trim the exterior of the house. The price turned out to be a little higher than he had thought, but it was still within reason, Jacob calculated. He also was able to locate window shutters which could be mounted on each of the windows. They could be closed in the winter or during storms to protect the windows and provide greater insulation against the cold. Besides, they would help dress up the exterior of the house.

When Jacob returned from his trip to Winneconne, he discussed the prices with his father, and together they determined that the prices were within reason and this was the time to complete the exterior of the house so it could be finished for Maren's wedding. There was no time to waste. The next day, Jacob yoked the oxen to their cart, and he and Terje drove off to Winneconne to buy the necessary materials. All of this negotiation was kept secret from Maren and the other members of the family. It was only when the cart returned, fully loaded with lengths of clapboard siding and lumber that the other members of the family had any inkling of Jacob and Terje's plans.

In the days that followed, the exterior of the new house changed dramatically as Jacob nailed the clapboards on to the squared surface of the logs. From time to time, he had to use his adze or draw shave to trim the log surface a bit smoother so that the clapboards would fit without unsightly bulges. Kittel was enlisted to help him, and it was necessary to erect a scaffolding to reach the higher places. After the clapboards were all in place, additional trim boards, especially under the eaves, had to be carefully fit, and the windows and doors and cornices required special and painstaking work.

Finally, after the exterior was completed, it was time to paint. Two coats would be necessary, and Jacob carefully mixed the white lead paint so that it would apply evenly. He had some experience painting when he had helped with Adam Cartwright's house, and Kittel soon became adept at painting as well. The weather held nicely, and within two days Jacob and Kittel finished the first coat of paint. It would take a day or two to dry, and then the final coat could be applied.

Within a week the exterior of the house was finished, and the shutters were attached. Jacob had selected a dark green paint for the shutters, and this contrasted nicely with the white siding. Jacob had first seen this combination from the train window as he traveled from Albany to Buffalo, and he vowed at that time that one day he would have a house of white clapboards with green shutters. Today this dream came true.

As soon as the paint dried on both the interior and exterior of the house, the family moved from the little log cabin into the spacious new house. It was a joyous day for the whole family as furniture and kitchen utensils were carefully transported the short distance into the cavernous space of the new house. Even after the last items had been moved in, the house looked spacious and empty. There was a small bedroom downstairs for Terje and Anna, a main room that contained the cooking stove and the kitchen items as well as the living and dining area, and an open stairway that led upstairs to two fairly large bedrooms, one for the women and girls in the family, and the other for the men and boys.

On October twentieth Adolph Preus came to the Neenah Settlement for his fourth visit. On October twenty-first there was a service with Holy Communion at Ole Saersland's barn, and on October twenty-second Preus came to Terje and Anna's house for a second time, this time to conduct the wedding of Johannes Baklistulen and Maren Terjesdatter.

During the morning there had been a rain shower, and so it was determined that the wedding should be held inside. The Risland girls gathered garlands of beautiful maple leaves in their rich, full color; and Maren wore her best brown dress with a few pink wild roses, the last of the season, in her hair. Jacob had always thought that his sister was very pretty, but on this occasion she was radiant. Gunder Tøvesen and his family were invited, and Sven Risland and Lasse were also included. Johannes' two brothers, Halvor and Kittel, both unmarried, were also present, as was their father, Anund Baklistulen.

Pastor Preus wore his cassock and ruff for the occasion, and Jacob noted that the ruff had been freshly starched. Anna was nearly overcome when she saw the pastor in his full regalia in her very own house. The ceremony itself was brief enough. Preus had some good words to say to the bride and groom, as well as to all the other people assembled. After the ceremony, he removed his cassock and ruff, and slipped on his coat and tie. He joined the family for the wedding dinner and the toasts that were proposed at the table. Shortly after dinner, he took Sven Risland aside once more, and they had a brief conversation outside. After greeting everyone, he bid the assemblage farewell because he had to conduct a service of baptism later in the afternoon, and tomorrow he would have to return to "Kaskeland."

Later in the afternoon Johannes and Maren were ready to leave. Maren had packed all of her personal items and she joined Johannes in the front seat of his "democrat wagon" which was pulled by a black mare. After all the farewells had been said, Anna had tears in her eyes as she waved good-bye to her oldest daughter, knowing that after this whenever her daughter would return to her home she would come as a visitor. Terje, too, stood by his wife as they waved the couple on their way, and he also fought back some tears. Maren was his favorite child in so many ways, and it was difficult to see her leave.

The House of Norton

When Maren stepped out of the democrat wagon which took her from her parents' house to the house of Johannes Baklistulen, she stepped into a bachelor's cabin. Johannes had lived alone ever since the death of his first wife, and he was indifferent to matters relating to housekeeping. Maren gasped a bit as she entered the cabin, but resolved not to show her emotions in front of Johannes. He had been so kind and thoughtful of her, and she respected him so much that she did not want to display any kind of disappointment over the disarray she saw all about her.

The cabin was slightly larger than the first cabin in which her family lived until they moved into their new house, but the worst of it was that it had a dirt floor. Nevertheless in the corner stood a lovely bed of hand-turned walnut, beautifully finished. It was the one piece of elegance in an otherwise primitive cabin, and in Maren's mind it was an omen that in good time more fine pieces of furniture might one day stand in a beautiful new home. In fact, Johannes had warned Maren that his cabin was very meager and primitive; but he made her a solemn promise that if she would consent to become his wife, he would see to it that within a year or two the miserable little cabin would be replaced by a new house, fully as fine as the one which Jacob had made for her family. To say that Maren had accepted the hand of Johannes on the basis of this promise would not be true, and Maren would be disturbed if anyone so much as gave credence to such a thought. She loved and admired Johannes without condition and was willing, if necessary, to follow him to the ends of the earth.

Maren had already promised Johannes she would accompany him to the lumber camp during the winter months, and he promised her generous payment in gold coins if she would help with the cooking for the camp. Maren thought this would be a good adventure, and she was pleased that Elias and Kittel would very likely be going to the camp as well as Johannes' two brothers. Johannes kept no animals on his farm other than his team of horses, and the horses would accompany them into the woods for the winter camp.

No sooner had Maren unpacked her things than she set about to dust and clean and try to bring order to the disarray that she found. She would have to ask Johannes what to do about some of the things she did not think really belonged in the cabin. There was a shotgun and other hunting paraphernalia, some hip boots and many of Johannes' tools. Perhaps some items could be stored in the shed or in the horse stable so the cabin could be put in order.

Next she made a list of items she intended to request Johannes to purchase on his next trip into town. The larder was rather meager, consisting mainly of flour and salt pork, and if she was expected to use her skill in preparing good meals for Johannes, the larder would need to be replenished. Johannes did have a good garden and was proud of his ability as a gardener, and there were still vegetables the garden had yielded – pumpkins, squash, potatoes, carrots and turnips.

The next morning Johannes hitched his mare to the democrat wagon and told Maren he would be home by sundown. Maren, in the meantime, was busy cleaning out the cabin. When Johannes returned, the democrat wagon was loaded with planks and other materials and supplies, many of which had been on the list Maren had made the previous day. Maren wondered why all of those planks were necessary, but when Jacob and Kittel appeared the next morning, the secret was out. Maren was going to have a plank floor in the cabin. Johannes, Jacob and Kittel moved everything out of the cabin, and then went to work putting in the plank floor. Maren was ecstatic. How very thoughtful of Johannes to make this improvement. When the floor had been installed, the entire interior of the cabin was white-washed.

Johannes and Maren returned with Jacob and Kittel to their home for the night because the cabin needed to dry out from its white-washing, and tomorrow they would return to move things back into the cabin. But there were still more surprises for Maren. When they returned the next day, Jacob loaded his oxcart with lumber left from the construction of the house, and when they came to the Baklistulen cabin, Jacob and Kittel erected a small lean-to on the back side of the cabin to provide storage space for many of the things which had been taking up space in the cabin.

Johannes had excused himself very early in the day and made yet another trip into town, and when he returned late that afternoon he unloaded a beautiful chest of drawers and a small horsehair sofa which would add a touch of elegance to their humble cabin. Maren was overwhelmed. Never had she expected to have such beautiful furniture. Now she could be proud of that little cabin and all it contained. She could hardly wait to play hostess, not only to her family, but to other neighbors and friends, including perhaps some of their Yankee neighbors

In the meantime, Anna missed her daughter very much, but gradually came to depend for many things upon Anna-Maria and the Risland girls, especially Berit, who was old enough to be of great help in the kitchen. Anna found her a willing helper and quick to learn how to do household tasks. The two younger sisters were sent to the Knott School. They had never been to school and knew hardly any English. It was not easy for them to adjust to the routine of school; but the teacher, Josephine Mary, was quite patient with them and tried to help them make an adjustment to their new environment.

Some of the Yankee children teased the girls mercilessly because they struggled so much to speak English. Their taunts made the girls not want to go back to school. Anna had to be stern with them, and from time to time had to put up with much pouting and crying. She wished that Maren could be there to deal with them, for she was about at her wits' end. At last she confided her frustration to Maren when she came home to visit. Maren talked to the girls, and it seemed to help for a day or two, but then they reverted once more to their pouting and crying.

But Maren returned later in the week. She had spoken to Johannes and he agreed that, for the time being, before they would leave for the pineries, the two girls should come to live with them. There was plenty of space in the loft, and it would be no farther for them to walk to the Knott School than it was from Terje and Anna's house. Anna was greatly relieved. It was understood that when Johannes and Maren left for the lumber camp, the girls would return. Meanwhile, Anna hoped Maren would be able to work her magic upon these girls. She had seen it happen before and believed this would be the best solution for all concerned. Berit Risland would remain with Anna and Anna-Maria. She had become a close companion to Anna-Maria and was relieved, at least for the moment, not to have the responsibility for her two younger sisters.

When Lambert Norton looked to the south from the front door of his log cabin home, he had an unobstructed view of the new house Jacob and his family had built. As long as it stood as a log house, Norton could dismiss it as such; but when Jacob suddenly took it into his head to apply clapboards to the building and paint the siding white and trim the building with dark green shutters so that it looked like a proper Yankee farmhouse, Norton became jealous of the Norwegian family that had come to this land so recently and taken up their claim several years after he had settled in the community.

This fine new house was a kind of affront to Lambert Norton, who perceived himself a community leader and thought he had been upstaged by this immigrant family. Had he given the matter a bit more thought, he should have realized that Terje had four able-bodied men in his household, plus two capable women and five more children, including the three Risland girls. Norton, on the other hand, had to hire any help he needed for the outdoor work. His wife and two daughters were quite capable of running the household, and this had included, until just recently, the care of his aged father.

Ezra Norton died on July third. If he had been conscious during his last week, he might have struggled hard to hold out until July fourth, but he slipped away unconscious of time and place. He was buried in the cemetery on the hill which the Norwegians had established because there was no other cemetery in the community. Several years later his body would be re-interred in a small township cemetery near the Norton farm which would serve as a resting place for a number of the Yankee families who were early settlers in the community.

Lambert Norton originally planned that he would erect his grand new dwelling on its prominently visible site in about two years. He and his family were comfortable enough in their log cabin, which was a bit more spacious than most, and fairly well built with a good plank floor. But Norton resolved, as soon as he saw those shutters installed on the windows of the house Jacob built, that he would build the kind of house that would tell the whole world he was a leader of men and a man to be reckoned with in the affairs of the community.

There was another incentive for building his house just now. When his father died, he left a safe-box in his bedroom which neither Lambert nor his brother Elijah had ever opened. Truth to tell, old Ezra Norton was somewhat of a miser, especially in his later years; and when Lambert Norton and his brother Elijah opened the box after they had properly buried their father, they counted out no less than one thousand six hundred and fifty dollars, mostly in gold coin. They summoned George Knott and Samuel Hopkins as witnesses, in case there should ever be any question about their father's estate, and Lambert and Elijah each received eight hundred and twenty-five dollars from their father's safe-box. This was a handsome sum and would go a good way in providing Lambert and his family with the house he felt should be prominently situated on the ridge overlooking the broad valley to the south.

It was now late October, but Lambert was intent upon beginning the construction of his house as soon as possible, before the winter set in. Lambert had hesitated making his decision for some weeks, but now was determined to summon Jacob for advice. He admired Jacob's skill and felt Jacob would be very capable of building the kind of house he wanted.

Jacob was summoned to Norton's place the day after he had completed building the lean-to for Maren.

Norton could hardly wait to speak to Jacob.

"Jacob," Norton said quite deliberately, "I believe you are the best qualified man I can find to undertake the building of my new house."

Jacob assumed that Norton was making some long term plans to begin his house project next year, perhaps late in the spring.

"I have decided that I want this house built as soon as we can possibly get to it. It should still be possible to get our foundation dug yet this fall, and perhaps we can even get most of the framing of the structure completed before winter sets in."

This was a sudden surprise to Jacob, and it took him a few moments to adjust his thinking to the possibility that Norton's idea of a building schedule could be accommodated.

"I think, Mr. Norton, it is very late in the season to undertake your project. Couldn't it wait until next spring? It will require quite a bit of planning and preparation, and I have already made some plans to work on the new university building in Appleton during the winter months."

But Norton was adamant. "It's important we get underway as soon as possible. What kind of wages do you expect to earn on that job in Appleton?"

When Jacob informed Norton of the wages he expected to receive in Appleton, Norton's response was immediate.

"I shall be happy to match those wages if you can start on my job immediately."

Norton then unrolled a large sheet of paper on which there was a fairly detailed sketch of the house he intended to build. Jacob immediately recognized it as very much in the same style as Adam Cartwright's house. It appeared somewhat larger than Cartwright's house, with two one-story wings on each side of a large two-story central section.

"I shall certainly need many helpers if you expect me to undertake a project of this size, especially if we expect to get the foundation fully prepared before winter sets in."

"I am prepared to hire as many men as you think will be necessary. I also will be responsible for buying all the necessary building supplies, either in Winneconne or Winnebago Rapids. I have a good wagon and team of horses that can be very useful for hauling lumber and other supplies."

"Our first task," Jacob said tentatively, "will be to dig out the cellar and get the foundation walls built. There is no time to waste, and we will need a crew of at least fifteen men to dig the hole as soon as possible."

"This is a slack time for most of our neighbors, and I can pay them good wages for the days that will be needed for the digging."

Norton then took Jacob out to see the large pile of stones which he had been gathering near the stable ever since he began clearing his land. Most of the stones were round grey granite stones of moderate size, but some of them were fairly large boulders. In spite of the size of Norton's pile of stones, Jacob wondered if there would be enough stones for the foundation walls.

Jacob also informed Lambert Norton that both of his brothers, Elias and Kittel, had promised Johannes Baklistulen they would go to his lumbering camp during the winter months, and Sven Risland also was planning to go to this camp as were quite a number of the other Norwegian settlers in the neighborhood. Perhaps if Norton could offer Kittel a good wage, he could persuade his younger brother to stay home to help him during the winter months. His father, Terje, might be available on certain days as a helper, but they would need to find one or two others who could assist, especially during the time when the frame of the house was erected.

When Jacob returned home after his conversation with Lambert Norton, his father and his brothers were amazed that Norton wanted to begin the project so soon. Why couldn't he wait until next spring and summer when the weather would be more favorable? But Jacob told them that Norton was insistent upon beginning the digging of the foundation soon, within the next day or two if at all possible. They finally agreed that if their Yankee neighbor was willing to pay them a good wage, they would all be able to help with the digging of the foundation almost immediately.

Jacob also went to a number of other neighbors, Yankee, Irish and Norwegian, and managed to recruit a crew of no less than fifteen men to begin digging the cellar for Norton's big house on the hill. Most of the men he spoke to thought Norton was foolish to rush into this project so soon, with so little time before winter was bound to set in; but they agreed to work for the wages and would try as best they could to get the foundation completed as quickly as possible.

And so they dug and dug, like so many moles and badgers, moving a vast amount of dirt in the first two days. They soon ran into a shelf of limestone rock and were forced to use mauls and picks to break the rock as they uncovered it. Fortunately, the limestone was soft enough to yield to the labors of the men who attacked it with such determination and muscle power. Within three days, the fifteen men had a huge gaping hole in the ground.

On the next day only five men would be needed, since Jacob planned to begin laying the stones for the foundation wall. Norton had procured the supplies of slaked lime and sand that would be necessary for the masonry work, and the additional limestone rocks that were broken out during the excavation would be useful in constructing the wall. Jacob built this wall as he had the foundation under his father's house, about twenty inches thick. Bag after bag of the lime disappeared, and Lambert Norton was forced to make a quick trip with his wagon to get additional lime and sand.

Kittel and Elias had done enough work on their father's house to be experienced helpers in laying the stone wall, and Sven Risland and Torger Landsverk were also good helpers, carrying the stones into place and helping with the mixing of the mortar. With such a determined crew, the great wall arose very quickly, but Jacob insisted upon checking the dimensions very carefully as row upon row of stones and mortar were added to build the wall higher and higher.

Fortunately, the weather held, although a rain shower threatened on the day the walls were completed. It would now take several days for the wall to cure. On the top of the wall, Jacob embedded a sawed timber, about eight inches wide and four inches thick, carefully leveling it and coating it with pitch to resist rot and moisture. This timber would provide the nailing surface upon which the framework of the house would rest.

On the day Jacob began to put the joists into place, the weather turned bitterly cold and raw. Jacob and Kittel, who was his chief helper for this task, struggled bravely to do their work; but in the middle of the afternoon a mixture of rain and sleet began to fall, and they were forced to give up work for the day. It was three more days before they could return because of the miserably cold and raw weather; and when they returned to finish setting the joists in place, their work was made more difficult because the lumber still had a coating of ice from the recent storm.

Norton was very upset that his bold plans for enclosing the house before winter set in seemed to be halted. It was late in November, and Jacob began to doubt that he would be able to get the entire building framed under these conditions. He hoped that early in December he might be able to make some progress with the construction.

Considering the odds of having to leave the entire work until next spring, Jacob proposed to Norton that they concentrate first upon one wing of the house; and, if possible, the second wing as well, leaving the framing of the central structure until last. If even one of the wings could be enclosed, it would provide a place in which to keep the lumber and hardware dry, and some of the interior construction could continue in the wings even in the dead of winter. It would, thought Jacob, be dangerous to attempt to work on the roof of the central two story structure during the middle of the winter, but the one story wings could be another matter.

And so it happened that the partially built structure began to take on a strange appearance, with two wings framed in by Christmas time, complete with their sawed cedar shingle roofs, while in the middle of the two wings there was only a large gaping hole. Jacob was able to install the windows in each of the wings and erect walls on the inner side of each of the wings where they would ultimately be joined to the main structure.

After Christmas, Jacob was forced to work alone because Kittel joined his brother Elias and a number of other men from the Neenah Settlement in the lumber camp run by the Baklistulen brothers.

On inclement days, Jacob worked alone inside at the tedious and time-consuming task of nailing lath to the permanent walls and partitions so that the plasterers could come to do their work. On mild days, Lambert Norton sometimes assisted him in nailing clapboard siding to the three sides of each of the wing structures. When the siding had been completed on these two structures, the appearance of Norton's house was stranger than ever.

Samuel Hopkins, known by his neighbors for his taciturn and sometime cynical wit, drove by one day on his way to pay a call on George Knott; and when he spoke to George, with a sly smile, he said that he had just had a look at "Norton's Folly!" From that moment on, the house was called "Norton's Folly" by all of his Yankee neighbors who were, in fact, a bit jealous of Norton. From the Yankees, their Norwegian neighbors learned also of the name, and so the word spread far and wide that the prominent and pretentious house on the hill was "Norton's Folly."

In the Deep Woods

The Skredderstuas celebrated their first Christmas in their new house with appropriate festivities. Elias cut a small pine tree, and Anna-Maria and Berit Risland enjoyed making trimmings for the tree from scraps of old Norwegian language newspapers, pine cones and bits of colored yarn. Anna Tøvesdatter prepared special delicacies for the Christmas festivities, baking lefse on her new kitchen stove, as well as other Norwegian specialties that brought back sweet memories of Christmases in their homeland. On Christmas Eve, and again on Christmas Day, Terje read from the thick old *huspostill* which he inherited many years before from his uncle, Mads Bjorvatn, and he sang from memory several beautiful old Christmas hymns.

But Christmas was also a time for neighborly sociability, and Terje and Anna had a party for relatives, including Gunder Tøvesen's family as well as Sven Risland and his family, Johannes and Maren, the other two Baklistulen brothers and their elderly father, Anund Baklistulen.

On another occasion they invited other neighbors, including the Torger Landsverk family, the Anton Møller family, and Ole Olson Strømme and his young bride, Yli Haugen. Anton had a reputation as a storyteller, and he amused the entire party with his tales about trolls and witches and the *julenisse*, holding the children spellbound all the while. When he told the story of the *Three Billy Goats Gruff*, he frightened little Knut Landsverk so much that he peed in his pants, and then the poor little boy was so ashamed of himself that he wanted to hide. Anna and his mother came to the rescue when Anna found a clean pair of pants her Klemet had outgrown.

Henrikke Møller chided her husband for exciting the children too much with his story telling, and she decided that the children should be taught to sing some of the old Christmas songs. How she wished she had her old pianoforte for this occasion, but she had an excellent singing voice and the children tried their best to learn the songs as she led them.

When the guests left after the party, Anna Tøvesdatter remarked to Terje that she couldn't remember having so much fun at a Christmas party since she was a young girl. The only thing that had been more fun in her childhood was when folks dressed up in ridiculous garb with masks and went from house to house *julebukking*. But this was America, and their Yankee neighbors would think they were crazy if they tried to carry on that way here.

Elias and Kittel were busy preparing for a nearly three month stay at the Baklistulen lumber camp in the pineries about forty miles north. They would be part of a crew of thirty lumberjacks recruited from the Norwegian settlers in the Neenah Settlement by the Baklistulen brothers who ran the camp. Maren and two other wives would be in charge of cooking the meals for all those hungry men. There were seven sleighs, four of them driven by teams of horses and three by oxen. The sleighs were loaded with supplies enough for the three months at the camp. The three teams of oxen started on the journey a day ahead of the horses. Halvor Baklistulen went with the oxen, together with five other men; his brothers, Kittel and Johannes, were in charge of the horse teams and the rest of the party. There was a kind of festivity in this adventure, as most of the men said farewell to their wives and families.

This was the first venture of the Baklistulen brothers in the woods as entrepreneurs. They were sub-contracted by the lumberman from Oshkosh who ran ten other winter camps comparable in size to the Baklistulen camp. The first task of the group was to construct a log barracks, a cooking shanty with enough space to serve the meals, and a stable for the horses and oxen. In the cooking shanty there would also be three small rooms for the three wives and their husbands who were an important part of the enterprise.

Maren was in high spirits as she left her log cabin on the crispy cold, sunny day when the party left. The other three horse-driven sleighs had assembled at her husband's stable, and she had hot coffee ready for the twenty-six in their party. She and the other two women rode in the first sleigh on a special cushioned seat which her brother-in-law, Kittel Baklistulen, had thoughtfully made just for them.

The men in the party could ride wherever there was space on top of the loaded sleighs. Some of the men preferred to walk part of the time just to keep warm, following the tracks made through the snow by the four sleighs. The sleighs were constructed by Kittel Baklistulen, with the help of his brother Halvor. Kittel was skilled both as a carpenter and blacksmith and had a clever and inventive talent.

It was necessary for the group to camp one night on the way to their destination. The Oshkosh lumber baron had furnished several large tents, as well as stoves which could be set up handily to keep the campers warm during the freezing weather. Maren was snug, wrapped in heavy blankets, with only the tip of her nose and her eyes peeking out, enjoying the outing as a grand adventure into the unknown.

She chatted merrily with the other two women who were her companions, but when the caravan halted at noon time, they had the task of feeding all those hungry men. They quickly built a fire so that water could be heated to make coffee to warm their frozen companions. Several of the men, out of sight of the women and of Johannes and Kittel, passed around a bottle of whisky and took generous gulps. One of the rules of the camp was supposed to be no drinking, but some of the more thirsty fellows didn't want to follow such silly rules.

After two days of traveling over snow-covered trails through heavy forests, frozen marshes and occasional clearings, the Baklistulen party finally reached its camp site. The horse teams passed the group which had set out a day earlier with the oxen on the second day of the journey, and arrived at the camp site about four hours ahead of the oxen teams. The tents were erected immediately, and Maren and the other two women immediately began the task of providing food for the hungry crew.

The very next day, the workers began to fell the trees, tall beautiful white pines, which would be used to build the cooking shanty and dining place. The sooner the women had a good place to work, with their large cook stove and their supplies readily at hand, the sooner the camp could begin to function in a normal way.

Within two days, the cooking shanty was completed. There were planks enough brought on the sleighs to make good floors, both for the cooking shanty and the men's barracks. During the first week in camp, the log structures were erected; even the animals now had shelter from the worst blasts of winter cold. Two of the sleighs had been loaded high with hay cut from Halvor Baklistulen's marsh for the animals, and on a third sleigh was a good supply of oats for the horses.

After the camp was constructed, the work of felling the trees began in earnest. The logs were to be cut to a specified length, loaded onto sleighs, and brought several miles to a site on the east bank of the Wolf River. After the spring thaw, they would be floated down the river to the sawmill which was owned by the enterprising lumberman at Oshkosh. From time to time visitors came to the Baklistulen camp, especially foremen who supervised several of the camps.

The pristine silence of the forest was broken by the steady sound of axes and saws and the loud yelling of men, warning of falling trees or just communicating with each other in the dense forest. The entire landscape began to change as the tallest and most elegant trees were brought down, one by one, leaving only the smaller undergrowth to take the place of the giants. There were large areas where the pines were so thick there was practically no undergrowth. When these areas were cleared, the land looked suddenly ugly and naked, marred by the presence of numerous stumps which would remind a later generation of the elegance and beauty the forest once had.

The men put in long, hard days, mercifully made a bit shorter by the longer dark hours of mid-winter. At night, they rolled into their bunks exhausted and slept soundly on their straw-tick mattresses. The bunkhouse reeked of human sweat, for there was little opportunity to bathe or even to shave; most of the men grew long beards and began to look like so many trolls and ruffians. Their wives would have had difficulty recognizing these fellows if they were to stumble into the camp, and their children would be frightened by their unkempt appearances.

It was exhausting labor, and the men certainly earned the modest wages they were paid. But their muscles hardened; and, thanks to the good food which Maren and the two other women prepared, they ate well, consuming prodigious quantities of flapjacks floating in maple syrup, which they had purchased from some Indians, as well as salt pork, boiled potatoes, and corn bread.

From time to time a gunshot would ring out in the woods, and someone from the camp would signal to his fellows to help him bring to the cook shanty a newly killed deer. Within hours, the menu would be varied by the addition of venison. Usually Johannes himself was the hunter, but several of the other men in the camp also brought their firearms with the intent of hunting in order to provide fresh meat for the camp.

Two years earlier, the first week of April 1850, a tragedy had occurred in the deep woods much closer to the Neenah Settlement. The white settlers had learned from the Indians the secrets of making maple sap into maple syrup, and a small party of Yankee settlers from the eastern edge of Ball Prairie had encamped in the deep woods on the north edge of the Neenah Settlement as their "sugar bush." Little Caspar Partridge, age five, and his sister, seven-year-old Loretta, were taken to this location deep in the woods by their parents, Alvin and Lucia Partridge. In the midst of gathering and boiling down the maple sap. little Caspar was suddenly missing from the encampment. Frantic cries went out as the parents and other folks who were there combed through the thick woods to try to find Caspar. But they searched in vain.

Soon word went out to nearby settlers and spread back to Ball Prairie. Lambert Norton was among those who left their work behind to join in the search for the missing child. The searchers tramped through the frozen marshy woods until their bones ached from exhaustion, but still there was no sign of the missing child.

Then an ugly rumor began to circulate among the searchers. There had been a band of Indians gathering sap and making syrup and maple sugar near the encampment from Ball Prairie. Was it possible that these Indians might have kidnapped the child, and then vanished? How else could their sudden departure be explained? As the men began to tire of their searching, the rumor gained credence among them, and they were finally forced to call off the search.

Several weeks later, a cousin of Mrs. Partridge claimed that he saw a white child with a band of Indians in the vicinity of the new settlement at Waupaca. Word spread rapidly that the missing child had been found as a captive, viciously abducted by a rogue band of Indians. Little Caspar's parents were ecstatic with hope that their lost son had finally been found. But when the child was brought to Lucia for closer examination, she was convinced that the boy was not hers.

Matters might have rested had it not been for the persistent efforts of Frederick Partridge, Alvin's brother, who was convinced by evidence based upon phrenology that the child really belonged to his brother and his wife, not to the Indian squaw named Nahkom. Finally, nearly two years after the initial disappearance of Caspar Partridge, the sheriff invaded the Indian encampment and seized Nahkom's child, against her vigorous but futile protests.

Emotions flared as Nahkom and the child were brought to the circuit court at Oshkosh on February 12, 1852. No court room was large enough to contain all the people who wanted to be a part of the proceedings, so the court secured the use of the newly erected Methodist church for its sessions.

Jacob attended the court procedings for two days at the beginning of the trial, but among the most ardent of those attending the proceedings was Lambert Norton, who was absolutely convinced that the treacherous Indians had committed a dastardly and cowardly deed by kidnapping the innocent little Partridge child. Norton knew the Partridge family well and was intent upon giving them every support that he could. However, on the basis of the information Jacob was able to get, he had his real doubts about the validity of the claims of the Partridge family.

The court finally ended its proceedings on March 27th by declaring that the boy legally belonged to his Indian mother. By any objective standard of judgment it could be seen that the Waupaca child was several years older than the missing Partridge boy, and the child's physical features betrayed his mixed Indian and white parentage.

But what was done by the court aroused the emotions of many in the Yankee community, including Lambert Norton, who avidly followed the proceedings, taking valuable time away from the construction of his new house to attend the long and often tedious sessions of the trial in Oshkosh.

In the hectic days that followed the trial, Alvin Partridge sold his farm to his father, and suddenly the Indian boy was abducted by the Partridge family and taken to parts unknown. The abduction of the child brought great consternation to the Indians who saw the whole episode as evidence of the white man's deceit.

Over a year later, in May of 1853, hunters in the woods where the Partridge boy disappeared discovered the skeleton of a child, presumably that of the Partridge child. But, in spite of what seemed like overwhelming evidence to the contrary, Lambert Norton insisted that the Partridge claim to Nahkom's son was both lawful and legitimate; and many of his Yankee neighbors were also of this opinion.

During the last week in the Baklistulen camp, Elias and Kittel were loading a sleigh with logs, using cant hooks to maneuver the heavy logs into place. It was a tricky business, and logs often slipped out of place, rolling free down the ramp of smaller logs. Sometimes the movement of one log would be sufficient to jar loose several others, and suddenly several logs could roll topsy-turvey from their place on the sleigh onto the ground.

On the day that Elias and Kittel were helping load one of the sleighs, a log suddenly rolled from its precarious place on the sleigh and brought down with it two other very heavy logs. Elias was able to jump free, but poor Kittel was struck by the second log which veered off in a different direction. Kittel could easily have been killed by this terrible accident. He managed to survive, but was knocked unconscious and badly bruised, and when the rogue log was lifted from him, his rescuers discovered that his left leg was badly broken.

It was not a simple break. Elias and the others realized that Kittel would need to be taken immediately to the nearest doctor. Johannes and Halvor Baklistulen, together with several other men, hurriedly made a bed of hay upon one of the empty sleighs, and Kittel was lifted, as gently as possible, onto this sleigh to be taken as quickly as possible to Mukwa, where a doctor who had been educated in Denmark recently arrived to set up his practice.

Maren insisted upon accompanying her brother; the other two women could easily handle her duties at the camp. Elias also went along with Johannes and Halvor on the sleigh, as it sped across the frozen landscape as fast as the horses could be prodded to go. Kittel was wrapped in heavy blankets, and Elias had attempted to straighten his broken leg as well as he could, tying two crude splints around the injured leg.

To Kittel and the others, the journey seemed interminable, but they managed to get to Mukwa well before dark. Unfortunately, the Danish doctor, Dr. Christian Linde, was not at home when they arrived, but was expected back from a call in the country within the hour. The doctor's housekeeper advised Johannes and Elias that Kittel should not be moved from the sleigh until the doctor returned, but she offered hot coffee to everyone in the party. She also gave Elias several extra blankets and pillows to make Kittel more comfortable on the sleigh; and she gave him a small bottle of brandy and a spoon, suggesting that Kittel should take some in order to stimulate his circulation and keep him warm.

The Danish doctor returned from his call in the country about an hour later than expected, so Kittel had a long and chilly wait out on the sleigh. Maren stayed by his side every moment, concerned that her brother should not freeze as the temperature began to dip further as darkness closed in.

When the doctor came, he instructed Elias and the others how to carry Kittel into his house. Very carefully, they hoisted him onto a cot in the corner of the tiny room which served as the doctor's office. The doctor carefully untied the crude splints which Elias had put around Kittel's leg and decided that the pant leg and heavy underwear that Kittel was wearing would need to be cut away. Kittel swooned with pain as the doctor pressed his hands on various parts of his bruised and broken limb. At one point he screamed out in agony, and this confirmed the doctor's opinion about the seriousness of the break.

"It is, I'm afraid, a very nasty break. The bones were crushed by the impact of the log in such a way that we can't be sure they will heal again as they should. I shall need to put a tight splint on his leg, and we must have him stay here, right on this cot, for at least a week, so I can see how his leg will mend before he is allowed to go home. It may take at least three or four months before he can walk on this leg, and then he may need to use a cane for quite some time. Of course, he is very young, and that is in his favor, because young bones heal much quicker than the bones of old folks. But his leg will probably never be the same as it was before, and he will likely walk with a considerable limp."

All of this was somber news to Elias and Maren and the others. It was hard to imagine this strong and vigorous young man as an invalid; and, if what the doctor said was true, this injury could really cripple poor Kittel for the rest of his life. Only time would tell how serious the consequences of this unfortunate injury would be.

Finding a New Name

When Terje and Anna were disheartened by the news of Kittel's serious leg injury. He had been such a healthy and strong young boy who had never been sick a day in his life, and now it was possible he would be crippled for life because of this terrible injury. It would have been so much better if he had stayed home to help Jacob with the building of Lambert Norton's house. Jacob had wanted him to, but Kittel was determined to go to the woods with Elias.

Terje insisted upon going to Mukwa at once to be with his son. Anna also wanted to go, but Terje would not allow her to journey by foot that entire distance, especially during the uncertain weather of the last several days. Besides, Anna would be needed to look after the house and the animals during his absence. So Terje set out on foot to Mukwa; and after a long day's walk, he arrived at the home of the Danish doctor where he was welcomed by the doctor's housekeeper and Maren, who had stayed on with her brother.

Terje was concerned about getting Kittel home as soon as possible, but he realized that the doctor would need to tell them just when the time was appropriate to make the journey. Johannes and Elias had returned to the camp because the camp was about to disband for the season. Maren found a place to stay with a German family who lived next door to the doctor, and they also made a place for Terje. But Terje and Maren spent most of each day and part of each night with Kittel.

Each day Kittel was gaining in strength, but he was not yet able to stand. According to the doctor, it would be about two weeks before his bones would be mended sufficiently to take him home. The hours were long and tedious for Kittel, but Maren proved a helpful companion both for Kittel and her father. She managed to borrow a child's English primer and another book of simple stories in English, and she took advantage of the idle hours to tutor both her brother and her father in the mysteries of the English language. Kittel caught on to her instruction quite rapidly, but Terje often only shook his head and muttered something to the effect that he was much too old to learn this complicated new language.

Terje paid several gold coins to the Danish doctor, with whom he was able to converse quite readily, expressing his gratitude for the excellent care the good doctor had given. He also promised he would bring provisions to him later in the summer, when the roads would be better and the crops would be in.

At last the day came when Elias and Jacob arrived in Mukwa with the oxen and the cart. By this time thawing had occurred so it was no longer possible to use the sleigh. But now the problem was the mud. It was with considerable difficulty that they were able to make their way north to Mukwa. Halvor Romme had shown them a place where the oxen could ford the Rat River, in spite of the high water, but this meant a meandering route several miles through thickets of brush and high brown marsh grasses, remnants of the last season's lush growth. Jacob remembered his experiences with Adam Cartwright when they first traveled together from Sheboygan to Fond du Lac, and how the oxen could pull through just about any obstacle because of their stolid persistence. This same persistence made this journey possible.

Finally they arrived home, after spending the first night of their return journey at the Halvor Romme farm. Kittel was propped in the cart with Maren at his side as it jogged roughly over ruts and through nearly impassable stretches of mud up to the hubs of the wheels. It was a tedious journey, but they were able to make it in a day and a half. When they arrived home, Anna immediately took charge of seeing to it that Kittel would have a warm meal and a good bed, which had been prepared for him on a special cot. She shed tears upon seeing her injured son and showered him with motherly solicitude.

Kittel made a painfully slow recovery, and at times his family wondered if he ever would be able to walk again. But he was persistent. Using the crude crutch Jacob had fashioned for him, he hobbled around, at first only in the house, but as the weather turned mild, in the farmyard. Gradually, he was able to help with some of the household tasks and the chores of looking after the animals. Sometimes when Terje saw his son hobbling about so painfully and awkwardly, a tear would come to his eye, but he would conquer his thoughts enough to be cheerful and optimistic to Kittel.

When the first settlers came to the Neenah Settlement, they settled in what at that time was the western edge of Neenah township. As a consequence, they called their new community the Neenah Settlement, and it continued to be called by this name for many years. But many of earliest Norwegian settlers took up land west of Neenah township in what was first called Winnebago township and later Winneconne township. As the population grew, new townships were authorized by the County Board, following the township definitions which had been established previously by the surveyors.

In the autumn of 1851 a public meeting was held in which the residents of the area voted to request the County Board to recognize them as a properly constituted township. Lambert Norton had been the prime mover in getting the township properly organized, and he had also made contact with the chairman of the County Board to make sure that the proceedings would be proper and in order. In fact, Lambert functioned as the temporary chairman of the organizing meeting. The first issue faced by this assemblage was what the new township should be called.

About two weeks before the meeting, Lambert Norton approached Jacob with the problem of finding of a proper name, and he wanted Jacob to make a motion to the meeting that the new township should be called "Norton." But Jacob objected to this kind of pressure from Lambert Norton. In Jacob's mind it would mark him as Norton's lackey. But to Lambert's way of thinking

"Norton" was a proud old Yankee name with many distinguished forebears in the early history of this country, especially in New England. Because he had no sons to perpetuate the name properly, he had latched on to this idea of naming the new township "Norton." After Jacob's refusal, he came to realize that this suggestion would probably be resented by many of his neighbors, whether they were Yankee, Norwegian, German or Irish.

All the Yankee farmers were present at the meeting, but they found, somewhat to their chagrin, that they were outnumbered by the Norwegians. A number of the Norwegians were scarcely able to speak or understand English, so Johannes Baklistulen had to translate for their benefit. There were also seven German farmers present at this first meeting, and Friedrich Winckler had to translate the proceedings for them, as best he could. As a result, the meeting proceeded very slowly.

When the business of the name of the new township was brought up, Helge Mathison suggested that since so many of the settlers had come from Telemark in Norway, the name "Telemark" might be appropriate. It was, he suggested, a name that could easily be pronounced by everyone, but it was also a name that was very special to many of the Norwegians who had come to these parts. There were objections to that suggestion, not only from the Yankees and the Germans and the Irish, but even from some of the other Norwegians who came from parts of Norway other than Telemark.

Samuel Hopkins then suggested that since there were so many oak trees in the township, perhaps a name like "Oakwood" would be appropriate. But Charlie Jones, one of Samuel's nearest neighbors and friends, said he was so tired of chopping oak trees that he didn't think he liked that name very well. Charlie's response evoked boisterous laughter from all of those assembled.

Frank Neville then asked for the floor. Frank had only arrived within the last month, and he and his family had come directly from England. Frank's wife was a cousin of Samuel Hopkins, and that connection had led to their seeking out this community as their new home. Most of the men at the assembly had never met Frank.

"I've listened to your deliberations with interest," Frank said, "I've come to this community only recently, and so I must speak as somewhat of an outsider, but I have a suggestion for a good name for our new township. In England I lived very near the old town of Winchester. It is one of the oldest towns in all of England, and the site of a famous cathedral and an equally famous college. Since coming to America I've learned that the name 'Winchester' has been used in various communities in America because it is a good name with venerable historical associations. This land is such a new land, but those of us who have come here, whether from other states or from foreign lands, come with memories of our former homes. Like many of the rest of you, I have some good memories of my old home in spite of the poverty and lack of opportunity I experienced there which drove me to seek my fortune in this bountiful new land. With these thoughts in mind, I suggest the name 'Winchester' for our new township."

There was a bit of buzzing as people reacted to Neville's suggestion, but when Lambert Norton called for a vote, twenty-six were in favor of Neville's suggestion, and only twelve were opposed. Norton ruled that the name of the new township would be "Winchester." Even those who had voted against the name finally agreed it was probably a good choice.

With the establishing of the new Winchester township, the Norwegian settlers of the Neenah Settlement found themselves living in several townships. In 1851 the townships of Clayton and Vinland had been formed in territory originally a part of Neenah township; others were located within the new boundaries of Winneconne township; and a few others who lived in the "Tangen" part of the settlement to the northeast of other settlers found themselves in Outagamie County. But the largest number of Norwegian settlers were included in the newly constituted Winchester Township.

In April of 1852, the first township election was held at the Knott School. Lambert Norton made it known that he was a candidate for town chairman. He coveted a position of leadership in the community and felt that the office of town chairman legitimately belonged to him and that he was eminently qualified for the job. He had, he felt, sufficiently befriended many of the Norwegian settlers to deserve their votes; and he also felt that the Yankee voters would support him. He had little contact with the German settlers in the western and northern reaches of the township, but they were so few in number he felt he could rely upon Yankee and Norwegian support and this would be sufficient for his election.

But Lambert Norton was due for a bitter disappointment. In spite of the fact that he had presided at the first assembly of voters, many of the Norwegians had already determined that Johannes Baklistulen was their man. They solicited some of the German settlers to get their support, and when the time came for nominations, Lambert Norton was startled to notice the enthusiasm in the crowd when Johannes Baklistulen was nominated for the office. Lambert had also been nominated by Samuel Hopkins, but he was disappointed when Jacob failed to second his nomination. He thought he could count on Jacob's support, but Jacob had a real dilemma: Should he support his employer or his brother-in-law? In the end he supported Johannes as enthusiastically as the others. As a result, Lambert's ambitions were defeated by a vote of thirty-four to eighteen, and Johannes Baklistulen was declared the duly elected chairman of the township.

If the township acquired a new name, many of the Norwegian settlers also found themselves trying to find new surnames, and, in some cases, new Christian names, by which they could more readily be known and identified by their Yankee neighbors. Johannes Baklistulen was entirely too awkward a moniker for Yankee tongues; and, as he launched on his new career as a political leader, he became known more and more as John Anunson.

Likewise, Terje and his family had been called the Skredderstua family, but more and more his sons were called "Larsen," in spite of the fact that according the traditional Norwegian usage they ought to have been "Terjesen" or even "Torgerson." Strangely enough, it was Maren who continued to use the name "Terjesdatter" when she was with her Norwegian friends, but she was "Mrs. Anunson" to her Yankee neighbors. As a result of these name changes, the Winchester community was soon overburdened with Petersons and Hansons and Olsons and Johnsons and Larsens and many other kinds of sons, all of which was confusing to the Yankee neighbors and sometimes equally confusing to themselves.

There were other offices to be filled by the first election. Samuel Hopkins and George Knott were elected supervisors, and together with "John Anunson" constituted the new Town Board. This assured the Yankee settlers a majority voice in Town Board decisions, and although Lambert Norton was unhappy with the election results, most of his Yankee neighbors were not. It was decided there should be three justices of the peace, one for each of the ethnic groups represented in the township: Ole Olson Strømme was elected, as were Friederick Winckler and Frank Jones. Both Strømme and Winckler were sufficiently fluent in English to deal with other township officers and yet able to deal with those in the township who were yet unable to make their needs known in English.

Gradually, as the spring weather set in, Jacob was able to frame the middle section of Lambert Norton's house. What had previously been called "Norton's Folly" as a term of derision by his jealous neighbors continued to be called "Norton's Folly," but with a new ring of respect. The two wings were now united by a handsome two-storied structure in the Greek revival style that was so popular at the time; and the whole structure graced the horizon with its new majesty. When the clapboard siding was nailed on and painted and the windows decorated by apple-green shutters, the result was very pleasing to the eye. The Yankee neighbors could remember houses like this that graced the landscapes of the communities from which they came in New England, York State or the Western Reserve.

When Jacob completed the tedious task of nailing laths to the interior walls, Norton brought two German-born plasterers from Oshkosh. When they finished their work, Jacob returned to install the interior woodwork which had been furnished by the new millwork factory in Oshkosh. There were elegantly paneled doors of black walnut with bright brass doorknobs, but most of the woodwork was pine. It would be painted by another German immigrant from Oshkosh who had established a good reputation for painting in some of the more pretentious and elegant homes now being erected in that city.

Near the end of August, after the house had been completed, several wagonloads of new furniture were delivered. They included finely carved bedsteads, horsehair chairs and sofas, and a beautiful dining table with twelve chairs and an elegant sideboard for the spacious new dining room. There were also carpets and curtains, all of which had been selected under the careful eyes of Norton's wife and his two daughters.

When the house was completely finished, it was by far the largest and most elegant home in the whole community. With the exception of Jacob, very few of the Norwegian settlers ever had the opportunity to venture over the threshold into the interior of this grand home, but there were parties for the Yankee neighbors, and Norton's friends and acquaintances from nearby communities were invited to housewarming parties. Some of these invited guests pulled up to the house in fancy carriages pulled by nicely groomed horses. Others came in the typical "democrat wagon," often pulled by an old nag too decrepit to be consigned to the heavy work of plowing and other field work, and still others trudged on foot to make their first visit to this fine house.

On Terje's farm, Elias and Terje planted a larger field into wheat than they had the previous year. There were two new calves, luckily both heifer calves this time; and Elias and Terje, with occasional help from Jacob, were able to erect a tight rail fence around a partially cleared small field for use as a sheep pasture. Anna had wanted a herd of sheep much earlier so she could have a good supply of wool for the spinning wheel which had been idle in the immigrant trunk ever since they arrived. But when Terje and Elias brought the first three ewes with their lambs into the newly enclosed field, Anna was ecstatic. The ewes had been sheared by their previous owner, a Yankee farmer in the township of Vinland, so Anna would have to wait nearly a year for the fleeces which she coveted so dearly. But she was patient, and the very presence of these sheep provided her with such new delights that the nostalgic memories of the sweet cherry tree at Skredderstua faded away.

As the weather turned warmer in the springtime, Kittel was able, with the use of his crutch, to hobble about the farmyard quite handily. He spent a good deal of his time tending the animals, and relieved his mother and sisters entirely of the task of milking the cows. He limped noticeably, but seemed to gain strength in his broken limb as the season progressed. He claimed, as the doctor had told him, that it would be good to exercise the muscles of his leg regularly, even though the bone structure would never heal perfectly. He began to regain some of his carefree and buoyant spirit, and even began to joke a bit about his injury.

The land office had been transferred from Green Bay to Menasha, and Elias made a journey into Menasha as soon as he had completed sowing the wheat crop in May to lay claim to the eighty acres southeast of their farm. He had saved enough cash from his work in the woods to make the purchase of the land, sixty dollars for each of the forty acre plots. The area was heavily wooded with hickory, elm and oak trees; and some areas would need drainage ditches before the fields could be cultivated properly; but Elias had a sharp eye for fertility and saw some good possibilities for this land as a farm which escaped the more casual observations of others. When he returned with the documents in his own name, he had an inner satisfaction that he was now a landowner in his own right, and when he had the opportunity he would begin clearing some of the land.

At the last service at Ole Saersland's barn, he caught the eye of an attractive young lady, Dorthea Funer, who lived with her parents on a farm in "Tangen," about five miles from his home. He had some opportunity to converse with this young lady and was pleased with her pleasant responses. Perhaps he should pay a courtship call in Tangen before long. If he had read her feelings correctly, she would welcome his visit, and, perhaps in due time he would have a partner when he was ready to settle on his own land. "All in good time; all in good time," Elias thought to himself; yet he realized that there were many more young bachelors than marriageable young ladies in the Neenah Settlement. Perhaps he had better not be too slow about this business lest someone else put in a bid for this attractive young lady ahead of him. He really should talk to Maren about this; perhaps she could advise him. But he certainly did not want any of the other members of his family to know anything about this, at least not yet.

The Whims of Roberta

On a beautiful Sunday early in June, Elias put on his best clothes and made his first journey to Tangen to pay his call upon Dorthea Funer. He was received cordially by Dorthea's parents, Gregar and Gunhild Funer. Dorthea had two younger sisters and one younger brother, but her younger siblings were visiting at a neighboring farm where they were playing with children their own ages. Dorthea was, in fact, a half-sister of her younger siblings; she was the daughter of Gregar Funer's first wife who died in Norway when Dorthea was a young child. Gregar and Gunhild emigrated from their small farm in Hjartdal in 1847, settling temporarily at Muskego, and came to the Neenah Settlement in 1848 with some of the other earlier settlers from Muskego.

The Funer family lived in a small but cozy log cabin. Gregar had cleared several fields and planted a good crop of wheat, but he had to do most of the outside work alone. Gunhild and Dorthea helped him as best they could, but Gregar insisted they should not be expected to do the hard work of clearing the land.

Dorthea Funer had a sly smile for Elias when he paid his first visit to her home. She was by nature shy; but once the barrier of her shyness was broken, she revealed a good sense of humor. Her stepmother, Gunhild, had been kind to her, treating her as her own daughter in every respect; and so there was a strong bond of affection between the stepmother and the stepdaughter.

Dorthea was confirmed in the Hjartdal Church just a year before the family emigrated. Now she was nineteen years old and

[186]

within a few more weeks would celebrate her twentieth birthday.

Other young men had noticed her slender beauty and her sly smile, but she had not encouraged any of her earlier suitors. However, when Elias called upon her on this beautiful Sunday in June, he found Dorthea responsive and interested in learning to know him better. She asked him many questions about his family and his experiences. She spoke the Telemark dialect, but she did so in such a charming and pleasing fashion that Elias was overcome by the very tone of her voice. She also had learned a good deal of English because she often attended the school in Tangen with her younger siblings. There was a special mischievous flash in her eyes from time to time, and she did not hesitate to tease Elias a bit now and then.

Elias made many more Sunday visits to the Funer family, and soon Anna Tøvesdatter insisted that the Funer family should be invited to their place so that she could have a chance to meet this young lady who had so charmed her son, When Gregar Funer saw the fine house Jacob built, he could not believe that a Norwegian family could live in such a fine style, just like a rich Yankee family, with white clapboards on the walls and green shutters on the windows. All the houses in Tangen were still log cabins, and Gregar thought it would be quite some time before any of his neighbors would be able to afford anything better. He was a bit envious of all the help Terje had from his capable sons in getting settled in this new land. The thought had already occurred to him that a strapping healthy young son-in-law like Elias could be of help to him, now and then, even if he lived some miles away.

The more Elias saw Dorthea the more determined he was to begin work clearing his own land and planning his future home. It was not long before he began sharing his plans with Dorthea, and she soon became enthusiastic and excited about their future together, and they began to discuss their plans for marriage. Elias insisted he should have a nice log house ready for her so that when they were married, he could bring her to their new home. There were so many things to consider, Elias discovered, when one had to begin from scratch to establish a new farm and a new home. His father and his brothers pledged their help, and soon they were busy felling trees on Elias' land, some of which were put into a special pile to be used in constructing a suitable first cabin for Elias and Dorthea.

At last, late in October, the cabin was ready. Jacob had been a great help in building a good cabin for his brother. It was not large, but it showed the same careful craftmanship Jacob had used on his parents' home.

When Herman Preus, pastor of the Spring Prairie parish north of Madison and cousin to Adolph Preus, paid his second visit to the Neenah Settlement in mid-November, Elias and Dorthea spoke their vows publicly, in front of the whole congregation, on the second day of his visit. Anna Tøvesdatter was delighted to have such a lovely daughter-in-law. Perhaps it would not be so long before she would have a grandchild because now both her Maren and her Elias had found their lifemates. Life indeed was much better in this new land than she had dreamed it could be when she first heard about the plans to emigrate to America back at Skredderstua.

Jacob, in the meantime, had spent most of the summer finishing Lambert Norton's big house and working on several smaller outbuildings. But he took a considerable amount of time away from his labors on the Norton place to help his brother clear some of his land and build his first small cabin, and during the harvest season he took time away from his carpentry to help Lambert Norton harvest his large crop of wheat.

Early in June, Lambert and Jacob had traveled together to Fond du Lac. Jacob had told Lambert so much about Adam Cartwright's place, and Lambert wanted to talk to Cartwright about his wheat harvesting machinery, both the reaper and the thresher. He also wished to see the barn which Jacob helped to erect before his family arrived on that wonderful day of reunion in July of 1850. So Lambert and Jacob took a steamboat from Winneconne to Oshkosh and then caught another boat from Oshkosh to Fond du Lac. It was a great adventure for Jacob who remembered all too well how he and his family had to trudge all of those miles from Fond du Lac three years earlier with their oxen and cart. Now, with steamboats operating on regular schedules, the journey was like a pleasant holiday.

When they arrived in Fond du Lac, Jacob was astonished to see how the small city had changed and grown during the three year interval since he had last seen it. When he and Lambert arrived at the Cartwright farm, Jacob was greeted like a long lost son, and Mrs. Cartwright insisted upon their staying as guests instead of taking lodgings in the hotel as they had planned. Adam proudly showed Lambert and Jacob his harvesting machinery, taking care to explain in great detail just how both the machines operated. Lambert was impressed with everything Adam showed him, and admired Adam's farm greatly. Like many other folks, Lambert was amazed at the wonderful black walnut staircase in the Cartwright house. Jacob had told him about this great staircase; but now that Lambert saw it, he regretted he had not taken more time in planning his own new house to include a staircase like this one.

Jacob was curious about Peter Smith and asked Adam of his whereabouts. Adam said Peter had moved to Madison where there was a good deal of construction going on. Jacob was sorry he would not be able to see Peter; but apparently he was well on his way to success as a building contractor, according to Adam's best information. Jacob thought someday it would be interesting to visit Madison, the city that had both the state capitol building and the new university. Perhaps then he would be able to renew his friendship with Peter, and they could reminisce upon their days together working for Adam Cartwright.

Adam also told Jacob that his daughter Edith was engaged to a young businessman in Beaver Dam by the name of Charles Swan, and the wedding was to take place at Christmas time, right here in the parlor of the Cartwright house. Jacob remembered, with some discomfort, the circumstances under which Edith was hurried away when he was working on their house. Now she had found her Yankee beau; that should make Mrs. Cartwright very happy. But Jacob did not want to bring up the subject in her presence. He was glad it was Adam who broke the news to him, and not his wife.

After spending one night with the Cartwrights, Jacob and Lambert caught an early morning steamboat for Oshkosh, and later in the day another boat to Winneconne. Late that evening, they drove Lambert's horse and wagon back to the Norton farm, arriving after midnight. It had been an interesting interlude for Jacob, awakening some good memories; and for Lambert, it had been most helpful because he had now placed an order for a reaper and a thresher, similar to the ones Adam had shown him. He negotiated the order while they were in Oshkosh awaiting the later boat that would take them back to Winneconne. The dealer assured Lambert this equipment would be ready for him in time for harvest. The items were costly enough, and no other farmer in the Winchester township had this kind of equipment, except Kittel Baklistulen who cleverly rigged up his own homemade version of a reaper. But even Kittel did not have the ingenuity to make his own thresher.

During the entire time Jacob had worked for Lambert Norton, a special relationship existed between his youngest daughter, Roberta, and Jacob. Perhaps the relationship could best be described as a flirtation, and it was initiated entirely by Roberta. Jacob was amused by Roberta and actually grew quite fond of her. They spent a good deal of time together, especially during those times when Jacob stayed overnight at the Norton house. Roberta was fond of card games and found Jacob a willing pupil as she attempted to teach him. Her sister, Lydia, on the other hand, tended to regard the games as frivolous and a waste of time. Lydia spent a good deal of her spare time sewing and reading. Unlike Roberta, who was a chatterbox, Lydia was quiet and reserved. Jacob often wished he could get to know Lydia better, but Roberta was always the one in the forefront.

It happened one early spring day. Roberta insisted that Jacob take time away from his work to help her gather some wild flowers, and Jacob submitted to her wishes without questioning her motives. When they were out of sight of the house, walking through the woods, Roberta suddenly thrust her hand into Jacob's large and calloused hand, walking close to him and chattering about how happy she was to be alive and how the spring flowers brought her to a point of ecstacy. She suddenly darted away from Jacob when she spotted a cluster of dainty pale flowers and gathered them quickly.

After she placed the flowers jauntily in his hair, she suddenly gave him a quick but passionate kiss.

Jacob was startled by her audacity, yet he had to admit it was a pleasant sensation to be kissed by such a charming young lady. After the kiss, she begged Jacob to hold her tight, and she pressed her body close to his.

"Do you find me pretty, dear Jacob?" she purred into his ear.

Jacob was a bit taken aback by Roberta's advances. It was pleasant to hold a girl in this fashion. Was Roberta really serious about him as a lover, or was she only teasing him? Jacob was so startled and perplexed that he suddenly broke away from their embrace.

"Have I frightened you, dear Jacob? I didn't mean to. You're my very special Viking abductor, carrying me off into the woods with your charms."

She threw her arms about him once more, and this time Jacob embraced her with determined intensity and ardor. This strange girl had inexplicably awakened some strong and primitive passions in him, and she sensed the difference in his manner of embracing her. At once, she began to fend him off just a bit.

"Not so fast, my dear boy! I am still your virgin princess, and you cannot possess me like a common woman. Our love must be more discreet and subtle. Do you understand what I am telling you?"

Suddenly, inexplicably, she broke into tears. Jacob was perplexed. What had he done to provoke her tears? Clearly, his relationship with Roberta was becoming more and more an enigma to him. Why did she tease and provoke him so much? What did he really mean to her that she could toy with his feelings in such a manner?

After that day in the woods, their relationship grew a bit more distant and cool. To be sure, Roberta often seemed to revert to her same carefree and spontaneous self when she was with Jacob, but there seemed to be a tacit understanding between the two of them that there should never be another encounter quite like the one in the woods when they were hunting wild flowers together.

During the summer of 1853 there was a great stir of excitement during harvest season when Lambert and Jacob drove out into Lambert's large wheat field to harvest his crop with a brand new reaper. Instead of a crew of men swinging cradles and scythes, the reaper cut a neat swath as it slowly made its first round. Jacob instructed several hired hands on how to gather the bundle from the apron of the reaper and how to tie each bundle as it was raked from the apron. Within a surprisingly short time, Lambert's field was transformed from a field of standing grain into a field of grain shocks, neatly stacked to dry his bumper crop of golden wheat. Several neighbors, including Terje, Elias and Kittel, stood by watching as the reaper did its magic work. Terje could only shake his head in wonderment. He had never imagined he would live to see such a machine as a reaper. It was almost as exciting as that first train ride from Albany to Buffalo.

But if the neighbors were amazed at the reaper, they were mesmerized by the thresher. The horses were harnessed to a circular power source and the thresher began to make strange whirring sounds. As soon as the bundles were carefully fed into the machine, clouds of dust and chaff encircled the machine, and straw emerged at one end while the golden grain flowed into a sack on the side of the machine. Soon the large bin, which Jacob had just finished in Lambert's granary in anticipation of this bumper crop of wheat, began to fill. Within several days, Norton's crop had been completely harvested, and within a few more days Norton could begin hauling his wheat into Winnebago Rapids for sale at the flour mill. This great crop would provide him with nearly enough cash to pay for his new reaper and thresher.

After his own crop was harvested, Norton was able to hire out his threshing machine to several of the neighbors, including Terje and Elias. Elias cut their entire crop with his scythe and cradle, but once the bundles were put into shocks, he was eager to try the new machine for threshing. Never again would Elias need to use the flail in order to thresh grain; however, because of his stump-infested field, it would be several more years before it would be feasible to use a reaper. Elias could, however, anticipate that the day would surely come when his father's fields and his own would be sufficiently cleared of the stumps to use it. In the meantime, as long as Lambert Norton was willing to thresh for several of the neighbors, it was well worth the price to hire the use of his machine. Elias and Terje also harvested a bumper crop; it had been an excellent growing season for the wheat, but their crop was only about one-third the amount of Lambert Norton's abundant harvest.

In the weeks and months after that exciting harvest season, Jacob came to realize gradually that Roberta was indeed a spoiled child, much pampered by her tolerant mother and indulgent father. She spent many hours reading silly romances which filled her head with nonsense; and, in retrospect, he began to see that his encounter with her in the woods had been a by-product of her literary obsessions. Jacob had been cast, in her mind, into the role of a Viking hero, abducting the fair maiden; and as long as the magic of her imagination sustained this role, Jacob could be her very own hero. But when Jacob's suddenly aroused ardor burst her bubble of self-deception, she was forced to reckon with the reality of the situation. Jacob was really only her father's hired man, not her romantic Viking hero.

High on the Hill

By the end of 1853 nearly all the lands in Winchester township, except some of the marshlands, had been claimed; and the adjacent townships also were nearly entirely settled. New settlers who arrived, in some cases family members or close friends of the earlier settlers, were forced to press on either to the north or west in their search for available lands.

One sizable group of Muskego Norwegians came to the Neenah Settlement; but when they discovered the unavailability of good land, they decided to press on. Knut Luraas took the time to act as their guide to the lands well beyond the Wolf River, into what became known as the Waupaca Settlement. Soon large numbers of Norwegian settlers, many of them from the Pine Lake Settlement near Oconomowoc, moved into that settlement; but they followed a trail west of Winnebago County, through Waushara County, to get to the open lands of what was called *Indielandet,* the "Indian Country," by the Norwegians. More new arrivals, coming directly from Norway, also settled there, with new families arriving every month during the seasonable weather.

It soon became evident that this Waupaca Settlement would become much larger than the Neenah Settlement. Strong ties of kinship existed between the two settlements, especially among the folks who came from Telemark. But there were also many families in the new Waupaca Settlement who came from Gudbrandsdal and other sections of Norway which were not represented in the earlier Neenah Settlement.

When the Rev. Olaus F. Duus arrived in America in 1854, his colleagues advised him to settle in the Waupaca Settlement. They arranged to have him officially called and installed as parish pastor so he could serve that burgeoning new settlement as well as the Neenah Settlement and a few other scattered preaching places. A congregation was organized and named the Scandinavia Lutheran Church, and Duus and his wife were provided with a log cabin parsonage. It would no longer be necessary for pastors to come from several southern Wisconsin parishes to provide occasional pastoral service to these more northerly locations. By this time great numbers of new immigrants from Norway were also settling in southwestern locations in Wisconsin and pressing across the border into northeastern Iowa and southeastern Minnesota. The Norwegian Synod was officially organized in 1853 and the Rev. Adolph Preus elected its first president. Several additional pastors had arrived from Norway so that new settlements could be provided with at least a minimal amount of pastoral care.

When the first child in the Neenah Settlement died in the autumn of 1849, even before the congregation was officially organized, a site had been selected for a burial ground with the thought that it would also be a suitable site for a church. It was located on the highest hill in the whole township and was visible for many miles where the view was not obstructed by smaller hills and ridges.

At a meeting of the congregation in the autumn of 1853, it was finally decided that a subscription should be taken from all the members of the congregation in order to finance a simple church building. A committee of three was chosen, and because of his reputation as a carpenter, Jacob Larsen was the first name put into nomination. He was joined by Ole Halvorson Uvaas and John Helgeson. During the winter these three men met several times to draw up plans for the building, but they were hampered by a lack of funds because the solication of the members had not been completed by the trustees.

When, in March of 1854, the trustees completed their solicitation, the results were disappointing, especially to the members of the building committee. Jacob and his colleagues had envisioned a proper church, replete with steeple and bell; but it soon became obvious to them that a much simpler structure would be all that the congregation could afford at this time. The steeple could be added later. Also, the dimensions of the building would have to be reduced from their original sketches. This also meant the building would not contain a proper chancel, but this could be added at some future date.

When Jacob told his family there could be no steeple on the building, Terje was bitterly disappointed. He could not imagine a church without a steeple because to his way of thinking the building then would be little more than a barn. He also thought the trustees had not encouraged folks to contribute as generously as they should, but he also acknowledged that most of the folks in the settlement had little extra cash. Perhaps the trustees had done as well as could be done, given these circumstances.

The committee suddenly had a bit of luck when they discovered that Nehemiah Hopkins, the brother of Samuel Hopkins, had changed his plans for building a new barn; and the framing timbers which he had purchased and prepared the year before were of a suitable dimension for the church. This meant that for a very reasonable price they were able to purchase a suitable frame for the structure; and with the help of members of the congregation, the frame could be erected as soon as the foundation could be prepared.

On a warm day at the end of March, before the farmers were able to get out on their land, about twenty volunteers from the congregation assembled at the site of the church building to dig trenches for the foundation walls. The soil was light and sandy, yielding readily to the shovels of the workers. At the end of the first day a trench about four or five feet deep was dug around most of the perimeter of the building. Tomorrow these men and others would return, some of them with wagonloads of round granite rocks and flat limestone rocks; and after finishing the digging, work could begin on setting the rocks into place for the foundation.

When the men came the next day, some of them worked hard to complete the digging, while the others were busy unloading stones, carefully placing some of the larger rocks at the bottom of the trenches. But just as they were in the midst of their tasks, it began to rain, at first very lightly; but soon the clouds opened and the work party was deluged with a soaking spring rain. Work would have to be delayed for several days. Several of the men left for their homes in the middle of the heaviest rain, but others decided to huddle under the protection of their wagons, hoping to wait out the storm.

Jacob and Elias sought shelter under the wagon of Gregar Funer, father-in-law to Elias. Six or seven other men also huddled under Gregar's large wagon; and as they waited out the rainstorm, they lit their pipes and began to exchange stories, most of them old stories from Norway they loved to tell each other from time to time when there were those rare occasions of leisure. One of the men had a jug of whisky and passed it around to the others, suggesting that a good shot of whisky would be helpful to ward off the "damps" and keep them from catching their deaths from colds and fevers. He found ready takers as the jug was passed from man to man.

Gregar Funer was in a good mood for story-telling and he suddenly remembered a great old troll story from Heddal:

"Have you ever heard the story about Valfinn the clever troll and the building of that old stave church at Heddal?"

He searched his audience carefully, but no one had heard that story.

"As you may know, my wife Gunhild is from Heddal; and we were actually married in that beautiful old stave church. At the time of our wedding, Gunhild's brother told us this story."

He stopped for a moment to clear his throat and look several of the men in the eye to make sure they would be good listeners.

"It seems that in olden times, before there were church bells in Norway, this clever troll, Valfinn, lived under the steep hill in Heddal which today is just a short distance east of the stave church. He had lived there for as long as men could remember, but now something new was happening in Heddal. The people had taken it into their heads to build a church. Five men of Heddal, led by Raud Rygi, were supposed to build this church, but they found it would be a difficult task, especially with all of that fancy carving and those gables and all the trim they felt would be necessary if they were to have a proper church."

At this point the jug was passed around another time, and Gregar paused to take a healthy swig.

"Just after their meeting when they had pondered these matters, Raud Rygi was suddenly confronted by Valfinn the troll. Valfinn had a proposition for Raud. 'If you will let me, I can build that church in three days!' Raud knew, of course, that this troll was a clever fellow, not at all like those stupid trolls that lived in the high mountains, but he could not believe that this church could possibly be built in such a short time. But, Raud thought, if anyone could do it, this clever troll could; yet he also knew that there was usually some kind of condition attached to any bargain made with a troll."

At this point Elias interrupted his father-in-law. "I never realized there were clever trolls. I just assumed they were always stupid fellows."

Gregar cleared his throat once more, and continued.

"Now, you must understand that while you and I know the name of this troll as Valfinn, Raud Rygi and the other folks at Heddal never knew his name. Trolls were a bit jealous about this knowledge, and so when he spelled out the condition to Raud Rygi he said, 'I will build your church in three days, and after it is completed, if you can guess my name, you will have won. I will leave Heddal forever and move to the mountain at Lifjell. However, if you cannot guess my name correctly, I shall have your head, Raud Rygi, as a plaything for my little troll son in his crib.' Raud pondered this bargain. Now he was a daring fellow, willing to take a chance, and so he said to the troll. 'Agreed. If after three days I fail to guess your true name, you may take my head. But if I guess your name, as I believe I shall be able to do, you will have built the church, true to every specification, and then you will leave Heddal forever.'"

One of the men huddled under the wagon said, in a muffled voice, "I'm glad we don't have to make that kind of bargain to get this church built."

"And so the bargain was sealed. The troll went to work immediately. On the first day he gathered all of the timber from the forest. On the second day he prepared the foundation and erected the frame of the building, and on the third day he finished the stave church at Heddal, complete with all of those carvings and fancy gables. At the end of the first day, Raud Rygi marveled at the energy of the troll and the amount of work he had done, but Raud had no hint yet about the troll's name. At the end of the second day, he also was astonished to see the progress; and he was getting more and more concerned that he would never find out about the troll's name. And he was beginning to get an uneasy feeling about his neck."

The jug was passed around one more time, but Gregar ignored it and continued with his story.

"But in the evening of the second day he wandered next to the small mountain inside of which the troll lived, and in the stillness of the early evening he suddenly heard a voice from deep within. It was the voice of the troll wife singing a lullabye to her troll child. *Tomorrow my child, you shall have a new toy. It will not be the sun or the moon, but the head of Raud Rygi, as surely as you are the son of Valfinn.*' At once Raud Rygi knew that he had the secret to the riddle of the troll's name, so when, near the end of the third day, he came to inspect the nearly completed church, he called the troll's attention to one of the supporting timbers: 'Here, Valfinn, don't you think that this vertical stave is just a little bit askew?'"

Gregar broke into a fit of coughing and had to pause a moment before continuing.

"At once, upon hearing his name from Raud Rygi's lips, the troll nearly exploded in anger, and poor Raud thought for a moment that he would destroy the whole church in his violent rage. But he soon simmered down. 'You have won, Raud Rygi! A bargain is a bargain. Now I must take my family and move to Lifjell, high in the mountains and away from the sound of church bells. Soon you will be mounting a bell in that bell tower which I have just completed in the church yard, and you know that no trolls can live within the sound of a church bell.' And with that the troll and his family disappeared, never to be seen again, and Heddal had its beautiful stave church and Raud Rygi still had his head on his shoulders."

At the end of the story, the men who were huddled under the wagon applauded Gregar for his good troll story.

"We could use a troll like that Valfinn for this job, couldn't we?" one of the fellows exclaimed.

Another man said, "We don't need a troll; we have Jacob, and he's almost as clever as that Valfinn fellow."

A third fellow piped up, "Yes, but Jacob is too handsome to be a troll. They're ugly fellows, aren't they? Our Jacob is so handsome that I hear all the young girls in our settlement can't keep their eyes off him."

And so the banter went on and on. The jug was passed around one more time, but then the rain suddenly stopped, and the men clambered out from under the wagon and were soon on their way home. They promised to return in several days, after things had dried out. Right now the trench for the foundation wall was half-filled with water, but in this sandy soil that water would soon disappear.

It was three days later when the men returned to continue their work on the foundation, and when it was completed and the mortar had dried sufficiently, the day finally came when the framework could be erected. It was a festive day, and many of the wives and children were also on hand. Jacob was the foreman, and he had several experienced assistants who also were carpenters. The men carefully raised the timbers into place by pushing them upward with poles. After the first wall was temporarily tacked into place with supports and the second wall put into place, it was time to install the cross beams, using augers and wooden pins. Jacob had to straddle the beam eighteen feet in the air to make the first connections.

It was an exciting moment when the last beam was lifted into place, and the framework of the building stood completed. Someone handed Jacob a small pine branch which he tacked into place at the apex of the structure. The women had prepared a picnic lunch for all to enjoy on this festive day when the church building was first raised in the Neenah Settlement.

In the days that followed, most of the farmers were busy getting in their crops for the season, but Jacob and several other men continued to work on the church building. Soon the building's walls were framed and sheathed and the roof boards were in place, ready for the shingles. It was a simple rectangular building. The only unusual feature in its design was the rounded top of each of the side windows. When Jacob ordered the windows from a glazier in Oshkosh, he determined that he could quite easily construct the special frames which would be necessary for more suitable windows, and the cost of the glass would not be much more than if the windows had been square at the top. Jacob spent a considerable amount of time fashioning these special windows, but he was determined that they would give the building an appearance appropriate for a church so it would not look like just another school house or town hall.

But Jacob and the other members of the building committee soon discovered that nearly all the funds which had been gathered for the building had been expended. There would be enough money to buy shingles for the roof, clapboards for the exterior siding and the windows and double front doors; but for the time being there was not money enough to put in a floor or finish the interior walls.

When the time came to hold the first church service in the new building, the congregation had to be seated on temporary plank seats on a dirt floor, and the people stared at unfinished walls. A simple table had to serve as an altar. To be sure, the building was larger than Ole Saersland's barn, but otherwise it was not much of an improvement.

But most of the folks were pleased that the building had at last taken shape. They were especially pleased with Jacob's windows, and many of them told him so. After the first service, conducted by the Rev. O. F. Duus, John Helgeson, who had officiated as the *klokker*, spoke to a group standing about after the service:

"It's not as grand a church as we'd hoped to have, but at least we now have a House of the Lord. Perhaps we shall have good crops this year, and our people can afford to be a bit more generous so we can make some improvements very soon. Jacob has worked out a scheme for making church pews, so after we get our floor in place, and our walls finished, we can have a more proper church. But it was for me a joyful day, just the same, to be able today to worship in a church building of our very own after all those temporary locations we've had to use."

On the way home from that first service in the new building, Terje still regretted that the church had to be built without a steeple and a bell.

"It's not really a proper church," he said, "until one can hear the church bell ring out every Sunday morning."

The Night Visitors

During a lull in the busy activities of the pioneer farmstead, an invitation came to Terje and Anna to attend a party at the house of Anton and Henrikke Møller. Jacob happened to be staying at home with his parents; and he accompanied his parents, at their request. He was needed to help find the way in the dark and protect his parents from any danger they might encounter during the two and a half mile hike through the dark woods to the Møller cabin.

With five young and half-grown sons, the Møller household was perpetually a noisy and busy place, but Henrikke managed to keep her cabin neat and orderly. She had acquired the part-time help of one of her neighbor's young daughters to assist with household chores and food preparation for her hungry young sons and their father.

Anton was a good farmer, and he carefully taught his boys the skills of husbandry. The older sons, Hans and Eric, were nearly grown and worked alongside their father day after day, especially during the busiest months of the summer; but in the winter months, both Anton and Henrikke insisted that the boys attend school as regularly as possible.

When Terje, Anna and Jacob approached the Møller cabin, they were startled to hear strains of music emanating through the open windows. They heard both children's and adult's voices singing to the accompaniment of piano music.

"Now I know the reason for the party," Anna exclaimed, "Henrikke Møller now has the piano she's wished for so long."

When they entered the Møller cabin, Anton greeted them warmly. Henrikke was so busy playing her new piano that she didn't notice their entrance, but when she heard her husband greeting these newest guests, she quickly stopped playing and greeted them.

"See what my clever husband bought me when he made his last trip to Oshkosh. This lovely piano belonged to the wife of a merchant in Oshkosh; and, sadly, the wife died quite suddenly. Anton says that the merchant made up his mind after his wife's death to sell his business and all of his personal goods and return to Ohio, the state from which they'd come. Anton was fortunate to be in Oshkosh on the very day of the sale and was able to buy this beautiful piano for me at a fraction of the cost one would pay for a new one. And so it seems the ill fortune that struck one family has turned out to be good fortune for us."

Anna added to Henrikke's thoughts, "Yes, we often find that one person's misfortune can somehow turn to another's good fortune. But I don't think, dear Henrikke, that you should let your thoughts dwell upon the misfortune of that family in Oshkosh. You have waited so long for this wonderful gift of a piano, and now we can all hear how well you play it."

Anton hastened to add, "Henrikke should have told you that she also received some news of ill fortune. Her elderly father, we learned, died on February fifteenth, and in the letter which told of his death there was also a draft for some money from his estate which provided us with more than enough to make this extravagant purchase. I asked Henrikke if we should not use the money to help build a fine new house like Jacob built for you, but she assured me a house could come later. Right now, more than anything else, she wanted to have a piano so that her boys could grow up with music ringing in their ears."

"That is true. More than anything else I want my boys to grow up with music ringing in their ears." Henrikke asserted with an enthusiastic smile on her face.

"Henrikke also said this piano would be a suitable memorial to her father because he loved music so very much. When she was a little girl, he took such pleasure in her musical abilities. So, here we are, with this fine aristocratic piano in our humble log cabin!" Anton laughed aloud as he made this last statement. Other guests soon arrived and crowded into the small cabin. Gunder and Aase came, together with Sven Risland. In spite of their religious differences, Gunder and Anton remain good friends and neighbors here in the new land. They frequently exchanged labor, and occasionally Sven Risland was also involved in these work exchanges. After Sven experienced the tragic death of his wife, many of his neighbors were solicitous of his welfare. Henrikke often invited Sven and his son Lasse for a good home-cooked meal.

But Terje, Anna and Jacob met one family this night they had never seen before: Andreas Børthe and his wife Ingrid and Ingrid's elderly aunt, Pernilla Semb. The Børthes recently arrived from Norway and purchased a forty acre plot of land from a Yankee farmer near Anton Møller's place. Andreas and Ingrid were young, in their upper twenties, and had been married only a few weeks before leaving Norway. Ingrid's elderly aunt, her deceased mother's oldest sister, emigrated with Andreas and Ingrid because she had no other close relatives left in Norway.

Both of Ingrid's parents had died some years ago, and Ingrid lived with her aunt in a small cottage in Heddal before her marriage to Andreas. Pernilla never married and earned a small livelihood as a seamstress, but her failing eyesight made that work increasingly difficult for her. She was reluctant to come to America, but both Andreas and Ingrid insisted she should join them; and in the end, she relented. She survived the long journey quite well and was now contented to be in her new home with her beloved Ingrid and her strong and clever young husband. She was also pleased that there were so many of her countrymen in this new neighborhood, and when she had this opportunity to come to Anton and Henrikke's place, she was happy to accept the invitation.

After all the guests had arrived, Henrikke returned to her piano and began to play more songs. She had taught her sons to sing some familiar old Norwegian folksongs, and her guests were delighted to hear those familiar melodies once more. Then she began to play some favorite hymns, much to the delight of Gunder who was beginning to think the party was much too frivolous for his taste. But Gunder joined in singing those beloved old hymns with great gusto, even though he was used to singing them at a different tempo. He had difficulty following the piano accompaniment, typically dragging about a half a measure behind Henrikke's confident pace. Never before in the entire Neenah Settlement had there been so much music played and sung as during this wonderful interlude in the Møller cabin.

Finally, after many songs and hymns, Henrikke turned to the others and asked if they had any special songs they wished to share. Terje, who had a fairly keen musical ear, sang four stanzas of an old soldier's ballad he had learned during his days in the barracks at the fortress in Christiansand, carefully omitting several other stanzas he knew would be offensive to the ladies present. Aase sang a delightful little children's song that she said her children were fond of, especially when they were very young.

Just as Henrikke was about to give up getting any more responses to her request, Pernilla said that she had a special song she would like to sing, a song which brought memories of her old home in Norway. It had been passed on to her many years ago by her own mother in Heddal, and it was very ancient, she said.

The song was entitled *Draumkvedet*, meaning "The Dream Song," and it dated back to medieval times, telling of the saintly King Olav and of the way to life eternal and the way to death, hell and destruction.

Pernilla sang the old song without any accompaniment, but with a remarkably clear voice for an elderly woman:

> *Vil du meg lyda, eg kveda full kann*
> *um einkvan nytan drengjen*
> *alt um han Olav Åsteson*
> *som hev'e sovi så lengje.*

Jacob had great difficulty understanding the words because they were in such a strange and archaic language. According to his best guess, the Olav "Åsteson" of the song must have been Olav Haraldson, Norway's ancient sainted king. The song seemed to be saying, "If you will listen to me, I shall sing you a song about a beloved young man, Olav Åsteson, one who has now slept for so long." But the stanzas went on and on, describing a panorama of life and death, and the uncertainties of the passage from this world to the next. There were vivid allusions both to the saved and the damned, and the whole was sung in such a haunting melody that Jacob found himself entranced by the very manner in which Pernilla rendered the many stanzas of the ancient song.

As Pernilla was singing, the thought came into Jacob's mind: "Here we are in this new land, so untouched by history and tradition, so raw and new and unspoiled; yet we come from an ancient line, an old culture that has a memory that goes back a thousand years or more. It is exciting to embrace the new, but there are those moments when it is well to contemplate how deeply our roots are sunk into the culture of that Old World that we supposedly left behind. But now we must be prepared to forget much of that ancient past as we embrace these new American ways."

Jacob wondered if anyone else at Anton and Henrikke Møller's cabin that beautiful night had similar thoughts. He looked over at the older Møller boys. They were obviously bored with the old lady's singing and could hardly wait until she was done, but they stayed in the cabin out of politeness. When she finished, they darted out into the openness of the evening air. It had been too much for them -- too confining. Like Jacob, they hardly understood the language enough to grasp the full meaning of the song. But in spite of the difficulty of the words, the haunting melody remained in Jacob's mind for days.

Pernilla's song was the last musical selection of the night. Henrikke had prepared some coffee for her guests and served some of her newly baked bread with apple butter and wild plum jam with the coffee. Within a short while, the guests began to take their leave. It had been a most interesting and inspiring evening. On the trek back through the woods, Terje continued to hum some of the tunes he had enjoyed singing so much, and Jacob found himself joining his father in some of those old and familiar melodies.

Terje, Anna and Jacob arrived home very late that evening. It was nearly midnight by the hands of Terje's old clock which stood so proudly on the shelf near the stove. Just as Terje and Anna were about to retire to their bedroom for the night, they heard a loud knocking on their door.

"Who can that possibly be at this time of night?" Terje cried out to Anna in a startled tone of voice. "Here, let me go to the door!"

When Terje opened the door, he was surprised to see an Indian man with a young Indian boy in his arms standing on the doorstep. Indians had knocked on their door before from time to time, usually begging for flour and salt pork. Anna had been frightened nearly out of her wits when they made their calls during that first winter they lived in their small cabin, but now she had come to understand that they intended no harm. She always tried to find something to give to these poor beggars. But this Indian man was no ordinary beggar.

"Saw light," the Indian said in his brusque manner. "Boy hurt. Need help."

Anna and Terje could not quite make out what he was trying to say, so they called for Jacob to come down from the bedroom upstairs to help them interpret the language of this dark-skinned stranger. Jacob at once perceived the situation and understood the pidgin English which the Indian spoke. He motioned for the Indian to bring the boy into the light. The boy, about ten years of age, was obviously in pain because of a break or bad sprain in his ankle, but he uttered not a word.

"Take furs to Butte des Morts, to Grignon. Leave boy here two days. Will return. Will pay."

Almost before they realized it, the man had disappeared into the night, trusting the care of the young Indian boy to these strange white folks. Anna's solicitude took over. The boy looked up at her with his large brown eyes as if to search her intentions. He had been left seated on one of the kitchen chairs, his left leg dangling painfully.

"Jacob, we must put cold compresses on this leg to bring down the swelling. Can you go to the well to get the coldest pail of water that you can possibly fetch. Terje, we must make a pallet for the boy to sleep on right here in the kitchen. We have some extra straw ticks upstairs. Please fetch one as quickly as you can."

Anna was obviously in command. She had treated injuries before, but this was either a bad sprain or a break near the boy's left ankle. How or why it happened she did not know nor did she need to know. All she knew was that she was needed to care for this boy who suddenly was thrust into her house like some injured wild creature which had to be taken indoors temporarily in order to mend.

By Anna's standards, the boy was filthy dirty, but that would have to wait. First things first. The ankle had to be treated as soon as possible with cold compresses. As she was applying the compresses, she realized that the boy was probably ravenously hungry, so she told Terje to fix a cup of hot herbal tea for him and get a slice of bread with some butter and jam from the cupboard. The boy drank the tea and ate the bread and jam greedily, seeming to understand that this kind lady meant him no harm. Yet he spoke not a word.

"I do not think that his ankle is broken," Anna spoke to Terje and Jacob. "I think he has a very bad sprain. I have massaged his ankle sufficiently so if a bone was broken we would know it."

The boy stretched out on the straw tick that Terje had put on the floor and finally seemed relaxed enough to get to sleep. Jacob told the boy, "Sleep! Sleep until morning!" and the boy seemed to understand perfectly. It was obvious that he was very tired and needed the rest.

Two days later the Indian man returned as he had promised. To Anna he presented a pair of mocassins and to Terje he gave two dollar bills, but Terje refused to take the money. The Indian boy had recovered sufficiently from his bad sprain to hobble about with the aid of a homemade crutch Jacob had fashioned for him. The Indian man lifted the boy onto a scraggly pony; and, without much communication, the man and the boy on the pony disappeared into the thickest part of the woods northwest of Terje's farm. Jacob waved at the boy, but the boy did not wave back.

Anna prized her mocassins and found them both comfortable and useful. When other folks asked where she got them, she replied only, "A friend gave them to me."

About six months after the incident, the man suddenly appeared at Anna's door again. This time he presented the carcass of a deer to Anna, and he was gone again before Anna had a chance to thank him properly. Anna sent word to Maren about the venison she had received, begging Maren to help her prepare it. From the hide of the deer, which he sent to Oshkosh to be properly tanned, Terje used his shoemaking skills to fashion another set of mocassins large enough to fit himself, and he used the remaining leather to patch an old pair of boots.

Loss and Grief

Jacob returned to Lambert Norton's employment in the late spring of 1855. Not only did Lambert need Jacob for the usual round of spring work; he also had plans to erect a suitable barn to house his stable of horses as well as his growing herd of red-brindled cattle. Again, Jacob went to Friederich Winckler and Heinrich Meyer to secure the necessary long pine logs for the framework of the proposed barn. As always, Lambert Norton was in a hurry to get the structure built. Jacob had to warn him that freshly cut pine logs could not immediately be put to use as framing timbers. They needed time to dry and cure.

Fortunately for Norton's restless ambitions, Jacob discovered that Heinrich Meyer was willing to sell, at a fairly reasonable price, pine logs that had been cut the year before and were piled near his cattle-shed. Norton was ecstatic when he heard that these logs were available and instructed Jacob to purchase them, make arrangements to transport them back to Norton's farm, and begin shaping them into the timbers needed for the new barn.

In mid-June, Jacob finished preparing the timbers for the framework of the barn, and Norton invited all the neighbors for a barn-raising, the first such event in the community. Many people responded to Lambert's invitation -- all his Yankee neighbors, most of the Norwegian neighbors, three or four of the Irish families who had settled about two miles west of Lambert's farm, and Friederick Winckler and Heinrich Meyer and their families who received special invitations to attend. The wives outdid each other in preparing food for the occasion, loading the tables set up in Norton's yard with all sorts of delicious food. Norton had provided a young steer from his herd for meat. Samuel Hopkins and George Knott were in charge of roasting the steer over an open fire fueled by charcoal. They had started their task the night before to ensure that the steer would be well-roasted by noon.

Jacob was in charge of the barn-raising. He enlisted his brother, Elias, as well as Sven Risland and Kittel Baklistulen to go aloft with him to make the necessary borings with augers and drive in the hardwood pegs that would hold the entire structure together. The other men were assigned to lift the framing timbers aloft with poles, taking great care not to push too vigorously, lest they overshoot and cause the frame to come crashing down. Lambert Norton took personal charge of the ground crews, asserting his authority as he gave command in a loud voice.

At last the critical pegs were driven into place, and the framework of the barn stood intact. A great cheer arose from the whole assemblage, and Jacob fastened a small pine tree at the apex to mark the achievement of the morning. The men aloft clambered down, and the meal was soon ready to be served. It was an occasion long to be remembered by all who participated. The framework of the first real barn in the community had been erected. Before the decade ended, a number of other barns of this type were built to house the growing herds of cattle and stables of horses, replacing the primitive log structures often built in haste.

During the summer of 1855, the trustees of the congregation made another solicitation, and they received enough funds to proceed with a plank floor for the church as well as the construction of the pews; this in spite of the fact that the price of wheat had dropped during the year so that most of the farmers were hard pressed for cash.

Jacob was in charge of the project, assisted by several other men who had carpentry skills. On one fine Sunday in late August, when Pastor Duus came from the Waupaca Settlement to hold a church service, the members of the congregation were finally able to sit in the new pews and put their feet upon a wooden floor instead of a dirt floor. There was still much to be done to finish the church building properly, but this was an important improvement, and many of the church members expressed to Jacob how happy they were that they finally had the floor and the pews.

In the late summer of 1855, Dorthea's pregnancy became visible, and she and Elias were ecstatic over expecting a child. Anna and Terje were pleased that at last they would have a grandchild, and Anna began to knit small items of clothing in anticipation of the birth, which was to occur late in October or in November. It had not been an easy pregnancy for Dorthea; she had been subject to much nausea, and she wished that the weeks could pass quickly until the time of her delivery. She had already spoken to Mrs. Ole Bjørnstad, the best midwife in the whole Neenah Settlement, and it seemed that all the arrangements were perfectly in order.

On October fourteenth, Dorthea began to experience labor pains, and Elias hurried to fetch Mrs. Bjørnstad. They had not expected the labor pains to come so soon; but, fortunately, the Bjørnstad farm was only about a mile away and Elias was able to complete his errand quickly, before the pains became too intense.

Mrs. Bjørnstad soon sensed that something was wrong, but she did not want to alarm Elias prematurely. She insisted, however, that Elias should summon his mother and his sister Maren to come as quickly as they could. When he returned with his mother and sister, he saw immediately that Dorthea was in great agony, and he began to fear for her life as well as the life of the child. Anna and Maren became aware of the seriousness of the situation as soon as they entered the cabin.

Dorthea writhed in agony with each pain, and Elias had to step outside the cabin because he could not bear to hear his beloved Dorthea in such pain. Maren stepped outside to be with her brother, trying to reassure him that women often had to endure this kind of pain before birth occurred.

At last, after what seemed like hours of delay to Elias, his mother came out of the cabin and spoke to Elias and Maren in a serious manner,

"Our joy is turned to sorrow, Elias. The child died shortly after birth, a lovely little boy child. It was a hard time for Dorthea. Fortunately, she is still alive, but she is not out of danger because she is very weak and has lost a good deal of blood. We must nurse her carefully during the next days and pray for her recovery. As soon as I saw that the child was struggling to live, I took some water and poured it on the poor baby's head and said the words for baptism, just as it says we should do in the hymnal. I don't know if that was the right thing to do or not, but I thought it might be of some comfort to you and Dorthea to know that I did it."

Elias listened to his mother's words stoically. He seemed too stunned to be able to react. It was Maren, in her gentle and sisterly way, who was able to bring consolation to Elias. She tried to point out to him how grateful they should all be that Dorthea was still alive and had a good chance of making a recovery in spite of her weakened condition.

Anna and Maren stayed on in Elias and Dorthea's cabin for a number of days, carefully nursing Dorthea back to health. After some days, Dorthea's stepmother, Gunhild Funer, came to relieve Anna and Maren, and they were able to go back to their homes.

As soon as Jacob heard the news of the death of his little nephew, he sorted through his supply of good lumber and fashioned a small coffin. The following day Terje, Jacob and Elias took the small coffin to the graveyard where they were met by John Helgeson. Helgeson was told of Anna's baptism of the child, which he duly noted for the congregation's records. When he asked if the child had been given a name, Elias responded that he thought the child should be named "Terje" after his grandfather. Then John Helgeson read the Christian rite of commital, and the little grave was quickly covered with soil.

The three men, Terje, Elias and Jacob, left the graveyard with somber faces and scarcely spoke a word until Elias said, "I suppose the next time I go to Neenah, I should buy a small stone to mark the grave."

Johannes Baklistulen had determined to raise horses on his farm. He had no cattle, but he needed more horses for his lumbering operations, and so, in addition to his team of two mares, he bought another young mare from a Yankee farmer in Vinland. On the very day Maren returned from caring for her sister-in-law, Dorthea, he brought home a fine spirited black stallion from a farmer near Thompson's Corner. He was proud of this animal and planned to breed each of his mares to this stallion. "Soon," he thought, "I shall have a paddock of young foals, and then I shall soon have a stable full of horses, enough horses to pull those sleighs to our winter camp so that we need no longer rely on those pokey oxen!"

Several days after he brought the stallion home, Johannes had another errand in town and needed to be gone the entire day. Maren was left home alone. It was mid-November, and the weather suddenly turned nasty, with a miserable mixture of rain and sleet and a furious wind. Maren was concerned about whether or not Johannes would be able to get home in such terrible weather, wishing he had never gone, even though early in the day, when Johannes left home, the weather was not too bad.

Just as Maren was regretting her husband's absence, she heard a terrible commotion coming from the stable. The stallion was making all sorts of noise, and as she peered out of the window, she saw the stallion break down the stable door and make his escape. At once she grabbed her coat and her boots and dashed out the door, hoping she could catch the animal and lead it back into its stall in the stable.

The stallion still had on its halter, but the rope which tied the halter to the stall had been severed. Maren quickly grabbed another rope and a whip from the stable, and ran as fast as she could after the stallion. But each time she got close to the animal, it would suddenly bolt off in another direction and gallop away, leaving poor Maren far behind. Meanwhile the rain and sleet were pelting down, and both Maren and the animal were soon soaking wet. But she was determined that this fine animal should not escape.

The chase went on and on, for what seemed to Maren like hours. Finally she was able, through sheer luck, to corner the animal where two rail fences came together to form a right-angled corner. The stallion reared up, but Maren had been around horses enough to know how to use the whip, and in a quick movement she was able to grab the animal's halter and tie the rope onto the halter. Soon the animal was docile enough to be led back into the stable. She took precautions to tie the stallion more securely to its stall, and finally she was able to return into the cabin.

During all this time, she had scarcely a thought for her own safety or comfort. She was absolutely soaked through by the freezing rain. When she stepped into the cabin, she took off the wet clothes and attempted to dry and warm herself as best she could, but she had sustained a nasty chill; and she continued to shiver, in spite of the warm and dry clothes which she put on.

Then she suddenly became nauseated and had to vomit. She decided, after firing the stove, that she had better lie down. The shivering continued, even though she pulled all the heavy blankets she had around herself. She got up once more and reached to the upper shelf of the cupboard where Johannes kept a bottle of brandy. She poured some of the brandy into a cup of hot water, thinking it would help take away the terrible chills. She was even conscious that her teeth were chattering and she felt weak in her entire body. After stumbling back into her bed, she finally fell into a deep sleep; and when she awakened, Johannes was standing over her. She must have slept for many hours, she thought.

When Johannes felt her forehead, it was clear to him that his wife was burning with fever; and when she attempted to talk, trying to explain to Johannes about the escape and chase of the stallion, she suddenly had a bad coughing spell. Johannes became alarmed and decided that Maren's mother should be summoned as quickly as possible. However, he did not want to leave Maren alone in the house for very long, so he decided to make a quick call upon his brother, Halvor, who lived in a small cabin with their father, Anund Baklistulen, less than half a mile away. Halvor could hitch up one of his horses to his democrat wagon and bring Anna Tøvesdatter back with him.

When Halvor drove up to Anna's door, she sensed immediately that something was not right, and when she heard that her daughter was desperately ill, she went into a flurry of activity, packing clothes and medicines in a large basket, taking care to anticipate what might be needed for the next few days. She scarcely had time to tell Terje, Kittel and the others why she was leaving in such a hurry. Suddenly the whole house was in an uproar. Terje demanded to know more about his daughter's condition, but Halvor couldn't tell him much except that Johannes had said she was desperately ill with a high fever and a bad cough. At this point, Halvor and the others in the family knew nothing of the adventure which Maren had with the errant stallion.

When Anna finally entered the cabin, she saw that her daughter was indeed seriously ill. Maren was scarcely conscious and between coughing spells sometimes mumbled incoherently. Johannes was at his wife's side, attempting to relieve her fever with tepid water washings of her face and limbs, but the high fever raged on.

Anna immediately drew from her basket several large onions, peeled and sliced them into a frying pan, and prepared a hot onion poultice which she applied to Maren's chest, hoping to break the congestion. Anna turned to Johannes, speaking in low tone, hoping that Maren would not be able to hear her.

"Maren is very sick, and I fear she has a bad case of pneumonia. I think we should summon Gunder Tøvesen's wife, Aase. She has some good skills in caring for sick folks, and I shall need her assistance because it's obvious we must be prepared for a long and arduous vigil if we are to save Maren's life."

The very tone of Anna's speaking frightened Johannes. He had tried to put out of his mind the possibility that Maren's illness could be fatal, but Anna left no doubt that Maren's condition was life threatening.

Later that day Aase arrived in Halvor's wagon, which was loaded with supplies; and toward evening, Terje, Kittel and Jacob also stopped by to see if they could do anything to help the situation. Terje nearly broke down as he saw his beloved daughter struggling to breathe. Maren had always been so strong and healthy, and now to see her in this condition was very sad and shocking.

Terje resolved that he and Jacob should go to Oshkosh as quickly as they could to fetch Dr. Linde who had recently moved back after living several years at Mukwa. He had been so helpful at the time of Kittel's accident; and, furthermore, Terje could understand his Danish. Besides, Linde was really a properly educated doctor, not a quack doctor like some of those Yankee charlatans who knew how to get money out of people but couldn't really cure anybody.

The cabin was very small, especially when so many crowded in, so Anna told Terje and the others that it would be better if they left, leaving only Anna, Aase and Johannes to spend the night with Maren. They might return early tomorrow morning for a short visit, but too many visitors would not be good for Maren.

Anna and Aase were tireless in caring for Maren, hoping the high fever would break and the congestion in her chest would break up. But after five days of keeping vigil day and night, Maren's condition only grew worse, and Aase began to hear in Maren's breathing what she described as the "death rattle." She had heard this ominous sound before in persons who were dying from pneumonia. Maren was now unconscious, but there were moments when she temporarily gained consciousness.

Terje and Jacob made the journey to Oshkosh by driving a horse and cart, which they had borrowed from Johannes, to Winneconne and then taking the steamboat to Oshkosh. When they got to Oshkosh they discovered from Dr. Linde's housekeeper that the doctor was not at home and was not expected back for at least another week. Terje and Jacob had to return on the next boat to Winneconne, bitterly disappointed that the doctor was not available.

Aase suggested that since there was no pastor to call, it would be good to have Gunder come and offer prayers for Maren, and Anna agreed. Terje and Jacob accompanied Gunder into the cabin, and Jacob afterward recalled that Gunder prayed a most beautiful and appropriate prayer. Much as he sometimes disagreed with his uncle on religious matters, he was grateful at this moment for his uncle's sincere piety and his way of praying. Years afterwards, Jacob could remember, almost word for word, much of the prayer that Gunder prayed that day by Maren's bedside.

It was now clear that only a miracle could save Maren's life, and as they stood by her bedside, they were reconciled to the fact that she was slowly dying and it would likely be only a matter of hours before death would come. Maren opened her eyes just once and made some effort to try to speak, but before the words could come out, she lapsed again in unconsciousness, and within a few moments, her breathing suddenly stopped.

Those who stood around the bedside -- Johannes, Anna, Aase, Gunder, Terje and Jacob -- were too overcome by grief to speak to each other. For many moments they stood in absolute silence, stunned by the burden of sorrow which they all felt. All of their lives would be profoundly changed from this moment on.

Jacob was the first to leave the room, followed by Aase and Gunder. It was only proper that Maren's husband and her parents should have some time without the others.

Aase spoke to Jacob about some of the tasks they would now confront. She and Anna would prepare Maren's body for burial. Jacob would need to make a coffin for his sister. They would have to ask Johannes about arrangements for the burial, but Aase assumed that John Helgeson would be asked to make arrangements for digging the grave and would also be called upon to read the burial service.

Jacob had to excuse himself from Aase and Gunder's presence, and he ran most of the way back home. It was almost as though by escaping from the cabin of death, he could somehow escape from the hard reality that Maren was actually dead. Elias and Dorthea would have to be told, and Kittel, Anna-Maria and Klemet would need to know as soon as possible. He would have to be the messenger of this terrible news to everyone else in the family, and he did not relish this responsibility. He stopped first to tell the news to Elias and Dorthea. Dorthea had recovered sufficiently from her own tragedy, but broke down into tears upon hearing the news of Maren's death.

"It seems but yesterday that Maren was here, caring for me. She was so strong and I was so weak. I don't think I could have survived without Maren's strength and help. And now she is gone. I just can't believe this terrible thing has happened. Why did it have to be Maren?"

She went on and on, until Elias at last had to admonish her that it would do no good to keep on in that manner. He, too, was profoundly overcome by grief, so much so that he wasn't able to talk about it.

Jacob's younger siblings also broke down in their grief. Anna-Maria sobbed uncontrollably until Jacob embraced her firmly and admonished her that everyone in the family would have to be brave and strong. Maren had meant so much to the entire family, and they would need to help each other through these sad days.

After Jacob broke away from his siblings to be alone, he began to sort through the pine boards he had stored above the rafters in the stable. Then he remembered some black walnut boards he had stored in Lambert Norton's barn. Those boards really belonged to Norton, but perhaps he would let Jacob use several of them to make a cover for the coffin. Just as he was about to head off for Norton's place, he was confronted by Kittel and Klemet.

"We would like to help you make the coffin for Maren. She was our sister, too."

When Kittel spoke these words, Jacob realized that this request was important to his two younger brothers, and he could not deny them this last opportunity they would all have to do something for their dear sister. He selected several of his best pine boards and suggested Kittel could begin making some simple cuts with the saw and using the plane on the boards. In the meantime, he and Klemet would go to Lambert Norton's place to fetch the black walnut boards. He would need Klemet to help carry those heavy boards, and Klemet suddenly felt needed as Jacob's helper.

During most of the next morning, the three brothers were in the stable, finishing the coffin. Jacob had built other coffins, but never before had he put so much care into building one. He carefully polished he walnut boards and painstakingly carved Maren's name on the cover, *Maren Terjesdatter Baklistulen, 1832-1855.*

On the day of the burial, a throng of people came to the graveyard on the hill. It was a beautiful day for so late in the season; the sun shone brightly. Many came because they wanted to show sympathy to Johannes and to Terje and Anna and their family, but most of all they came because of Maren herself. She had been well-known and widely respected in the community. In addition to the Norwegian folks, quite a few Yankee families came, and even Heinrich Meyer and Friederich Winckler were there. The burial service was read by John Helgeson in Norwegian. Then Halvor Baklistulen spoke in English to the people assembled, thanking them for their sympathy and support for his brother and for Maren's family during this time of grief. Most of the people came up to Johannes and to Maren's family to personally extend their condolences. Jacob had never seen some of these folks before, but graciously accepted their condolences nevertheless.

Maren's death was especially hard on Terje because Maren was his favorite in so many ways. For a long time, he believed that if Dr. Linde had been able to come to see her, he would have been able to save her life.

About six months later, when Terje and Anna were in Oshkosh, they paid a call on Dr. Linde, who was at home when they called and was pleased to see them. Terje needed to find out if they had done everything possible to save Maren's life. After questioning Anna carefully about the progress of Maren's illness and the treatments that she and Aase used, Dr. Linde turned to Terje and reassured him that he could have done no more for Maren than the two women had done. Pneumonia was a terrible scourge, he said, and once it gained a foothold, there was little to be done except keep the patient comfortable and allow the disease to take its terrible and inevitable course. This relieved Terje's mind of any lingering guilt he carried about Maren's death and any resentment he may have had against Dr. Linde for not being available to care for Maren when he was needed so badly.

On the day of Maren's burial, Johannes did not shed a tear. He hid his feelings behind a stoical mask. For the second time in his life, he had to bury a spouse; and, if one could probe behind the mask, it would be apparent that he was devastated in his grief to the point of despair.

When he finally returned to his cabin alone, he carefully took out his gun and methodically loaded it. Then he went to the stable, led the black stallion out to a remote corner of his land, tied the stallion to a tree, stepped back some paces, took aim and shot the stallion dead, hitting the animal directly in the heart. It was a senseless thing to do; but, for Johannes, it was necessary.

No one ever called him to account for this deed, even his brothers who might have had occasion to admonish him for this needless waste of a good animal. They respected the grief Johannes felt on that day and his need to assuage his grief by sacrificing this animal which had so innocently caused the death of his beloved Maren.

Recovery and Discovery

In the days following Maren's death and burial, Terje was silent and morose, wandering off aimlessly into some of the yet uncleared portions of his farm in spite of the frigid weather. Anna began to worry about his wanderings and his ominous silences. Often he would only stare into space, apparently oblivious to all those around him. The loss of Maren, while keenly felt by every member of the family, seemed to devastate Terje more than anyone else. Anna worked out her grief by tackling her numerous household tasks with Herculean energy, but there were times when her energy waned and she would sit on a small stool in her pantry, weeping, until, by force of her indomitable will, she would summon the energy to return to her work once more.

The Christmas holidays were truly a test for the entire family. Anna insisted that Klemet should go to the woods where the small pine trees were growing to pick out a suitable tree, and she mustered the help of Anna-Maria and the Risland girls in trimming the tree and making other necessary preparations for Christmas. Just as the girls were in the midst of trimming the tree, they heard a loud knock on the door, and Anton Møller stepped in from the cold, his boots covered with fresh snow.

"Henrikke and I wish to invite your whole family to come to our place for Christmas Eve. This year has been such a year of sorrow for you good people, and Henrikke thought that if you could all help us sing some of those wonderful old Christmas hymns it could bring some cheer to you."

Anna was pleased by this invitation, and Terje even managed a smile of approval at the thought of a nice evening of music at the Møller house where they could once more hear Henrikke play so beautifully on her piano.

"The Risland girls are invited too. Their father and Lasse will come, but Gunder and his family prefer to have their own observance of Christmas Eve. It is perhaps just as well because our house is not as large as yours, and it would be difficult to include so many folks, especially now in the wintertime, when we must all be inside together. Anna, Henrikke has instructed me to tell you that you are to bring nothing to eat for she has been busy preparing a mountain of food, and she will be insulted if you do not all bring hefty appetites to help consume all that good food."

"Thank you. But surely Henrikke would not mind if I brought some sweet things that we have been baking in preparation for our own Christmas."

"Well, all right. If you insist. We all know that you can bake some delicious Christmas treats. We have tasted them before. But just bring a few of your sweet things because Henrikke has already provided so many of her own."

"Elias and Dorthea will not come with us, They already have made plans to go to Tangen to be with Dorthea's family. But Jacob will probably wish to join us. He is now staying at the Norton house, but I know that he enjoyed his last visit to your place and will want to come again."

After Anton Møller went on his way, Anna turned to Terje and spoke.

"It was very kind and thoughtful of Henrikke and Anton to invite us. I think we all need to escape this house of sorrow for a little while."

Terje nodded his head in agreement, and as he did so, Anna saw a tear streaming down his left cheek. It was the first time that Terje had been able to shed a tear since Maren's death.

It was a pleasant evening for everyone in the Møller cabin. They all joined in singing the Christmas hymns. Anton read the Christmas gospel, and the Møller boys sang several special songs their mother had taught them. Henrikke, with her sons as helpers, prepared a delicious meal, and Anna's sweets were served at the end of the meal. Terje made a little speech, thanking the Møllers for their wonderful hospitality. On the way home, Anna was pleased when she heard Terje humming some familiar Christmas hymns as they sat on the sleigh together.

Johannes turned more and more to his work as township chairman during the days and weeks following Maren's death. He called the supervisors together for meeting after meeting to discuss what should be done to improve the roads in the township. Most of the roads were mere trails in the dirt, filled with muddy ruts every time it rained. Fortunately, there were several good deposits of gravel right in the township, but payments needed to be made to the owners of those gravel deposits in order to use the gravel to improve the roads. Most of the farmers contributed their labor rather than pay a road tax in cash. They hauled the gravel in their wagons to fill the worst spots on the most traveled roads, but the task of improving the roads seemed never-ending, and much planning and discussion had to precede the actual labor.

Shortly after Christmas, Johannes received a visit from several Norwegian farmers who had settled in a far corner of the township. One of their neighbors, a man who had recently arrived with his family from Norway, was clearly insane and was a danger to his wife and family of four young children. It was a desperate situation, according to these neighbors, and something needed to be done immediately to protect the wife and children from the insane violence of this man. He had been a heavy drinker, the men said, but now he was totally out of control. Johannes summoned two of the constables and several other men, and together they were able to subdue the man and take him to Oshkosh, where he was committed to the county jail for temporary custody until county officials could determine what should be done with him.

On the second night the man was in jail, he used his bedclothes as a noose and hanged himself in his tiny cell. In a tragic way, the situation had resolved itself, but Johannes now realized that the poor widow and her children would be utterly dependent upon their neighbors. They had no money and very few possessions.

After discussions with the distraught woman, it was agreed that the entire neighborhood should be solicited to provide enough funds to purchase passage back to Norway for this unfortunate family. In Norway she had a family who would care for them. So Johannes and some of the other officers of the township went from door to door begging for contributions to help these unfortunate people. Somehow, the very act of helping this family helped Johannes deal with his own oppressive burden of grief.

Shortly after Maren's death, Johannes determined that he would not go to the woods after Christmas as he had done for several previous years; he turned over his leadership in the lumber camp to his two brothers, Halvor and Kittel. During the early spring of 1856, he immersed himself more and more in local and county politics, making many trips to the county seat in Oshkosh. He came to know many of the county officials and other township officers quite well.

Earlier he had come to know an ambitious young attorney in Oshkosh by the name of Coles Bashford. Bashford had been active in promoting the newly-founded Republican party, both within the county and in the state at large, and in the November election of 1855 he had challenged William Barstow for the governorship of the state. In a nasty and hotly contested election, the state board of canvassers, Democrats loyal to Barstow, declared that Barstow had won the election by a mere 157 votes statewide. Bashford and the Republicans contested the count; and when gross irregularities in the election count were discovered, on March 24, 1856, the Wisconsin Supreme Court declared Bashford the winner of the November 6, 1855, election.

Because of the growth in population of the state, the legislature and governor of the state determined that the size of the state legislature should be expanded to the total number authorized in the state's constitution, but up until this time not elected to office. As a result, a number of new seats were available for the state assembly and the state senate. Members of the newly established Republican party, especially under the vigorous leadership of Governor Bashford and some of his cohorts, were anxious to take advantage of the situation and hoped they would then be able to control the majority in the legislature after the next election in the autumn of 1856.

In Winnebago County, three seats in the state assembly were authorized: one for the city of Oshkosh, one for Neenah-Menasha and the northern tier of townships, including the township of Winchester, and one for the central and southern townships. In the Neenah-Menasha and northern townships district the name of John Anunson was mentioned more and more as the leading candidate for the Republican nomination, but the official caucuses were not scheduled until October.

Governor Coles Bashford was lavish in praise of his Norwegian friend, John Anunson. According to Bashford, it was time that the Norwegians and other immigrants from Europe should be elected to office, and the Republican party was the party that should include these good folks. The Republican party was especially anxious to repudiate any connection with the "Know Nothing" movement which had cast aspersion upon all foreign-born elements in American society, and the candidacy of John Anunson was advanced in Winnebago County to counteract the claims of the Democrats that the Republicans were really the party of "Know-Nothings" in new garb.

Elias joined Halvor and Kittel Baklistulen at their winter lumber camp after Christmas in 1855, but Jacob continued to stay in the employment of Lambert Norton. Terje and Kittel were left at home to take care of the winter chores. Kittel had recovered quite well from his bad accident, but continued to walk with a decided limp. His youngest brother, Klemet, was now nearly full grown, and the two brothers and their father spent a good deal of their time during the winter chopping down trees in order to clear more land; but during the coldest days they had nothing to do but sit around the house.

Terje subscribed to *Emigranten,* a Norwegian language newspaper, and spent hours reading and re-reading to keep from being totally bored. Kittel and Klemet spent a good deal of time chopping firewood, keeping the fires burning on the coldest days of the winter. Kittel was clever at whittling wood and interested his younger brother in the skill, just to pass the time indoors.

Anna and Anna-Maria and the Risland girls managed to keep busy with the normal routine of household tasks; but after the sheep had been sheared of their heavy fleeces, all the women and girls in the household were very busy with an endless round of carding, washing, spinning and weaving.

When spring finally came, Terje, Kittel and Klemet were suddenly taken up with bringing more land under the plow and the endless task of grubbing out stumps with the help of their team of oxen. Elias had purchased a new team of horses the previous summer, and he and his father and brothers often exchanged work on each other's farms. Elias also purchased a new mower so much of the tedious work of cutting hay and grain could be made easier, and he intended to use his horses to pull the mower instead of those pokey oxen.

Dorthea spent many days alone during the winter in her cabin while Elias was working in the woods; but she also came, sometimes a week or so at a time, to stay with Terje and Anna, helping with the spinning and weaving that was continually going on in their household. Rarely was Maren's name even mentioned in conversation during the first months after her death; it was simply too painful to recall her memory. But, as time went on, her parents and brothers and sisters began to talk more freely of Maren, recalling, sometimes with great sadness and at other times with light-hearted humor, the many memories they all shared.

Jacob spent the entire winter with the Norton family. He was very busy constructing a small tenant house that Lambert Norton was anxious to have finished as soon as possible. He had hired a young Irishman by the name of Jim Rooney to help with the farm work. Jim was married to a red-haired girl by the name of Rosie, and they had two very small children and were expecting their third child. They came to this country late in October of 1855 and were living with Jim's sister and family, Bonnie Nesbitt, and her husband, Mike. The small Nesbitt farm was about a mile west of Norton's place. Jim and Rosie had no money to buy land and were pleased to have a place to begin life in the New World working for Lambert Norton. Jim was a jolly fellow, full of jokes, and Jacob became quite fond of him as they labored together on the small house into which Jim and his young family would soon move.

Lambert insisted that this tenant house should be constructed, not of logs, but from lumber which he earlier had purchased from the sawmill in Winneconne. This made the task of constructing the house easier for Jacob and Jim. In spite of the winter weather, which sometimes delayed the construction for a day or two, they were able to get the building framed during a mild spell in January; and after the sheathing was put on, they were able to work inside most of the time.

The house was small, only sixteen feet wide by twenty feet long, but many of the neighboring farmers were still living in log cabins of smaller dimensions. There was a stairway to the loft, which would provide sleeping quarters for the children as they grew older. Jim and Rosie were thrilled to see this neat little house take shape. They were very crowded in the Nesbitt cabin and looked forward to the day when they could move their meager belongings into this new little house.

During his stay in the Norton household, Jacob became aware of several visits to the Norton home by a banker from Oshkosh named Abner Hutchinson. Abner was about forty years old and had recently lost his wife. It suddenly dawned upon Jacob that Abner was courting one of the Norton daughters -- but which daughter, Lydia or Roberta? Jacob began to surmise it was Roberta when she suddenly packed a suitcase and a valise and left for a visit to Oshkosh which lasted for several weeks.

In the days immediately following Roberta's departure, Lydia began to unfold the story to Jacob. Her father, Lydia said, had come to have more and more business dealings with Hutchinson during the last several years. She did not say so, but she implied that her father had needed to borrow money from Hutchinson's bank from time to time; and he had come to know Hutchinson very well, especially after the death of Hutchinson's wife.

Abner Hutchinson came to visit the Nortons on a number of occasions. He had a sixteen year old son by the name of Jonathan and a ten year old daughter named Lucinda. Roberta grew especially fond of Lucinda during their visits, and recently her father made it known to Lambert and Emmeline Norton that he wished to court Roberta. He, too, had become fond of Roberta and noticed how strongly attached his daughter had become to her. Both Lambert and his wife were shocked to realize that Abner Hutchinson could well become their son-in-law. But what about Roberta? How did she feel about marrying a man twice her age? These were questions foremost in Jacob's mind as he discussed the situation with Lydia, and Lydia had no ready answer, confessing that she had no way of reading her sister's mind.

Hutchinson owned an elegant house on the most fashionable street in Oshkosh, and Lydia hinted that perhaps her sister might find life in the city much more to her liking than life in the country, especially if she could have access to the wealth and social position which a marriage to Abner Hutchinson could give her. Then there was also the matter of the strong bond with Hutchinson's daughter, Lucinda. But Lydia was as puzzled as Jacob as to what Roberta's feelings were for Abner Hutchinson. Jacob remembered all too well the romantic fantasies which seemed to possess Roberta as he knew her. How could she enter into a marriage with anything less than overwhelming feelings of love and total commitment?

In the weeks following Maren's death, after Jacob returned to live in the Norton household, he found that it was Lydia who was most solicitous of his feelings and needs. Lydia and her mother often sat conversing with Jacob during the long winter evenings, and these conversations were helpful to Jacob in dealing with his grief over his sister's death. He began to discover that Lydia was in many ways similar to his sister Maren. She had a great capacity for empathy with people in need; and, like Maren, she had a subtle sense of humor that often was not apparent at first glance. Like Maren, Lydia was capable in all that she undertook. Jacob began to see more and more that she was the serious and capable and responsible elder sister, while Roberta was the volatile and somewhat spoiled younger child.

When the pleasant days of spring began to beckon and tempt Jacob to spend some of the evenings out of doors, he was frequently joined by Lydia. They took long walks together and conversed, sometimes on serious topics and sometimes light-hearted ones.

On a warm Saturday afternoon in June, Roberta Norton and Abner Hutchinson were married, not at "Norton's Folly" as Lambert Norton might have wished, but in Hutchinson's Oshkosh mansion. Jacob was not invited, nor had he expected to be. As the event was related to him afterwards by Lydia, Jacob was just as happy he had not been. The house was crowded with Hutchinson's friends, and Lydia felt out of place. Even Lambert Norton, her father, felt somewhat out of his element among all the merchants and lawyers and bankers and lumber barons and their wives.

But Roberta was radiant in her happiness, Lydia told Jacob. She seemed to relish each prominent person to whom she was introduced as another conquest on her social calendar. Lydia had, of course, been asked to be her sister's maid of honor, so she had been drawn into the receiving line and introduced to all of the elite. She confessed that she couldn't remember many of the names, and further confessed to Jacob that she would rather meet the simple country folk who were her neighbors, whether they were Yankees, Norwegians, Germans or Irish, than that bunch of pompous and inflated and egocentric socialites that filled Abner Hutchinson's house on the day of her sister's wedding.

About two weeks after Roberta's wedding, during a lull in the farm work just before the harvest began, Johannes Baklistulen invited Jacob to accompany him on a quick trip to Madison. Johannes, as a likely candidate for the state's legislature, had been invited to a special political meeting there. They drove to Winneconne where they caught a steamboat that took them to Oshkosh; from Oshkosh they managed to get onto a steamboat headed for Fond du Lac just before it was ready to cast off from the dock; and at Fond du Lac they paid a call at the Cartwright farm where they were invited to spend the night.

Early the next morning they boarded a train which took them to Horicon. This was the first train ride Jacob had taken since the ride from Albany to Buffalo seven years earlier. At Horicon they boarded another train to Milwaukee, and later that same day they took a third train from Milwaukee to Madison. They spent their first night in Madison in a noisy, filthy boarding house near the train depot. Both Johannes and Jacob were tired from their long journey, and the railway cars had been stifling hot. They both vowed they would find a better place to stay for the next two nights.

Jacob had obtained Peter Smith's address in Madison from Adam Cartwright, and after he had breakfast with Johannes and walked with Johannes to the State House, they parted company for the rest of the day. Johannes spent his entire day at the State House, but Jacob asked directions to Peter Smith's house. When he arrived, he was met by a lady whom he promptly discovered was Peter Smith's wife. He had not realized that his friend had married because somehow Adam Cartwright had neglected to tell him, probably because he thought that Jacob would surely have known.

Not only was Peter married; he and his wife had two small children, both tow-headed little fellows. The oldest one could hardly have been more than two years old, and the youngest was less than a year. Peter's wife, who introduced herself as Maggie, invited Peter into the house and apologized for the clutter and disarray. The care of the small children, she said, made it difficult to keep an orderly house fit to entertain strangers.

Jacob found out from Maggie that Peter was busy as a contractor, building new houses in an area east of the State House where lots had recently been plotted. It would be nearly a mile for Jacob to walk, so Maggie insisted that Jacob take a cup of tea and a piece of bread spread with apple butter before he left her house. She was anxious to chat with him a bit about when he and Peter had worked together at Cartwright's farm. Peter had told her a few things about those days, and he had mentioned Jacob's name to her a number of times, and now she seemed to relish every bit of information which

Jacob could give her as they sipped tea together at her kitchen table.

After leaving Peter and Maggie's house, Jacob walked in the hot sun for nearly an hour before he found the building which Peter and his men were constructing. When Peter saw Jacob, his jaw dropped, and then he dropped his hammer and rushed over to greet him, pumping his hand vigorously.

"Jacob, you rascal! I never thought I would live to see you again. What are you doing here in Madison? Are you looking for work? I could surely use a fellow like you on my crew. I can never forget those good days we spent together at Adam Cartwright's farm, building his fine house. Come, you must tell me all about yourself."

Jacob spent the next hour answering a barrage of questions from Peter while watching him nail floor boards onto the joists in one of the upstairs rooms of the house. Jacob insisted upon grabbing a hammer and joining his old friend in pounding nails, but between the poundings they chatted on about many things.

Peter insisted that Jacob should spend the next two nights at his house. When Jacob explained that he was traveling with Johannes, Peter insisted that Johannes should also come.

"Most of the hotels and boarding houses in this town are bad, except the ones that are very expensive. As you can see, this is a busy town, and those of us who build houses can hardly keep up with the demand for new buildings. If I could hire more men, I could build twice as many houses, and still people would come to me and clamor and beg me to put them first on my list."

Again Peter, this time more seriously, begged Jacob to consider coming to Madison to work for him, promising to make him foreman of a crew with wages that were tempting. Jacob could only promise that he would give some consideration to the offer, but he warned Peter that he should not get his hopes too high because it would be difficult to leave his family and his friends at this time.

"Ah, perhaps you have a sweetheart up there in that north country! Now the truth comes out," Peter said teasingly.

Jacob blushed slightly at the suggestion, but he immediately denied Peter's assertion vehemently.

When the work day concluded, Peter and Jacob drove in Peter's wagon directly to the State House where Jacob sought out Johannes from the throng of people milling about, both outside and inside the building. Johannes was talking to several people, but summoned Jacob to join him.

"Jacob, I would like to introduce you to Hans Heg from Muskego. I have known Hans for many years, and now he is active in our Republican party here in Wisconsin. We are hoping to persuade some of our party leaders to put Hans on our ticket for one of the state offices."

Jacob greeted Hans Heg politely, and Heg began immediately to chat with Jacob in Norwegian about the Neenah Settlement, asking questions about folks he had earlier known in Muskego who had moved there.

It had been a long and exciting day for Johannes, and when Jacob explained to him Peter's invitation, Johannes willingly accepted. Soon the two men were able to break away from the crowd and together they sought out Peter who was waiting patiently in his wagon. Johannes carried with him a valise in which both he and Jacob had packed their razors and clean shirts, and soon the men were on their way to join Peter and Maggie Smith for a quiet evening of conversation and rest. Maggie was able to put on the table a simple meal for the three men who came into her house shortly after she had settled the children into their beds for the night.

Peter spent the next morning showing Jacob some of the sights of Madison, including the new university buildings located some distance west of the State House. In the afternoon, Jacob borrowed work clothes and joined Peter at work. Together they finished installing the sub-floor in the house under construction.

Just before Johannes and Jacob were about to board the train the next morning that would take them to Milwaukee, Johannes spotted Governor Coles Bashford and several of his friends who were ready to board the same train. When Bashford spotted Johannes, he motioned for him to join his party. Johannes introduced Jacob to Bashford, and on the journey to Milwaukee, Jacob heard a good deal of high spirited banter and political talk.

The whisky flowed freely and loosened the tongues of these politicians more and more as the journey proceeded. Bashford and several of his friends were engaged in a poker game, and from what Jacob could observe, they were gambling with fairly large amounts of money. From this experience Jacob resolved that he could probably never become a politician if it took this kind of behavior to pull off a successful career.

Jacob returned to Norton's farm just in time to roll out the reaper from its storage shed and get it ready for the new harvest season. Jim Rooney had never so much as seen a reaper before, so Jacob had to explain to him the workings of this wondrous new machine. After oiling the machine and checking it carefully, Jacob hitched the horses and within a few minutes made the first round of Norton's largest wheat field. Norton had hired three young neighbor boys, including Jacob's brother Klemet, to help with the binding and shocking of the grain, and, under Jacob's instruction, Jim soon caught on to his task of riding on the reaper and raking the grain from the apron into bundle-sized clumps that could then be tied by the boys.

When the reaping was done several days later, it was time to prepare the threshing machine for its annual workout. Quite a few of Norton's neighbors, including Terje and Elias, had spoken to him about hiring the rig to thresh their grain after Norton was finished on his own farm. After the grain had dried and cured sufficiently in the shock, the threshing season began. Jacob was in charge of hitching and driving the horses at the power source. Norton took charge of the operation of the machine itself, taking care that bundles were not fed into it too fast, lest the machine become clogged and the entire operation come to a halt until it was cleaned out.

It took a crew of twelve men or more to do the threshing, and the farmers' wives vied with one another in preparing good food for all these hungry men. There was a good deal of camraderie on the threshing crew, and the cultural and linguistic barriers that often kept Yankee, Norwegian and Irishman apart were broken down as they shared in this annual rite of harvest.

Unfortunately, the price of wheat had dropped severely in the last several years, and it no longer produced the bonanza of cash for the farmers that it had several years earlier. Some of the farmers were beginning to sow fewer acres into wheat and adding to their herds of cattle, but Lambert Norton still believed in wheat and each year added to his acreage. In the years of the best prices, he had managed to pay for both his reaper and his threshing rig, so now he was able to earn a fair amount each season by threshing for his neighbors, and this tended to offset the decline in the price he received for his own wheat.

The threshing took nearly a month to complete, but soon after it was done, Jacob made inquiries about a farm that was likely going to be sold in the near future. The husband had died quite suddenly, and the wife and her children intended to sell the farm and return to her parents in Muskego, probably early next spring.

Ole Halvorson Uvaas owned the farm adjoining this one, and Jacob spoke to him about the possibility of buying the farm from the widow. The man had been unable to clear much of the land because he had been in poor health during the last several years, and the house was a miserably small log cabin, only twelve by twelve feet, with a dirt floor. But the soil was rich, with the exception of one corner of the land which contained a gravel deposit that had already been used to improve some of the roads in the township. From this use, the farmer had been able to get a few dollars which helped to sustain his family.

Jacob asked Ole Uvaas if he intended to buy this land, but Ole already had a whole quarter section, much of which had yet to be cleared and said he was not in a financial position to buy more land at this time. Jacob and Ole discussed what might be a reasonable price for the farm, and Ole was of the opinion that $350 might be a fair price, since the land originally cost the man only $100 four years ago and not many improvements had been made.

Jacob discussed the matter with his father and Elias. They both agreed that $350 would probably be a fair and generous price to offer the widow. This would provide her with sufficient funds to get her family relocated to Muskego and have a fair amount left over.

After Jacob spoke to the widow, she agreed to sell to him, but wished to have a higher price. She told Jacob that she had thought of having an auction of the tools and plow and wagon. There was also a yoke of oxen. If Jacob was willing to pay her $425, she would let him have not only the farm but everything else as well, including the yoke of oxen. Finally Jacob agreed upon that price. He could make good use of the oxen and the plow was in good shape. The wagon was not in the best of shape, but it could be repaired and used until he could afford a better one.

Jacob had saved over three hundred and seventy dollars. He would need to borrow the rest from his father, who still had about four hundred dollars left from the sale of Skredderstua to Consul Lund. So the deal was made with both the widow and with his father. He would pay his father interest on the money which he was about to borrow, and would take possession of the widow's farm about March first of the following year.

Jacob's Wedding

Lambert Norton voted a straight Democratic ticket in the election of 1856. He had the satisfaction of seeing his candidate for the presidency, James Buchanan, win over John C. Fremont, the candidate for the upstart Republican party. But in the state elections the Republicans made a fairly decisive sweep into victory. John Anunson was elected to the state assembly from the Neenah-Menasha and northern townships district of Winnebago County. Norton was not at all pleased with Anunson's election, but he did not voice his displeasure to Jacob, knowing that Jacob had such a close relationship to Anunson.

Many of Lambert Norton's Yankee neighbors and friends jumped aboard the Republican bandwagon, in many instances because they were vigorously opposed to the fugitive slave provisions in the Compromise of 1850. But Norton stayed by the principle of "popular sovereignty" which was so convincingly stated, in his mind, by Senator Douglas of Illinois. In fact, he did not think that the holding of slaves was the vicious evil that many of the abolitionists in the North said that it was. After all, most of the planters in the South were reasonable men and looked after their slaves well enough because it was in their best interest, was it not? To be sure, some overseers might be cruel and even vicious in their treatment of the slaves, but Norton thought their number must be small because a responsible planter would not want such a man exploiting his slaves in this manner. These abolitionist propagandists were always painting the darkest side of things, he thought. George Washington had slaves, and so had Thomas Jefferson and dozens of other famous men who founded our nation. What would happen to all of those black slaves if they were suddenly made free? How could they possibly survive on their own?

Norton began to feel more and more that the rabble-rousers and abolitionists who had wormed their way into control of the new Republican party were playing a dangerous game. Fortunately, they were not able to get their man into the White House this time around, but who knows what could happen four years from now. The South would simply not stand for an abolitionist in the White House. It was a serious situation, and Norton dreaded the consequences if these upstart Republicans ever managed to gain control of the presidency and of Congress.

But the price Norton had to pay for his political convictions was that whatever political ambitions he may have had in the past now seemed out of reach. These northerners, whether Yankee or immigrant, would not listen to reason, and Lambert Norton found that he could not even discuss political matters rationally with some of his neighbors and best friends any more.

In spite of the progress he had made in establishing his new farm and in building his fine new house, he began to feel more and more isolated from many of his neighbors. It was, however, of some comfort to him that his new son-in-law, Abner Hutchinson, shared some of his political views, and through Abner he met other men in Oshkosh who were active in the Democratic party and held to its ideals of "popular sovereignty."

Jacob never discussed politics with Norton. Jacob's political views were influenced by Johannes and by the Norwegian language newspaper *Emigranten* to which his father subscribed and read faithfully each time it came. Many of the Norwegians in the Neenah Settlement earlier had a strong loyalty to the Democratic party, but this loyalty had shifted rapidly during the past several years, largely as a result of the leadership of Johannes Baklistulen in the Neenah Settlement.

After the harvest in the autumn of 1856, Jacob spent a good deal of his time clearing land on the farm he was purchasing from the widow. He had made an agreement with her that allowed him to do this work on the farm even though he would not take formal possession of the place until March of the following year. She and her two children continued to live in the cabin, but Jacob spent many days chopping down trees, clearing brush and grubbing out stumps in order to make larger fields in which to plant crops the following spring. He also made arrangements with Heinrich Meyer to cut a number of pine trees which he could haul out when the winter snow came and use for building a larger house. In all of these tasks, Jacob was frequently helped by his younger brother, Klemet, and sometimes also by Kittel, Terje and Elias.

Jacob spent less time at Norton's farm, but when he was there, he noticed that Lydia was anxious to spend time with him. On Sunday afternoons he frequently met her, and they would go for long walks in the woods if the weather was nice; if not, they would be forced to stay indoors at "Norton's Folly," but they felt less free to converse with each other under these circumstances.

Jacob shared with Lydia many of his plans for improving the farm he was going to possess the following spring, and Lydia took a great interest in every detail of the planning he shared with her. More and more Lydia seemed, in Jacob's mind, to fulfill the role that Maren had played in his life, and his first thoughts of Lydia continued to be "sisterly." But gradually he felt more and more drawn to Lydia for her own sake, and he began to feel strong affection and attraction to her. Remembering his earlier experience with Edith Cartwright, Jacob began to wonder if the Nortons, in spite of their openness and friendliness with him, might have some feelings that a young immigrant was not worthy of their daughter's hand in marriage.

Then, one day in the late autumn, while he and Lydia were walking in the woods on a crisp, sunshiny afternoon, Jacob, almost before he realized what he was doing, suddenly confronted Lydia with a proposal of marriage. Lydia smiled coyly at Jacob and responded by teasing him a bit, asking him why it took him so long to come to this decision. Didn't he know that she had already decided, some months ago, that if Jacob asked her, she would certainly respond favorably to such an offer of marriage. She had not always felt this way, she confessed. When she first knew him, he seemed so strange and foreign to her, but now that they had come to know each other so well, there was no question in her mind but they were destined for each other.

"But what about your parents, Lydia? Roberta got herself a rich Yankee banker with a fine mansion. What will they think of me, a poor immigrant boy, as a son-in-law? I can't give you a fancy mansion on the most fashionable street in town; I can only give you a humble farmhouse, much less pretentious than your father's house."

"But Jacob, don't you understand? I don't want the kind of life that Roberta chose for herself. You know me well enough to understand that I prefer life in the country to life in the city, and you, dear Jacob, are a clever enough fellow to build a good home for the two of us. You built my father's house, didn't you, and your father's place as well. I have great confidence in your future and our life together, Jacob."

When Lydia's parents learned of her promise to marry Jacob, Emmeline Norton was positive and supportive of Lydia's decision, but Lambert Norton had more than his share of misgivings. He had not really expected that his daughter would want to marry Jacob. It wasn't that he didn't have confidence in Jacob, but the idea had just never occurred to him either that Jacob would want to marry his daughter. He was not so much opposed to the marriage as surprised by the news. Emmeline chided her husband for being so preoccupied that he had not noticed how Lydia and Jacob had become so friendly with each other during the last months.

At last Norton reconciled to the thought of Jacob as a son-in-law. In fact, he began to look at the advantages this marriage would have for him in the future. Jacob was a clever fellow, and someday he would likely take over Norton's farm. When he talked to Jacob at the time that Jacob asked him to give his consent to the marriage, Lambert tried to persuade him that he and Lydia should stay in the big house and make their home with them instead of venturing off on their own on the little farm Jacob was planning to take over next March. But after talking it over with Jacob, he came to realize it probably would not be a good idea. The young people needed to be on their own. In time, children would likely be born, and it would be very inconvenient to have three generations all living together. To be sure, it would be empty in the big house with both of his daughters gone, but in Lydia's case, she would not be far away, and Jacob would also be on hand to give Lambert some help whenever he was needed. Lambert smiled to himself because it really was going to work out much better than he ever thought it could.

When Anna and Terje were told of their son's intentions to marry Lydia Norton, they taken by surprise.

"We had always supposed you would find a bride from among the young girls of your own kind here in the Neenah Settlement, just like your brother Elias."

These words of his father cut Jacob to the quick because they seemed to imply his disapproval. But then his mother hastened to add her own comments.

"Jacob, you must not take your father's words wrong. Neither your father nor I know Lydia Norton very well. We've only seen her a few times, and we cannot speak her language. I'm sure she is a very fine young lady. We've met her father a number of times, but we've scarcely seen the others in the family, even though we're close neighbors. But now we must invite these people to visit us so we may come to know them better."

It was a day late in November when Lambert Norton and his wife and his daughter drove into Terje Larsen's farmyard. Anna had been scurrying about the house, making sure everything was in order so these fine Yankee neighbors would get the right impression. She had prepared a delicious dinner, using one of the hams from the smokehouse as the main course. Poor Anna-Maria was flustered and nervous as she had to endure her mother's scolding for every little hitch in the preparations. At last, Jacob ushered the Norton family into the house. Terje, Kittel and Klemet stood stiffly in the background as the Nortons greeted Anna and her daughter first. Jacob had to translate the greetings to his parents. His sister and his brothers knew enough English to understand what the Nortons were saying.

Lambert Norton had inspected Terje's house when it was under construction, but this was the first time he had stepped inside after it was completed. He expressed his admiration for the workmanship of the log interior, and made some comments which Jacob translated to his father about how this house was the finest house of log construction he had ever seen. Terje glowed with pride over this compliment, but he wanted Norton to know this good workmanship was entirely his son's doing.

Emmeline Norton complimented Anna and Anna-Maria for the fine meal they had prepared. But there were awkward silences during the course of the meal, as though this entire occasion was something to be endured rather than enjoyed. At last the meal was over, and the time came for the Nortons to depart. After they left, Anna almost collapsed from exhaustion, and Klemet had to help his sister in clearing the table and washing the dishes in order to give his mother some opportunity to take a much deserved nap.

Emmeline Norton, on the way home, spoke to her husband and daughter.

"Oh, how I wish that I could speak to Jacob's mother. She is a good person, of that I am sure. His entire family is a good family. It is such a pity that we are so separated by language and culture."

In December Jacob was able to haul the pine logs from Heinrich Meyer's place. He preferred to build his house of logs in the same fashion he built his father's house. He explained carefully to Lydia the advantages of this kind of building over the flimsy "balloon frame" method that was so popular. The log house, he told her, would be much warmer and cozier than the drafty rooms Lydia had to live with, even at "Norton's Folly." At first Lydia was skeptical, but after visiting Terje and Anna's house on that brisk November day, she agreed that there were some advantages to Jacob's plan.

The house would be about the same size as the tenant house Jacob had built for Jim and Rosie Rooney and their family, but Jacob explained to Lydia that the house he was planning to build would eventually become a wing of their future house. Certainly this tiny house would be adequate for the two of them for several years to come.

It would take them several years to get ahead enough to afford a larger house, and in the meantime there would be other needs, such as a new barn and cattle and a team of horses. The list could go on and on. Then, too, Jacob was anxious to pay back the loan his father had made to him. Even if he was lucky enough to get a good crop of wheat the first year and able to sell it at a good price, it would still be several years before he could "get on his feet," as his Yankee neighbors would say.

Construction on his house could not begin until late in the spring after the crops were in. In the meantime, Jacob was busy hewing the pine logs into shape. He provided the widow with fuel by giving her the chips from his logs as well as split wood from some of the trees and branches he had chopped down in order to clear the land.

On March first, Jacob drove the widow and her children to Neenah, where they could take a steamboat to Fond du Lac to get railway passage to Milwaukee. There they would be met by her family from Muskego. Jacob returned from Neenah with his wagon loaded with supplies for the construction of his house.

The house took shape rapidly in late April and early May, after Jacob had completed sowing his small fields into wheat. When the time came to put the logs into place, his father and brothers were anxious to help him in every way they could. Then, one day late in May, Jacob paid a call on the Nortons and invited Lydia and her mother to come with him to inspect the nearly completed house.

"Within about three weeks I should have this little house completed so that it will be ready for occupancy," Jacob said proudly. "Now I think we need to discuss seriously the date for our wedding."

The dulcet clanging of the old Connecticut clock on the mantel aroused a flushed response on Lydia Norton's excited face. For weeks she had waited for this grand moment. In spite of the haste of their courtship, her Jacob now had the audacity to be late! To Lydia's prime sense of decorum and order, the easygoing ways of Jacob Larsen, immigrant and interloper into her Yankee world, were sometimes a source of puzzling exasperation. Late for his own wedding! How very like Jacob that was, and yet she could not bring herself to think of him harshly, telling herself that she loved him all the more for his casual tardiness.

Just then her father, Lambert Norton, burst in upon her room with the news that the Larsen party had arrived. They slipped in almost stealthily through the back door -- Jacob and his parents, Terje and Anna Larsen, and his brother Elias. Neither Elias' wife, Dorthea, nor his younger siblings came, in spite of the fact that they had been invited in a most explicit manner. Somewhere deep in the morasses of the Nordic soul there is a fierce pride which outlanders can never fathom, and the absence of Jacob's sister-in-law and his younger siblings had something to do with that inverted pride which often paraded itself as an excess of humility. It was Anna, Jacob's mother, who decided the younger siblings could not dress well enough for the occasion, but Dorthea's absence was another matter. She was in the final weeks of pregnancy, but this pregnancy had gone much better than her first which had ended so tragically. Both she and Elias were confident that all would go well this time, until she came to full term.

For Terje Larsen and his shawl-draped wife, the threshold of the Norton house was nearly as formidable as the entrance into a great and gilded throne room of some exalted monarch, in spite of the fact that their own son had built the house. From their house in the valley they had looked up to "Norton's Folly" during its time of construction; and now the house, gleaming white with its apple-green shutters, stood there like a sentry over the entire valley. In the reckoning of Terje, entrance into such a grand house seemed more unlikely than entering into the promised mansions of Paradise. Yet today he entered that big white house, clothed in his drab homespun, only to find himself suddenly accosted by the gregarious Lambert Norton who extended his fine hand in surprisingly egalitarian fashion into the gnarled paw of startled old Terje Larsen.

Will the wonders of this strange America never cease? To be sure, when Terje first arrived in this new land, he had been entertained in the grand house of Adam Cartwright in Fond du Lac, a house which, like this house, his own son Jacob had helped to construct. But only once before in his entire life, when he stood rigidly at attention at the garrison in Christiansand during his young days in the Norwegian army in the presence of a high-ranking Swedish general, did Terje feel so overwhelmed by pomp and high status as today when he crossed the threshold of "Norton's Folly."

Today his great Yankee neighbor, Lambert Norton, stretched forth his hand to greet poor Terje as a friend and equal, and welcomed the groom's party with effusive warmth. His words, of course, sounded like so much cackling to the ears of Terje and Anna, but Jacob stood by to translate Norton's eloquent phrases into Norwegian for his parents. Terje, sensing the dignity of the occasion, paused for a moment in the far end of the kitchen, and then intoned a humble greeting in Norwegian to his host.

Terje's guttural voice seemed to assault the gleaming crystal and hanging drapes and the genteel horsehair and velvet opulence of "Norton's Folly." The strange, high-pitched utterances of Terje were overheard by the awaiting guests of the Norton family in the great sitting room, and one silk-bedecked Norton lady, the wife of Lambert's brother, Elijah, was heard to mutter to her son, "I suppose that man was speaking Norwegian. What a strange and disgusting language it really is. Lydia might have found herself a nice Yankee beau instead of this foreigner she insists upon marrying."

But Elijah Norton's wife spoke her words so cautiously that even her son had difficulty hearing them, and her son softly reproved his mother, pointing out that the tall, handsome Jacob was easily the match for many a Yankee. Didn't Uncle Lambert himself speak of him with enthusiasm and high regard?

Roberta Hutchinson did not attend her sister's wedding because she had recently suffered a miscarriage, and it would not be wise to make the journey from Oshkosh in her weakened condition. Jacob was relieved when he heard she would not be there, for he feared meeting her on this occasion. Perhaps Jacob was just being protectively cautious about his new love for Lydia and did not want it shaken by the faint memories of an older passion. This new love was inexplicable, yet beautifully gentle and serene. Lydia, simple and good-hearted as she was, overcame Jacob's natural reserve and caution, and they had opened up to each other as friends and companions, but this friendship had quickly ripened into a full-blown love.

Today, on Lydia's wedding day, Lambert Norton was in fine form, ushering the Larsen parents into velvet plush seats in the parlor. Norton smiled as he saw Anna's fingers caress the soft velvet of the chair upon which she was sitting. In Anna's life there had been very little soft velvet to caress.

By the broad-arched doorway Jacob stood with his brother Elias. Elias, older than Jacob by only one year, was red-faced and bearded, in striking contrast to the beardless and blond Jacob.

At the mantel stood the Rev. Ezekiel Jackson, a Methodist preacher who occasionally conducted preaching services at Knott's school-house. Tall and awkward in appearance, Ezekiel Jackson's greatest endowment was a pious nasal drone which greatly impressed some of his more susceptible listeners. Mr. Jackson had ridden nearly thirty miles on his black and aging mare in order to perform this marriage of Lydia Norton and the young Scandinavian stranger.

But Terje Larsen looked at Mr. Jackson with eyes of suspicion. How could a marriage be truly valid if the minister wore neither ruff nor gown? He had been assured that the Rev. Mr. Jackson was as genuinely a Yankee preacher as Olaus Duus was truly a Norwegian *prest*, yet Terje still had lingering doubts about Jackson's legitimacy and authority to perform this marriage.

The Rev. Mr. Jackson's stance at the mantel was the pre-arranged signal for the commencement of the wedding. Lambert Norton vanished temporarily up the stairway and in a few moments emerged with his daughter Lydia upon his arm. She was dressed simply in a brown silk dress, and her light brown hair was parted severely in the middle and pulled back tightly. Flushed and nervous, she nearly tripped on the stairs, and then she caught the eye of her bridegroom who was waiting for her at the landing. Shyly she smiled, then reddened with a blush as she took Jacob's arm. Together they walked into the parlor and stood before the parson. Elias Larsen stood by his brother's side; and Lydia's friend, Sophia Hopkins, rose from her chair in the corner to stand by her side. Sophia had been asked at the last minute to perform this duty when it was learned that Roberta would be unable to attend the wedding.

Mr. Jackson read from a worn and tattered black book, entoning the vows with a kind of ominous chant. Terje wondered if this Yankee preacher was really trying to chant and couldn't bring it off, or if this was just the Yankee way of preaching. Next to the ruff and the gown, chanting was the mark of a true *prest* in the mind of Terje, and this poor stick of a Yankee preacher put on a poor performance, that was for sure. Why back in Austre Moland Church, in the days of old Pastor Sandberg, there was some real chanting then. Folks said that Sandberg chanted to put the devil asleep, and Terje was inclined to believe it. But in America it was different. Even the Norwegian preachers here weren't so great on chanting. Duus really wasn't much good at it, but at least he tried, which was more than some of them did. . . .

In the midst of Terje's reverie, it was suddenly all over, and before he knew what was happening, Lambert Norton handed a fine crystal glass to Terje, filled nearly to the brim with a reddish-brown wine.

"I propose a toast," Norton said to the entire company in a raised voice, "to the bride and the groom. May their days together be long and happy," and winking at Terje, who understood not a word, he continued, "and may we both live to become grandfathers."

Terje drank his wine down lustily, somewhat to the embarrassment and amusement of the other guests.

"Fine old Madeira," Norton spoke to Terje, forgetting momentarily that his words would not be understood, "I ordered it from Oshkosh last spring, hoping I would have a special use for it soon."

Terje and Anna were escorted into the dining room where they sat down at a long table spread with fine Yankee food. Amid the buzz of conversation all about them in a language they did not understand, they concentrated only upon their best table manners as they ate this wedding dinner in honor of their son and his bride.

Often, in the weeks and months which followed, Terje would look through the narrow panes of his snug log house and see the large white Norton house on the hill with its apple-green shutters just over a half a mile north of his own snug and cozy home, and he would reminisce about the wedding of his son. He would think about all of that velvet and fine crystal up there, and then he would smile contentedly, recalling that he had once, not so long ago, been an honored guest at that great house which was called "Norton's Folly."

Author's Afterword

This is a story for readers who have some regard for their own ancestors and some interest in the kind of world in which those ancestors lived and died. It is, of course, impossible to reconstruct the world of nearly one hundred and fifty years ago with total accuracy. The historian needs to strive for the highest degree of accuracy possible, but the writer of historical fiction is typically allowed some greater liberties.

As an example of a greater liberty, I point to the role which I chose to give to the Rev. Adolph Preus in this narrative. His initial appearance in the Neenah Settlement on October 25, 1850, at which time the congregation was organized, is factual. Some of the details of that organizational meeting, including the names of persons elected to hold office, are also factual; but I have taken the liberty to include other names, including some of the principal characters in the story, in such a way as to weave the whole into a coherent narrative. Likewise, the subsequent visits of Preus are made to conform to the narrative. The surviving church records show that the cousin of Adolph Preus, Herman Preus of Spring Prairie, came to the Neenah Settlement earlier than this story indicates. I took those liberties with the historical records in order to create Adolph Preus as a sympathetic character, a clergyman who could reach out to the needs of the people he was attempting to serve in a very positive manner in several episodes of the story.

Much of the base for the story comes from the experiences of my own ancestors, passed on by diaries and memoirs and by word of mouth from one generation to the next. The Terje Larsen of the narrative was, in fact, my own great-great grandfather, but his fictional reconstruction in this story may or may not conform in details to the surviving records and memories of his life, and his children bear only incidental resemblances to their real life counterparts.

I have also taken fictional liberties with other historical persons and events, deliberately scrambling names and inventing certain episodes which did not occur in the early Neenah Settlement, but which could very easily and typically have happened. For example, the suicide of "Anlaug Risland" and the death of "Maren" did not occur within the surviving family accounts. The false report of the sinking of the *Juno* did occur, but the ship was known by another name.

Jacob, the central character in the story, was a "builder" in the most literal sense of the word, and the reader may at times feel a bit burdened by details about building. Yet I must ask the reader to understand that this is a narrative about the "building" of America. There may be a kind of epic quality implied in this narrative, but it is certainly not intended to be an epic in the classical sense. I have not tried to create the characters as some kind of superhuman heroes, but as ordinary people who happen to be caught up in the challenge of building for themselves a new life in a strange new environment. Perhaps the term "saga" can more accurately describe my intention in the narrative than the term "epic."

I have attempted to write this story in a simple and straight-forward manner, with little thought for literary subtleties or complexities, because I would like thirteen and fourteen year olds to be able to read and comprehend it without difficulty. Yet I would hope that the story is compelling enough on its own terms to engage the interest of adult readers as well.

It is an old-fashioned and somewhat out-of-fashion theme with which we are dealing in this story -- the "land-taking" theme of pioneering days. I am suggesting, in this story, that it is very helpful, from time to time, to look back to our beginnings in America, to a world largely untouched by the manipulators of mass culture, to a world in which the American dream really motivated people in ways our cynical age finds it hard to understand. There was a refreshing innocence about these ancestors of ours that stands in sharp contrast to our contemporary agonies of self-doubt and self-pity. Yet, in their innocence, they were often tempted by vanities and foibles not unlike those which continue to plague us.

I have chosen, in this story, to focus upon how our immigrant ancestors acclimated to the new land; and how they inter-related with the dominant Yankee culture. Indeed, it must not have been easy to cast aside many old customs; and it must have been most difficult to learn, in their adult years, with little formal instruction, the complexities of the English language. Many of the older immigrants, of course, never did master the new language; but those who came as children or young adults were typically much more successful in making this transition.

It should be obvious from the context that the immigrants often spoke to each other in their native language, but when they attempted to speak English they undoubtedly spoke it with a heavy accent and probably made many mistakes in grammar and usage. Any attempt to replicate this broken English would only make the characters seem comic and ridiculous to the reader. As a result, there is no choice but to cast their manner of speaking into standard English.

I hasten to point out that these early immigrants from Norway came to this country well before the great national awakening of their homeland really took root. The names of Ibsen, Bjørnson, and Grieg were yet unknown to these people; a few of the more literate might have heard of Welhaven and Wergeland, but it is doubtful that the many of the early immigrants had been touched by these forerunners of Norway's great cultural awakening. The Norway which these immigrants knew was all too often marked by poverty and severe social limitations. To be sure, they brought with them some of those wonderfully painted immigrant chests and other remnants of a richly endowed peasant culture; but those remnants were typically cast aside -- sometimes with lingering regret and at other times with disdain.

Norton's Folly also focuses upon the Yankee neighbors of these immigrants, as well as immigrants from other European nations. The Yankees exhibited a variety of attitudes toward their immigrant neighbors, ranging from the nativism of the "Know-Nothings" of that era to genuine acceptance. The marriage of Jacob at the end of this narrative signifies the latter.

Unlike many of the settlements of Norwegian immigrants in Wisconsin and other midwestern states, the Neenah Settlement was small and surrounded by people of other ethnic backgrounds. This forced the immigrants in this community to interact with their neighbors much more rapidly than in those communities where Norwegian immigrants and their descendants prevailed in such large numbers that contacts with other groups were very limited.

There are only a few references in *Norton's Folly* to the Indians whose original territory had been forfeited to white settlement. This forfeiting of the land had been done well before the immigrant settlers came, but the immigrants did have some occasional encounters with the Indians. I deliberately included the Partridge kidnapping incident, a tragic occurrence which had its origins right on the edge of the Neenah Settlement, because it serves to illustrate both negative and positive attitudes toward the Indians.

Likewise, there are only a few oblique references to blacks in this story because they were so rarely seen in this region. Yet there was a strong awareness of the mounting sectional controversy in those years over the issue of slavery, especially in the wake of the fugitive slave provisions in the Compromise of 1850. These same immigrants who were so busy "building" their new communities in the early 1850's were destined to put aside their building tools in order to take up arms within just a few more years. It is my intention to write a sequel to this story which will extent the sagas of the Skredderstua and Norton families and others into the Civil War era.

Neil T. Eckstein

[254]

A Glossary of Norwegian Terms

Page 1

"tun" A farmyard, usually surrounded by farm buildings.

"odel" Primogeniture, where property is passed on to the eldest son in the family.

Page 4

"odelsrett" The law of primogeniture.

Page 81 (83) (116) (167)

"huspostill" A book of sermons intended for family use.

Page 83

"Ellinganer" The name given to the followers of Elling Eielsen.

Page 96

"barn" Child or children.

"fjøs" A cow barn.

"stall" A barn or stable, usually for horses.

Page 105

"candidatis" (Latin) The certification given a theological candidate by the university faculty, qualifying for ordination.

"kapellan" A curate or chaplain.

Page 108 (114) (201)

"klokker" A sexton or precentor who led the singing in church. This person was often also a schoolmaster.

Page 116

"bygd" Parish; country community.

Page 167

"julenisse" Christmas elf (similar to Santa Claus).

Page 168

"julebukking" The custom of going from door to door at Christmas, masked and costumed, begging for treats.

Page 194

"Indielandet" The "Indian country" in Waupaca and Portage counties, Wisconsin.

Page 247 (248)

"prest" Priest or pastor.